THE COURTSHIP TRAP

INCONVENIENT VENTURES
BOOK ONE

NINA JARRETT

ROGUE
PRESS

To Mr. Jarrett.

I would never have gotten this far without you.

PROLOGUE

Sweet maid, the blushes on thy cheek
With innocence and beauty speak;
May love and joy attend thee still,
And every wish of thine fulfill.

The New Ladies' Valentine Writer (1821)

* * *

EARLY AUGUST 1821, LONDON

"*A*nd speaking of scandal, you will never believe who was seen sneaking out of Lord Uppington's chambers at dawn—a certain countess!"

The Dowager Lady Harriet Slight arched her brows in response, her facial muscles shifting in polite reflex as Lady Cordelia Hammond prattled on about the latest *on-dits*.

They strolled along Piccadilly to shop, but Harriet was barely listening. She was feeling rather queasy—not to mention regretful—for having indulged in too many bottles of wine the night before. But it was all beyond the pale.

Last year, she had lost her paramour, Perry Balfour, to a country mouse named—of all things—Emma Davis. What a tritely provincial name! And the chit had matched it, being a tiny, frumpy thing from the countryside. Gauche. Clumsy.

Although, Harriet admitted, the girl did possess an impressive pair of diddeys. Which, at least, explained why Perry had abandoned her bed for the parson's noose with that mousy hoyden.

Cordelia continued as if a rapt audience hung on her every word. "A respectable married lady, no less. Of course, she claims she was merely seeking advice on a family matter, but really! At that hour? And in a state of such disarray?"

Gadzooks, her fellow widow did talk. Fortunately, Harriet's lingering inebriation made it easier to ignore the incessant chatter while she brooded over the events of the past two weeks.

Initially, she had sought revenge for Perry's defection by welcoming his friend, Mr. Brendan Ridley, into her bed and had enjoyed a few months of his avid pursuit across Town. It had restored her self-esteem to see the handsome heir to a baron enraptured by her, quite taking her mind off the humiliation of the year before.

Then, just as she was considering sending him on his way, another unsophisticated hoyden had appeared in her drawing room, demanding that Harriet provide Brendan with an alibi.

Her! An important viscountess! Expecting her to ruin herself to save Brendan from the gallows by testifying that he had been with her at the time of his father's murder? It had been all she could do not to collapse into peals of laughter.

Nay, Brendan had got himself into trouble, and he could damn well get himself out of it. Heroic rescues were the stuff of phantasy, and clearly, little Lily Abbott was nothing more than a deluded schoolgirl barely out of her short skirts if she imagined Harriet would leap onto a white horse to rescue a man she barely knew—then be forced into an unwanted marriage with a lowly baron to mitigate the ensuing gossip.

Only, the ridiculous girl had provided an alibi in Harriet's stead, thoroughly ruining her own pristine reputation to marry Brendan in the resulting scandal and become the new Lady Filminster.

"If her husband hears of it, she might find herself exiled to the Highlands before the Season is through," Cordelia continued, failing to notice that Harriet could not care a whit for her incessant tattling.

Were the gods mocking her? Was she to lose every future paramour to some dumpy, green girl? Harriet stretched her neck ever so slightly to relieve the tension. She was alluring, damn it! Incomparable! She could have any man of the upper classes merely by crooking her finger.

At that moment, just as they passed Hatchards, the door swung open, and indeed, the gods proved themselves fond of a jest—for out stepped Brendan Ridley and his prattling, small-breasted bride, deep in conversation, neither noticing that Harriet had stopped to consider them, bringing Cordelia to a sharp halt.

Lily Ridley, the new Baroness of Filminster, turned her head toward her husband, engrossed in their conversation, to trill a breathless question in his direction. Brendan—who had, just weeks earlier, been at Harriet's beck and call, utterly enthralled by her vivacious beauty—now did not even notice her standing three feet away, squarely in his line of sight?

It was not to be tolerated.

Harriet's resentment ratcheted up, and she decided it was high time the newlyweds paid her some mind.

"Well, well. It is the scandalous Lily Ridley, if my eyes do not deceive."

Silly Lily spun about, and Brendan found Harriet with a jolt of surprise.

Harriet drew her shoulders back in rigid pride, well aware that this posture lifted her breasts prominently. The short chit who had caused all of Harriet's recent botheration took an instinctive step backward, as if to avoid getting banged in the face by Harriet's well-admired bosom. Beside her, Cordelia was riveted, giggling coldly at Harriet's coy remark.

Harriet welcomed the small surge of smugness. She was still a force to be reckoned with.

For a moment, little Lily appeared unsure how to respond. Then, her elfish face firmed into lines of determination.

"Oh, do you mean the scandalous night I spent with Lord Filminster while his father was being bludgeoned to death?"

Reaching out, Lily seized Brendan's arm. He cooperated, stepping through the door and shutting it behind him before tucking her hand into the crook of his elbow.

"Or do you mean when I stepped forward to speak to the coroner in order to clear Lord Filminster's name of those dreadful accusations of murder?"

Both Harriet and Cordelia drew back in wide-eyed horror at the girl's unexpected temerity. Harriet had anticipated blushing, perhaps even suppressed tears—all of which would have served to alleviate the gnawing doubts plaguing her these past days. Not this.

"Or perhaps you mean our hasty marriage to protect my reputation?"

Lady Filminster paused, as if giving them a chance to answer, but no words were forthcoming. Harriet's wits scrambled at this brazen conduct.

"Perhaps you mean when our footman attempted to abduct me and my husband bravely offered to take my place? Before our butler shot the man dead, of course." The baroness tapped a finger to her lip as if thinking. "But, no, I think you must mean all of it."

Settling the matter, Lady Filminster dropped her hand to gesture widely. "If I think about it, I must confess that I am. I am scandalous. Scandalously happy, that is!"

Harriet's jaw hung open. The silly little chit who had confronted her not two weeks earlier was now transformed into a confident peeress. Could it be love that had prompted such a change? And was it true that Brendan had offered his own life in place of hers? Thus, Harriet's internal certainty that she enthralled the men in her circle began to crumble as she tried to think of even one who would risk life and limb to save her. Her doubts rose once again, like the tide returning.

Steeling her nerves, Harriet reminded herself that the young woman had a talent for assaulting one's senses with chatter, but her candor in the face of censure was … was … too damn provocative. How dare she flaunt her happiness so? This was not how ladies behaved in polite society.

Beside his wife, Brendan raised a hand to cover his mouth as he struggled not to burst out laughing. Lady Filminster herself appeared to be fighting the urge.

Turning to her husband, she lifted a hand to cup his neck. Tugging him down, she rose onto the tips of her toes.

Brendan dropped his hand from his mouth and leaned in, capturing her lips with his, more than willing to indulge his bride's performance. He deepened the kiss, wrapping an arm around her waist to pull her closer, and the young baroness was crushed against his hard chest. When he lifted his head, genuine admiration and true affection were painted across his features, a silent declaration that Lord and Lady Filminster were deeply in love.

Harriet gasped at the public display. It was not fashionable to like one's husband, let alone be seen enjoying his company, but the new baroness, apparently, did not care what others might think. She was radiant with joy, the very image of a young woman who had achieved her dreams, and Harriet could not quell the vicious grip of envy at the sight of such unbridled happiness.

Lady Filminster dropped back onto her heels before turning to face the widow.

"Whomever it was that my husband was with before me, I am ever so grateful that they set him free … so that I could catch him."

She tilted her chin in challenge, daring Harriet to speak. But Harriet could only open and close her mouth, grasping for a rebuttal to this brazen verbal assault.

And then—for just a moment—Harriet saw it. Pity.

It flashed in Lady Filminster's chocolate-brown eyes, making Harriet's mortification all the worse.

Releasing her husband, the baroness stepped forward and reached out, brushing the back of Harriet's hand. Harriet flinched as if seared by a hot poker.

"I wish you the boundless joy of truly connecting with another person."

The very ground shook beneath Harriet's feet as, somewhere in the recesses of her mind, a door cracked open.

"Of opening your heart to another, and finding that you care more about them than your own self."

The door yawned wider, even as Harriet fought frantically to slam it shut.

"I wish you a strong young husband and healthy children."

Somehow, it would not yield, widening inexorably to reveal the memories she had long buried.

"And I wish you a long and full life filled with laughter, Lady Slight."

The shell she had built over these many years shattered, and regret came spilling out, swirling around Harriet as the door now stood open, and she stared straight through.

A long-forgotten celebration of St. Valentine's … a man gazing upon her with the same deep affection that Brendan had just displayed toward his bride, while in the present the horrid Lady Filminster cursed her with her cruel wishes of love, marriage, and progeny.

* * *

MEANWHILE IN FLORENCE

"I need your help," Lorenzo implored, his lean face earnest in the low light of the drawing room. "I have tried for years to find a clue amongst these letters, but nothing. You are English. You might notice something that I cannot."

Sebastian Markham and his Italian friend had been working together for a year or more now, forming a lucrative partnership to trade in art to the titled and wealthy visiting Florence. So successful had they been that he had long since stopped collecting his annuity from his brother, the great and lauded Duke of Halmesbury.

It had been a brilliant day when he had relinquished his allowance, no longer beholden to his arrogant older brother. The great philanthropist who refused no plea for help … unless it came from his younger brother, in which case he was a coldhearted bastard. Sebastian gritted his teeth and willed the thought of his cursed brother to recede.

The fly in the ointment was that Lorenzo was obsessed

with his family history. Specifically, what had happened to his ancestor, Matteo di Bianchi, whom Lorenzo claimed had been a talented apprentice at the side of Sandro Botticelli before being taken on at the workshop of the Renaissance Man, the Master of all Arts—Leonardo da Vinci.

That had been before Matteo was commissioned by Englishmen for some sort of grand cathedral and left Italy, never to return. He had left behind a family legend of greatness never realized, and the mystery of what had happened to Matteo's work.

"What does this *Regis Aeterni* mean—Eternal King? These people who commissioned him ... could they have been entangled with this king of yours, Henry the Eighth? Perhaps they are the ones who encouraged Henry to break from the Catholic Church and declare himself as the divinely sanctioned ruler of Britain? I am not an expert in English history, but you grew up as one of the elites. The son of a duke. You might note something I do not."

Sebastian stretched out his legs and raked a hand through his mane of hair. It was time to get it cut, but he enjoyed the untamed appearance that greeted him in the morning. It was tangible evidence that he had walked away from the past to forge his own path. To be his own man.

"Just read them. Point out a clue. Anything that might unravel this ball of thread."

Sebastian huffed, responding with reluctance, "It has been three centuries since Matteo sailed from Italy, Lorenzo. Why expend your energy on this? Do you not appreciate the life we lead? We live in the greatest city in the world, surrounded by the art from the Masters. What does it matter?"

"It matters, *mio amico*! Matteo was destined to be a *Maestro*—a Master—I tell you! This *Regis Aeterni* did him foul! My family has long awaited the discovery of his work. The recognition he deserved as an *artista*! A great artist! A man of extraordinary talent."

There was despair in the black eyes of his closest friend, an appeal for help reminiscent of the one which Sebastian had once made to the duke. Sebastian did not like to think of that time, but he felt the echo of despair. Even after five years away from home, it still irked him that his grand ducal brother had not seen fit to wield his power in Sebastian's favor.

He did not wish to encourage his friend's preoccupation with the past, but it was difficult to ignore a plea for help when the favor was so easy to grant. Sebastian would read the letters, find nothing of import about a minor artist's departure three centuries earlier, and appease his good friend with his assistance. Perhaps then Lorenzo would finally come to peace and leave this family mystery buried in the past where it belonged.

So Sebastian relented.

"Give them to me, then."

* * *

MID-AUGUST 1821, LONDON

Lady Filminster's words still haunted Harriet. Ever since she had met the silly chit on the street, who had brushed her hand and uttered her curse, Harriet had been unable to think of anything else. It was as if a spell had been cast.

First, *her* Peregrine Balfour had deserted her to marry a country mouse with no fashion sense.

Then, *her* Brendan Ridley had married a ridiculous debutante flibbertigibbet who had uttered those dreadful words. The words that haunted not only her sleep, but her waking moments, too.

Not that she was sleeping very much. She tossed and turned all night, and none of the gentlemen pursuing a place in her bed held any appeal because of the shrew's tormenting condemnation.

I wish you the boundless joy of truly connecting with another person.

How dare she? Lily Ridley was a foul-mouthed demon.

Of opening your heart to another and finding that you care more about them than your own self.

Harriet knew that only pain and betrayal could come from opening one's heart.

I wish you a strong young husband ...

Husband! She needed no man in her life telling her what to do.

... and healthy children.

Children! They were loud and cumbersome and demanding of constant attention.

And I wish you a long and full life ...

Her life was plentiful, especially when there was no husband or children to ruin it!

... filled with laughter, Lady Slight.

Laughter was overrated. For years, she had practiced her laugh before she had allowed herself to do so in polite society. Only once she had cultivated the perfect little titter.

If she were back on that street with Lady Filminster, she would throw the tiny baroness's maledict back in her face and scream a counter-curse.

"You are a coldhearted bitch, Lily Ridley," Harriet mumbled, turning over to stare at the drapes. Morning had arrived. Again. And Harriet admitted the truth—it was no good. No matter how many assurances she uttered to herself, no matter how long she walked, or how many glasses of wine she drank, or events she attended, or company she enjoyed, the words returned to taunt her in the dark hours of the early morning. And the lit hours of the afternoon. And the gray hours of dawn when the sun rose to mock her for her state of misery where nothing provided solace from the regret and guilt.

She had with great deliberation encased her heart in ice years ago. Now the ice was melting, and the resulting beats were the deepest of agonies. There was no undoing what she had done, nor her selfish endeavors since that time. Even if she could undo the past five years, what use was recovering her heart if it was shattered beyond repair?

Regret for her past behavior was becoming a constant companion, and Harriet was growing desperate to find relief. Rolling on her back and staring at the crown moulding that framed her ceiling, she lay in her soft bed, which might as well have been a bed of coals for all the comfort to be found, and she racked her mind.

It could not be too late for her to change her course. She was yet young.

But how?

She tried to think if there was anyone she could speak to, dismissing the glib acquaintances she had spent her time with these past few years. Nay, she needed someone who had overcome the mistakes of their own past to carve out a sliver of happiness.

And, to her surprise, someone came to mind. An unlikely but estimable confidant, to be sure.

The person in question was not a friend, but now that she had thought of him, she knew he was the one person who could advise her on how to ease the torment in her splintered soul. The dogs of gossip may nip incessantly at his heels, but he had walked his path with fortitude and seemed to have found the elusive joy she had sought these many years despite the darkness of his past.

Calling on him would be a painful pill to swallow, but if it eventually cured what ailed her, it would be well worth it. However, one thing was for certain—the gentleman in question would not be pleased to see her. Which was unfortunate for him, because when Harriet set her mind to a task, it was difficult to thwart her.

* * *

SEBASTIAN WAS in his bedchamber in their rented rooms, reading the numerous letters from Matteo to his sister. A painstaking task due to the spider-like scrawl penned in a mixture of Tuscan Italian and Latin. It was evident that this Matteo fellow had worked for the great Leonardo, if the secretive nature of his letters was anything to go by.

Having read a year's worth thus far—full of Matteo's cryptic allusions to the great work he had been commissioned to do and the bewildering dealings of the association he served—Sebastian could confidently attest that he had no notion of what this *Regis Aeterni* was about. Only that they seemed to be well-connected, possessed far too much wealth and far too little sense, and that Matteo had been utterly engrossed in the mysterious work he was undertaking.

Sebastian returned the current letter to the leather portfolio and drew out the next with a weary sigh. He estimated he had another ten or more years of correspondence to read. Mildly entertaining from a historical aspect, but mostly numbingly tedious to wade through.

Deciding this would be his last for the evening, Sebastian smoothed out the aged paper on the desk, the words inked in Italian long faded.

15th September, 1515

My dearest sister,

I have completed my greatest work to date! Here in England of all places. Maestro Botticelli himself would be most impressed to

witness The Lady's Hidden Secret, which could rival his Birth of
Venus for the exquisite and elusive nature of its subject. Maestro da
Vinci would be enraptured to witness the discretion of her riddle.

Sebastian frowned, the words evoking a vivid recollection of a sublime painting that had once captured his imag-
ination. A masterpiece, unsigned, that he had discovered in
the attics of his family home, Avonmead. As a youth, he had
been so enthralled that he had asked his father if he might
have it for himself. His father had agreed, and Sebastian
had arranged with the butler to have it hung in his
bedchamber.

It was that very painting that had ignited his passion for
art. The very reason he had come to Florence. The reason he
had remained, with the painting still in his possession—until
the sight of it became too painful to bear, and he had sent it
away as a final gift. A farewell to the one who was too like
the angelic yet deceitful beauty portrayed by the talented
hand of the artist.

For a moment, Sebastian was lost in the memory of the
first time he had stumbled upon the painting and how it had
utterly bewitched him.

He blinked rapidly, shaking off the past before it could
awaken old wounds. With renewed focus, he turned back to
the letter, only to freeze at a single line.

A great lord, a descendant of the Norse gods themselves,
remarked that it was a masterpiece and insisted he keep it safe at
his estate in Wiltshire.

Sebastian's head shot up.

His gaze locked onto the looking glass that hung above
the desk, which doubled as his washstand. In it, he saw the
reflection of a man of thirty, with a mane of bronzed hair
and irises the color of storm clouds. Broad shoulders spoke
of strength and vitality. His Italian friends jested that he had
descended from the halls of Valhalla to toy with mere

mortals, towering over them as only a great Viking god could do.

Three centuries earlier, the first Duke of Halmesbury had been granted his title and taken possession of his Wiltshire lands, amassing a treasure trove of fine art, much of which had been placed into storage when Avonmead had been built atop the foundations of that duke's manor.

Sebastian swallowed hard.

The reason *his* painting had come to mind was because it was *the* painting.

Matteo di Bianchi had been the unsigned talent behind the brushstrokes that had shaped his very fate.

Apparently, his own great-great-great-great-grandfather had been affiliated with the *Regis Aeterni*, the very organization Lorenzo sought to unravel.

Sebastian exhaled slowly, his fingers tightening over the letter.

Curse the compact world of the British aristocracy—fate, it seemed, was the cruelest of mistresses indeed.

CHAPTER 1

In vain I seek to calm my mind,
And reason's aid implore;
For still, alas! I find
Thy image haunts me more.

The New Ladies' Valentine Writer (1821)

* * *

DECEMBER 8, 1821, LONDON

Sebastian drummed his fingers against the arm of his padded chair, doing his best to keep his voice low in respect for their host's home. He and Lorenzo had arrived in England a mere ten days ago, along with their Italian friends, Marco and Angelo Scott, after Marco had recently revealed himself to be heir to an English baron. Sebastian supposed he and Lorenzo should move into the duke's townhouse now that Marco had wed the day before, but the thought of being in such proximity to his older brother simply squashed any inclination to be considerate to the Scott household.

So he and Lorenzo remained, likely outstaying their welcome, especially when they continued to quarrel with such regularity. Drawing a deep breath, he restated his position in Italian. There were footmen in the breakfast room beyond the connecting doors to be mindful of.

"You must be patient, Lorenzo."

Lorenzo spun on his heel to face him with a glower, throwing out his long, lean arms in an effusive gesture that spoke to his dwindling patience. Not that Lorenzo was patient at the best of times.

The truth was that they were at a deadlock. Lorenzo had managed to convince Sebastian to come to London, but now that he was here, he had no desire to meet with the woman who had possession of the painting that Lorenzo was so frantic to view. His friend's obsession to uncover the truth about his ancestor had reached new heights in the past month, matched only by Sebastian's increasing reluctance to approach the widow.

"We have been here an eternity! Our friend has met a maiden and married, while you continue to delay!"

An eternity was a hyperbole. Only ten days, but Lorenzo was agitated, so Sebastian suppressed a grimace of guilt. Their lucrative partnership was straining as his friend was growing ever more frustrated, but ... Sebastian growled, mindful of the servants in the next room as he replied in his accented Italian.

"The time is not right."

Lorenzo sucked in air deeply, his exasperation written in every line of his tall form.

"The time is never right! What is it about this ... this ... this bit of muslin that has you hiding under the stairs like a schoolboy?"

Sebastian straightened in warning. Harriet was no bit of muslin, and he would not stand for any insult of her in his presence.

"Watch how you act!"

Lorenzo shook his head vehemently, his rapid Italian rising in volume to Sebastian's embarrassment as he glanced toward the doors. Grabbing a spindly chair from the corner, Lorenzo dragged it over to plop down with an earnest expression.

"No! Not this time, Sebastian! You keep delaying, and it is unlike you to behave so cowardly. We need that painting if I—"

Lorenzo broke off, his expression that of defeat. Sebastian knew it was momentary, and his friend would not let this matter go. But how was he to explain the torment of losing the woman he loved? How long it had taken for him to carve out a sliver of peace in Florence?

He did not wish to recall the dark days when he had left London in a heartbroken rage so many years earlier. When he had run from his past—from what could not be because he had been powerless to affect the rigid constraints of polite society in pursuit of his heart's desire.

If not for Florence, Sebastian well believed he would have just kept running until he had found the edge of the earth and dived into the infinite abyss. His return to London was as difficult as he had anticipated. Perhaps more so.

On the other hand, his conscience remonstrated that he had made a commitment to Lorenzo to assist him with the painting, and despite his troubles, he could acknowledge that he had been dragging his feet.

"You are right. My apologies, Lorenzo."

Lorenzo, wordless but fuming, scraped his chair back abruptly so that it teetered on its back legs. Sebastian hastily reached out to grab it as his friend stormed out, his footsteps sounding loudly as he retreated down the hall.

With regret, Sebastian took to his feet and made for the breakfast room, worried about the potential scene that had unfolded to those within earshot, and to his disappointment, he found Marco sipping on a cup of coffee. Stalking over to the sideboard and rifling around, Sebastian turned to take a seat at the table with a laden plate.

Marco refrained from commenting, watching him with a sympathetic gaze.

Sebastian stared at his plate but did not pick up his fork or commence eating.

"You overheard our argument."

It was not a question. Marco said nothing.

Sebastian leaned back to raise his arms and comb through his mane of hair, his elbows bracketing his head as he exhaled deeply.

"I know you were not the same after that English girl died of consumption. It makes me wonder how you have found the courage—" He stopped, overcome by a rush of memories. Returning to England had been hard. Sebastian rubbed his jaw and peered out at the garden, unseeing as he sorted through the cascade of memories England had resurrected. "How do you find the courage after your heart has been so utterly crushed beyond repair?"

Marco weighed his words carefully, his face thoughtful in Sebastian's peripheral vision.

"What choice do we have, my friend? We cannot give up on the future when it has so much more to offer than the past."

"You believe I should stop delaying?"

"I think you have an opportunity to close the door on an old chapter. As painful as it might be, it must be done if you are to … resuscitate."

Resuscitate. An interesting choice of words. The notion that Sebastian was being brought back to life. Or perhaps it was just his heart resuming its beating. Painful, but necessary to walk a path to the future.

Sebastian nodded, exhaling a puff of air as he finally reached a decision and announced, "Then the time has arrived to pay a call on Lady Slight."

* * *

HARRIET WAS SHOWN into the study by a servant she did not recognize to find Lord Bertram Hargreaves scribbling at his desk with a single-minded focus on the page in front of him. She seized the opportunity to shore up her courage, suppressing the wave of butterflies that had set flight as the door shut behind her with a decisive click.

It was difficult to credit that she was here. That she was going to have the conversation she was about to broach. Her palms were damp, and her heart pounding against her ribs like a frightened bird beating against the bars of a cage, but she was determined to make this stand.

Moving forward with as much insolent dignity as she could muster, Harriet took a seat, perching gracefully on the edge and fixing her skirts.

"Father," she greeted, feigning confidence she did not feel. Showing weakness would only make her mission more … more.

Lord Hargreaves raised his head, his cold ice-blue eyes skewering her with disdain, before putting aside his quill and leaning back in his swivel chair of wood and leather.

Harriet smiled benignly, feeling rather violated at how his attention had flickered briefly over her bosom as if to critique the demure modesty of her bodice. She wished to fidget, but she and her Mentor had discussed in detail how to attend this meeting, and it was imperative she not display any sign of nerves.

It was just that she felt so deeply invested in the outcome.

"Harriet."

He was dressed in a black coat, with a black stock tied about his snowy linen. His auburn hair was still thick, his face frigidly handsome. Only the white at his temples revealed his age. She had always thought that if Lucifer had an earthly form, he would resemble her ageless father, both in form and temperament. Which made it all the more incredible that she was here to discuss ... well, anything.

"I wish to inquire about Belinda Cooper."

His jaw tightened just a fraction, barely perceptible, but Harriet always made a point of studying him closely to ensure she did not inadvertently unleash the devil within.

"That is an inappropriate subject."

"I am an inappropriate widow."

Harriet nearly winced. Impudence was not quite the direction her Mentor had advised her to take, but now that the words were said, she must proceed without apology. Hesitation would only make this discussion worse, so she stared back at him, two pairs of matching ice-blue eyes attempting to freeze the object of their view, until finally, her father blinked and looked away.

Harriet resumed breathing, a surge of triumph making her mildly giddy at the small victory.

"Belinda is none of your concern."

"Nevertheless, you have caused quite the stir of gossip. It is not the done thing to cast off your mistress without honoring your agreements."

A thin smile spread across his face as he stared out the window, and Harriet's heart sank. She suspected that her little victory had been mere subterfuge, her father reeling her in to deliver a sharp cut. Her stomach tensed in anticipation of what cards he may hold up his sleeve.

"My dear, there comes a time when a beautiful woman

has passed her prime …" His leer found hers, and Harriet nearly flinched at the malevolence in their icy depths. "Belinda's time has passed as, apparently, has yours."

His gaze swept over her in contempt, a silent rebuke over the attire she now wore. Harriet shifted uncomfortably. She knew she was still elegant, Signora Ricci being an artiste of women's wardrobes, but no longer … alluring … since she had opted for a different presentation to the world.

Her father was venting his ire, she reminded herself as she steeled herself against his venomous cut. He had intended to use her as a pawn to make a second match that was advantageous—to him, not her—but Harriet was not participating in his schemes again. Not now that she was a widow of independent means.

Feeling rather desperate, Harriet lunged in a bid to end the meeting. "I wish to have her address."

Lord Hargreaves shrugged, his lean shoulders lifting with a deliberate nonchalance. "I could not say. I bid her to depart the house I keep, and I know not where she went."

"Then give me the gifts you took from her, along with the money owed per your arrangement, and I will find her." Harriet could hear her voice was a little shrill. It would not do to reveal any emotion, but her composure was eroding within his stifling presence.

"I would not concern myself if I were you." It was worded as advice, but the menacing threat caused the last of her cool resolve to crumble.

"I shall inform Mother if you do not honor your agreements!"

Her father arched an eyebrow before breaking into laughter, appearing genuinely amused at the thought.

"My dear, are you going to travel all the way to Wiltshire to upset your goose of a mother? I think not. From what I hear, she is too foxed these days to keep up her correspondence."

Curses!

He was right—that was a ridiculous threat to make. It was just so bloody appalling what he had done, but losing her temper would never work. Not with the Viscount of Hargreaves.

Trying to recollect the stratagem that her Mentor had advised, she tried again.

"Belinda Cooper is a gracious woman. She took care of your needs these many years. Surely, you wish to do right by her as her former benefactor. She earned those gifts, and you promised her a settlement when the time came to end the arrangement."

Lord Hargreaves stared at her, unmoved by this appeal to his better nature. Probably because it did not exist.

Harriet sought a different tactic, her mind working to find a more selfish reason for him to keep his commitments. "If word gets around, women will not be willing to enter similar arrangements with you."

"It is none of your business, Harriet, but rest assured my current mistress has already moved in, and she is delightful." He paused, piercing her with those irises of frost as he inspected her face in minute examination to deliver the killing blow to her self-esteem, his point as clear as crystal. "And young."

He was masterful—precise—in his attack on her vanity, Harriet forcing her hands to still in her lap lest she reach up to check the delicate skin around her eyes and ensure no lines were visible. She might be a widow, but she was yet a young woman—young enough to bear children. Somehow her father's razor-sharp barbs made her feel like an old hag.

It was his special gift to shred the confidence of any who dared confront him.

Blazes!

Harriet genuinely liked Belinda, having met her on several occasions at private events. The other woman often played cards with the Carlton Set while waiting for the viscount to return from discreet meetings in some quiet drawing room or tucked-away study within those aristocratic homes.

Harriet had truly hoped to mitigate the situation after hearing the whispers of her father's perfidy toward his loyal mistress of so many years. Perhaps assisting Belinda would finally assuage the gnawing shame of Harriet's past, representing an opportunity for redemption. But it had been a wager against the odds to attempt this. Appealing to his good nature was a laughable endeavor.

Despite the low odds of success, the disappointment still ran deep as she admitted failure. If she were to effect a rescue of the wronged woman who was the current subject of high society's whispers, she would need to find another way because the contemptuous viscount was not going to lift a finger in aid.

* * *

Sebastian walked up to the door, and raising the brass knocker brought it down with a hard tap before stepping back. He was a large man of six foot five and most were intimidated by his stature, so he usually did his best not to loom in doorways and startle others.

After a minute or two, he stepped forward to knock again, signs of activity being absent. As he raised his hand, the door unexpectedly swung open to reveal … well … he was not certain what had just been revealed.

Instead of the customary footman or butler, he found his gaze dropping to find a short, stout woman with a frizzle of gray hair escaping a limp white mobcap. An apron covered her gray-brown dress, and the dress sleeves were rolled up to reveal the scars of old burns on her strong arms, along with a faint scar curved around one of her eyebrows which were arched in question.

She tutted, craning her head back to view him with exasperated curiosity.

"Blimey, ye're a big 'un, ain't ye?"

Sebastian stepped back again, realizing he was towering over the ... servant? If he were not standing on the steps of a gracious townhouse just off Grosvenor Square, he would have sworn the older woman was a tavern maid.

"Lord Sebastian Markham, to see Lady Slight?" He proffered a card, wondering if he perhaps had the wrong address.

Just then, a waif of a girl, who looked no older than twelve, came darting up the hall.

"Missus Finch, Cook says she needs ye right quick!"

The servant—Mrs. Finch, apparently—harrumphed before spinning on her heel to hurry away.

"Take the gent to the painted room, Jem," she threw over her shoulder as she disappeared in the direction the waif had come.

Sebastian found himself staring down at the young girl, who barely stood four and a half feet tall, making him feel like a giant by comparison. Now that he had a proper look at her, he suspected she was a few years older than his original assessment.

Her large hazel eyes spoke of worldly experience, despite her slender frame. A shock of copper-brown hair and a crowd of freckles added to the impression of youth, but her gaze was inquisitive and steadfast. Even challenging, perhaps. She could easily be mistaken for a foundling, if she had not been dressed in the clothes of a maid.

"C'mon, then," she abruptly announced before leading

him down the hall. Stopping at a door at the far end, she swung it open, then skipped away without another word. Her skirts flapped soundlessly as she disappeared around a corner.

Sebastian shook his head, nonplussed. These were not the sort of servants one customarily expected in the home of a wealthy viscountess, but as the London Season had ended, perhaps Harriet's usual staff had left for the country to prepare for her arrival?

He set these musings aside to enter the drawing room and stopped in surprised fascination. The small, gilded parlor was simply beautiful, more of a private space for the owner's enjoyment than a public room. Every surface had been covered with intricately painted floral patterns and deities frolicking. On the smooth vertical space of the mantelpiece was a frieze of Romans going about their business while a musician strummed a string instrument.

It brought to mind a happier time, when he and Harriet had enjoyed the art in Avonmead's attic with avid debate over brushstrokes, colors, and the subject of the paintings they beheld.

Then he registered a presence seated in a regal blue-green armchair with a gilded frame. He frowned, searching his memory for the name of the dainty blonde woman who stared back at him with the same startled recognition that must be evident on his own face.

Finally, he broke the silence with a polite bow. "Lady Wood."

The noblewoman rose gracefully, setting her book aside. "Lord Sebastian. You have returned from Italy."

His lips curved into a polite yet warm smile. "I have. I was hoping to speak with Lady Slight."

"She is not at home at present," Lady Wood replied. "I cannot say with certainty when she will return."

A pang of unexpected disappointment stirred within him. After all the anticipation leading up to today, Harriet was not even at home?

"I see. Then perhaps you would be so kind as to convey a message?" His voice remained pleasantly neutral, though irritation threatened beneath the surface. "I will call again tomorrow."

Lady Wood regarded him carefully, her delicate features thoughtful, almost hesitant.

"I shall deliver your message, of course. But, Lord Sebastian, I feel compelled to say …" She paused, as if weighing her words.

Sebastian waited.

"Lady Slight … no longer entertains … visitors … in her home."

It was stated with deliberation, as if she were warning him away.

Sebastian's frown deepened ever so slightly as he tried to parse the meaning of her words. No longer entertained visitors? Had Harriet withdrawn entirely from society? And yet, here was Lady Wood, sitting alone in Harriet's drawing room, as though she belonged there. Why was Lady Wood unattended at Harriet's home? Was she in residence?

Before he could stop himself, he raked a hand through his tousled hair, an old habit of his when confronted with the tiresome subtleties of high society. After so many years abroad, he had forgotten how aggravating it was to navigate the things left unsaid.

"There is no need for entertainment," he said at last, his tone carefully measured. It seemed Lady Wood was warning him off from pursuing her hostess like some sort of besotted lordling. "I merely wish to put a question to her. About … just … something from our youth." He did not know how to explain why he was here. His expectations had been simple—

to be greeted by a pompous butler, to put his request to Harriet, and then to depart. Instead, he had found himself amidst a rather eclectic household, and Harriet was absent.

Lady Wood inclined her head. "Then I shall inform her of your return."

Sebastian bowed once more, his head swimming with odd observations as he made his departure and wondered about the strangeness of Harriet's home. Nothing about this visit had unfolded as he had imagined.

CHAPTER 2

When first our paths in life's vast maze did meet,
I felt the hand of fate had led my feet;
No chance, but destiny, had brought you near,
To be my own, my dearest, ever dear

The New Ladies' Valentine Writer (1821)

* * *

DECEMBER 9, 1821

*H*arriet had not slept a wink.

Evaline's news that Sebastian Markham had returned to England had sent her reeling, memories flying in every direction as she realized she would be forced to confront her first major misstep. She was not ready to face him.

If only she had more time—time to make amends for the many mistakes she had made since that fateful St. Valentine's

Day—then perhaps she might find it easier to confront him. But she had only just begun her crusade to set things right.

Had she already succeeded in finding and assisting Belinda Cooper with her predicament, Harriet might have summoned the extra courage required for this unexpected meeting. The older woman needed her, and Harriet felt the situation was personal. A chance to stand up to her father after too many years of cowardice.

"He gave no indication of what he wanted?"

It was the eleventh time she had asked since coming downstairs to break her fast, yet Evaline, to her credit, showed not a whit of impatience. Then again, she had long mastered the art of forbearance in the presence of irascible companions. Her late husband had been a brute of a man, from what Harriet had heard.

"Merely that he had a question to pose to you," Evaline responded, setting down her fork to converse properly. "Something about your youth."

Harriet shook her head in agitation.

The only question about their youth that came to mind was the one she dared not think about. The one that had haunted her for years. Her faithless behavior as a young lady had shadowed her every step since. But surely, he was not coming to ask her … that.

Pushing her eggs around her plate with the tines of her fork, she finally abandoned the pretense of eating.

"I will be having tea in the painted room," she declared, pushing her chair back.

Jem appeared at her elbow, her big, expressive eyes peering out from beneath a mop of thick hair. The sight softened Harriet's pounding heart, for the girl looked up at her with such profound admiration to which Harriet was still growing accustomed.

"Oi'll get the tea, m'lady."

Harriet smiled to show her appreciation. The young foundling had turned out to be a hard worker, and Mrs. Finch was well pleased with her addition to their rather unusual household of characters.

"Thank you, Jem."

Soon, Harriet was seated in the painted room, breathing deeply and sipping her tea as she did her best not to anticipate Sebastian's arrival.

Should she ask Evaline to join them?

No. That would only make their discussion all the more stilted.

While she waited, Harriet discovered—to her dismay—that her mind had begun to play tricks on her.

Optimistic thoughts toyed with her composure. Perhaps Sebastian did wish to resurrect the past. Perhaps, now that she was a widow, he intended to pursue what they had once shared.

She shook her head and leapt to her feet, pacing the room. But the space was small, and after only a few strides, she was forced to stop. Turning to the window, she gazed out toward the street.

Perhaps she should leave for the day, avoid this meeting altogether.

But her treacherous heart yearned to glimpse the man who had once loved her so thoroughly.

And then, her thoughts turned to their last day together.

"Come with me, Harriet! Leave with me in the morning, and we will wed in Calais. I have an allowance to maintain us, and we shall take my Grand Tour together."

She had been carried away, speaking of plans as if she truly intended to meet him.

But she had been afraid—terrified—of walking away from the marriage her father had arranged to Lord Slight. To turn her back on wealth and status, all the while knowing that Sebastian's brother might very well cut him off once he learned that his younger brother had wed the daughter of Lord Bertram Hargreaves—a match to which he had been firmly opposed.

So she had pretended. She had spent that last wonderful St. Valentine's Day with the man she loved, all the while knowing she would never summon the courage to leave Wiltshire with him.

A decision she had regretted ever since.

The clatter of carriage wheels brought her back to the present, and she tilted her head to watch as the vehicle rolled to a stop before her home. The coat of arms was vaguely familiar, but it did not belong to the Duke of Halmesbury or the Markham family.

Nevertheless, it was Sebastian who alighted from the darkened interior, and she inhaled sharply—fascinated to see him after all this time.

He was tall, his too-long mane of hair sun-bleached and his skin bronzed by the faraway sun of Tuscany. He was lean and muscular in his buckskins and coat, his white cravat loosely tied. Sebastian had matured into the casual perfection of a god—one stepped straight from the pages of a book on Norsemen, those infamous marauders who had sailed the seas in search of plunder.

Her heart skipped a beat.

And just as they had the day before, her palms grew damp. But this time, it was with excitement rather than the dread her father had provoked in the pit of her stomach.

Looking down, Harriet fussed with the folds of her gown before walking toward the elegant settee that commanded the center of the room.

Her painted retreat had been designed to accentuate her as a woman. Her vanity might be slowly withering in the pursuit of a greater purpose, but she needed this boon to her confidence for the meeting ahead. Settling down, she carefully spread her skirts to their fullest advantage, wondering —perhaps foolishly—if she ought to have worn one of her older, low-cut gowns from the Season.

She had dithered over the decision that morning, but in the end, embarrassment had won. The thought of Sebastian witnessing her past incarnation as a Merry Widow had been too much to bear. He had never known that version of her, and she had decided he never should because, deep down, she feared the judgment she might glimpse in those gray eyes —eyes that had once captured her very soul.

Sebastian had never looked at her with criticism. And if he ever did, Harriet was certain she would incinerate to ash.

Pulling her shoulders back into perfect posture, Harriet wondered where Sebastian was staying. The coat of arms on the carriage made it clear he was not at Markham House, where the duke resided with his duchess. With the duchess's father having died earlier this year in London, Harriet hazarded a guess that the young woman had elected to bear her second child in Town because word was that the ducal couple had not returned to Avonmead despite the holidays. But it appeared Sebastian was not a guest at their townhouse.

Waiting for her visitor to be announced, Harriet stilled her agitated fingers, which had been restlessly rubbing the fabric of her silk gown. Leaning forward, she took up a teacup and saucer, giving her hands something to do as she poised herself and sipped, composed in appearance if not in spirit.

What if he is here to propose a courtship? Now that we are both free to pursue the marriage of our choice.

She squashed the thought—the romantic musings of a girl who had long since ceased to exist, despite her best efforts to rise from the grave and plague Harriet with lamentations of what could have been.

But if I mend enough of my past mistakes ... Perhaps there is a possibility of—

Harriet seized the thought and shoved it into a dark room in her mind, bolting the door before it could escape—before it could unravel her carefully composed demeanor with foolish hopes and long-forgotten dreams.

She was some sort of addlepated fool to believe that one could undo so many lost years and so many poor decisions in a single meeting.

Mrs. Finch appeared in the doorway, and Harriet drew in a steadying breath, bracing herself.

Sebastian stepped up behind the housekeeper.

"Lord Sebastian be 'ere for ye."

With that blunt announcement, Mrs. Finch turned and brushed past their guest, slipping through the narrow gap between him and the hall wall before disappearing in the direction of the kitchens.

Harriet colored at the crude reception. Her new servants were competent in their duties but unpolished in their manners. She and Evaline had learned to take their rough charms in stride, but it was still a tad mortifying to receive Sebastian with so little aplomb.

Forcing a smile, she set her cup and saucer aside and rose gracefully to her feet.

"Sebastian, you look well."

"Lady Slight."

He bowed politely, and Harriet fought the urge to screech in frustration at the formal address. Were they to behave as polite strangers, then?

Clearly, she had been correct not to get her hopes up.

"Please, come in. Have a seat," she finally offered, licking her dry lips as she gestured toward a matching armchair.

He did not move, lingering in the doorway with an

uncomfortable expression on his handsome face, his square jaw tight with tension.

"Should Lady Wood join us?"

Harriet quelled a frown at the request for a chaperon, choosing instead to smile despite the thoughts crowding her mind.

"I thought perhaps you would prefer a measure of privacy. To put your question to me?"

Sebastian rolled his broad shoulders, the motion drawing Harriet's gaze to his lean form, the powerful thighs encased in his buckskins.

Her fingers itched to reach out and touch him as she once had, to trace the changes the years had wrought upon his frame, to press her lips to his. But she remained still, her feigned smile as unmoving as she was.

"I am here to put a request to you."

She waited for him to continue, alarmed by the clamoring of her foolish heart. All the signs indicated that this had nothing to do with their long-ago connection, yet she yearned for him to seize her, to declare himself.

"I sent you a painting some years ago."

And just like that, all her hopes came crashing down, deafening her with their roar of I-told-you-sos. At last, she accepted the truth. This was not a second chance at the past. Nay, this was merely a momentary encounter before they each resumed the paths they traveled now.

"I hoped I might prevail upon you to return it to me."

She drew a slow breath, staring at him.

The painting.

The one that had arrived after the death of her elderly husband, as if to taunt her with what might have been.

Gradually, though, it had become something else—a relic of her past, a meaningful solace when she had needed it most.

Just like Sebastian's letter.

The one she kept folded in the journal beside her bed.

The one he had written when he had gifted her the unsigned Italian masterpiece.

The one she had read a thousand times in the dark of night.

But she refused to choke on the lump rising in her throat.

If she were a good person …

But she was not.

She was merely a work in progress, trying to become a good person while battling her baser instincts—the ever-present urge to protect her own selfish interests.

What he asked was too much, too high a price, even as she sought her road to redemption.

So she reached a decision—to lie.

It was what she knew.

There was no doubt her Mentor would take her to task for it. They would debate the morality of her actions until he argued her into a corner, but at this moment, she had no desire to reveal the truth. She would put off that quarrel for another day.

The painting was hers, she reasoned. Sebastian had gifted it to her. It was her last remaining connection to the girl she had once been, and the thought of giving it up was more than she could bear.

So she pasted on a brilliant smile, even as her stomach clenched with the bitter knowledge that any last hope of reconciliation was shattered beyond repair. If Sebastian sought the painting back—

"That whimsical phantasy? I rid myself of it years ago, darling."

* * *

Sebastian gradually realized he had not imagined the dismissive words.

Harriet was even more beautiful than he remembered, and it had left him distracted during their awkward exchange. Her auburn hair was elegantly coifed, her ice-blue eyes as riveting as the vision that visited his dreams, her delicate features perfectly sculpted, reminiscent of a masterpiece from ancient Rome. She had matured into a lovely young woman.

He had been watching her so closely that he caught the slight narrowing of her eyes, the shift from ice blue to frozen frost when he had posed his question, followed by her haughty dismissal.

Even after all these years, he could still read the transitions of her mood. She had always possessed a volatile temper, even in their youth, and he knew he had upset her—though in what way, he could not quite place his finger on.

Unfortunately, not nearly as much as she had upset him.

To learn that his most valued possession—the painting that had stoked his love of art, set him on his current career with Lorenzo, and remained his constant companion across countries and months of travel—was now gone?

The very piece he had treasured for years, until the memories it evoked had become too unbearable to face. Until he had made the agonizing decision to send it to the woman he had once loved, accompanied by a letter meant to close the door on a past that still tormented him.

Only to now be told she had given it away?

And in that moment ... He hated her.

Hated her with the burning passion of a spurned lover who had never forgotten a single second of their time together.

Hated her with the fury of a bottomless ocean, bent on destroying the mortals who dared to traverse its depths during a violent storm. Much like the day he had sailed from British soils to begin a new life without her at his side.

Sebastian found he had nothing to say in response—nothing that would not leave him riddled with regret if he allowed the words to escape his lips.

So he turned and walked away.

As he sank into the well-padded squabs of the Scotts' carriage, Sebastian's mind churned with restless fury. Unfortunately, he needed to clear his head because he had made the greenhorn error of agreeing to meet with his brother immediately after this call on Harriet. There would be no time to cool the rage bellowing through his veins, no reprieve before facing yet another battle.

His fingers drummed an impatient rhythm against his knee as he forced his thoughts elsewhere—toward the things that made him happy.

He imagined walking the narrow streets of Florence, his boots clicking softly against centuries-worn stones, polished smooth by countless footfalls. The city would be alive with the hum of conversation, the distant trill of a violin, the scent of warm bread drifting from a bakery tucked beneath an ochre archway.

Yet it was not the bustle of the streets that drew him back again and again.

It was the art.

The soul of the city, immortalized in fresco and marble.

The Piazza della Signoria—where Perseus stood in defiant splendor beneath the Loggia dei Lanzi. How many hours had Sebastian spent here, sketchbook in hand, capturing the dramatic tension in the lines of Medusa's lifeless form? He had gone there as a younger man, restless and searching, and found solace from the personal history pressing upon his shoulders.

In his mind, he turned toward the Uffizi Gallery, that

hallowed temple of genius where Botticelli's *Birth of Venus* still stole his breath. He had studied her countless times—the delicate arch of her wrist, the ethereal way her golden locks curled about her shoulders, as if the wind itself were in love with her. It was here, beneath the soft glow of candlelight reflecting off gilded frames, that he had first understood the power of color, of form, of light and shadow whispering stories only the soul could hear.

Yet of all the places that belonged to him in this city, it was the quiet halls of San Marco that beckoned most.

Here, masterful frescoes adorned the cells of long-departed monks, each painting a private window into devotion.

He had stood in the silence of those narrow chambers, the scent of old plaster and incense clinging to the air, and traced his fingers just above the painted surface—never touching, only feeling.

Florence was a city of masterpieces, but it was also a city of discovery.

Of dreams he had once chased … and perhaps still did.

And though he had left, though his loyalty to Lorenzo had drawn him back to England, he knew that no matter where he wandered, Florence would always be waiting for him.

When the carriage drew to a stop, Sebastian opened his eyes, a small measure of peace restored.

He had traveled so far, yet he had never found another woman who captured his heart as Harriet once had.

But that was the past. A past he suspected, unfortunately, he would be forced to revisit when he spoke with Philip.

His brother had insisted they meet in private, something Sebastian was loath to do. The duke would demand to know why he had returned to London. And he would not like the answer.

Alighting from the carriage, he strode up to Markham House. Best to get it over with. He knocked on the door.

Soon, he was ushered into the study by Clinton. Tall and slim, with a distinguished air and graying hair, the butler had greeted him with a glimmer of humor, likely recalling the many scrapes he had rescued Sebastian from as a boy. Sebastian vaguely realized he was musing to distract himself from the conversation ahead.

Philip stood at the window, staring out at his private garden, hands clasped behind his back. This was Sebastian's second visit to Markham House, but they had exchanged few words the last time. That visit had been about meeting the new duchess—an intelligent young woman with chestnut hair and brandy eyes, already well-rounded with their second babe. He had also spent time with his nephew, Jasper, who shared his mother's coloring. Sebastian had wondered whether the boy would grow to match his father in stature, and then, before he could stop himself, his mind had strayed to another possibility.

What if Harriet had left for Calais with him all those years ago? Would they have had a son or daughter by now? Would their child have shared Harriet's auburn hair and ice-blue gaze?

Apparently, hopes for the past still lingered in the present.

Philip turned, his expression stern as he crossed the room.

He greeted Sebastian with a clumsy pat on the upper arm. "Thank you for coming."

The corners of Sebastian's mouth flexed in the hollow imitation of a smile.

He and Philip were similar in build, his brother taller by an inch, and looking at each other was like staring into a mirror. Except staring into a mirror did not usually unsettle him as much as this.

"Of course."

The duke's study was a sanctuary of quiet elegance, a place where power was wielded not with swords, but with ink and careful deliberation.

Lined with towering walnut bookshelves, displaying a wealth of leather-bound volumes, the room bore the unmistakable scent of aged parchment, polished wood, and the faintest trace of coffee from afternoons spent in contemplation. African masks were mixed with ormolu clocks and marble statues, speaking to their family's storied legacy.

A large, ornately carved desk of dark mahogany commanded the center of the room, its surface impeccably arranged—a heavy silver inkstand, stacks of correspondence meticulously aligned.

Behind the desk, a high-backed leather chair bore the faint creases of frequent use—the only sign that the duke allowed himself true comfort amidst his responsibilities.

The true marvel of the study, however, was the expansive window overlooking the private garden beyond. Unlike the manicured precision of a country estate, this London retreat was a carefully cultivated oasis under the pale December sky —a stone pathway winding through bare bushes, leafless vines climbing the trellises, and a wrought-iron bench nestled beneath the shade of an ancient oak.

As the soft golden light of a winter afternoon slanted through the glass, the faint scent of fresh-cut pine and holiday greenery drifted into the room.

To the side of the window, a small sitting area offered respite—two wingback chairs upholstered in deep red velvet flanking a low table, where a silver coffee service gleamed in the light.

Here, matters of state and personal intrigue alike were

discussed in hushed tones, a place where whispered secrets could be as vital as formal declarations in Parliament.

A marble fireplace, its mantel adorned with delicately carved cherubs and classical motifs, cast a gentle glow with its cheerful fire, while an exquisite portrait of one of their ancestors surveyed the room with imperious regard.

On a nearby side table, a single vase of winter greenery—an indulgence maintained by the household staff—was the only softness amid the room's otherwise stately grandeur.

This was a space that balanced duty and retreat, intellect and authority—a place where a duke might command his affairs with the measured precision of a strategist, or sit in rare solitude, gazing out over the garden, contemplating the path ahead.

Philip gestured to the wingback chairs, and Sebastian dutifully took a seat, leaning forward to pour himself a cup of aromatic coffee.

His brother sat opposite, his expression grim, and Sebastian knew they would finally have to clear the air. This discussion had been inevitable the moment he had decided to return to England. He only hoped Lorenzo would one day appreciate the lengths to which he was going to assist him, because, given the choice, he would never have left Florence.

"You no longer accept the allowance I have been sending."

Sebastian could almost detect a note of hurt in his older brother's tone. But perhaps that was whimsy on his part.

"I have no need. Business in Florence has been good."

Philip breathed in, his expression stern.

What did His Grace, the lauded Duke of Halmesbury, make of his little brother engaging in commerce? Considering they were not close, Sebastian had no notion of his brother's thoughts on the matter.

"I am told you trade in art?"

Sebastian nodded. "Renaissance art. My partner, Lorenzo

di Bianchi—whom you met at the Scotts' residence—is quite the expert."

A shadow of a smile passed Philip's lips. "You are quite knowledgeable yourself."

It was a compliment, and the unexpected warmth Sebastian felt on hearing it caught him off guard. Despite their differences, they were still family. Blood.

And for all that they did not see eye to eye on one essential subject, Sebastian respected that Philip was a good man. One who took his responsibilities to heart.

"I mostly provide introductions and credentials. The Markham name carries weight, even in Europe. Lorenzo is the true connoisseur. It runs in his veins. He had a great-great-something uncle who worked in the workshops of both Botticelli and da Vinci."

Philip nodded.

A handful of years older than Sebastian, the duke shared his features, but his brother's hair was closely cropped, his manner more serious. A clash of temperament—Philip, ever the duty-bound peer, and Sebastian, who considered the *de rigueur* customs of high society to be of negligible importance.

That was the prerogative of a spare. Although, with the duke now having an heir, he supposed he was a spare no longer. Just a wayward relation who had left for his Grand Tour and never returned.

Philip nodded again, appearing momentarily at a loss for words as he leaned over to pour his own cup before settling back in his chair.

Sebastian watched closely, noting the subtle tightening of his brother's broad shoulders.

As if he were bracing for battle.

"Why are you here?"

"I am doing a favor for Lorenzo. Retrieving something. Hopefully, we will depart from London soon."

Especially if the painting was lost.

Which was when Sebastian realized that, in the heat of his anger, he had stormed out of Harriet's home without learning whom she had given it to.

Bloody fool.

He wanted to smack himself for his stupidity. Once Lorenzo heard the news, he would be relentless, harassing Sebastian into returning to Harriet for more conclusive information.

Deuce it!

It was as if London had grabbed hold of him in its suffocating embrace, refusing to release him until he drowned in memories and regrets.

After all this time, why had he not found another woman to capture his heart? Was it because he no longer had a heart to give?

"Does it have anything to do with Lady Slight?"

Philip's baritone interrupted his scattered thoughts, yanking him back to the contentious subject that had severed their affinity years earlier.

Sebastian stiffened, setting down his cup. "Why do you ask?"

"She is why you left. I wondered if she is why you have returned."

"I think, perhaps, we should not discuss Harriet."

Philip growled, setting his cup down with a decisive clink before rising sharply to return to the window. "I should never have allowed Lady Hargreaves and her daughter to visit Avonmead as often as they did."

"We are neighbors. It is the way of things in the country."

"It was a mistake I have long regretted."

"But why?" Sebastian's fist clenched, his carefully maintained equilibrium threatening to shatter.

"Lord Hargreaves. The man is poison. And the water drawn from that well is logically compromised."

Sebastian ground his teeth in an effort to squash his frustration. More than five years had passed, yet they had resumed this argument as if it had begun only this morning.

"For a nobleman known for his philanthropic works, you have always been most uncharitable toward Harriet, who cannot be blamed for her father's failings."

The duke snorted, an uncharacteristic display of ill humor for a man renowned for his composure. "Failings? The man is evil incarnate. He exploits his tenants, discards his mistresses without recompense, not to mention seducing his servants. If I had known what he was about, I would never have allowed his wife and daughter so much access to Avonmead."

Sebastian rose, unwilling to hear Philip censure Harriet yet again. Truly, it was as if they had begun this argument only minutes earlier, rather than back in 1815, when Sebastian had first approached him for help in courting Harriet.

"It is not like you to condemn an entire family by mere proximity! I could never understand why you held Harriet accountable for Hargreaves."

"Because I saw the same weakness of character when you did not. The self-absorption. The disregard of servants. The naked ambition."

"Harriet is no angel, I will grant you, but she was just a young woman under the influence of a foul parent. And her mother is weak. If she had had the opportunity to walk away —she is intelligent and lively, damn it!"

Sebastian wanted to fall to his knees and howl to the heavens, the despair of a man trapped in an infinite argument. Was he Sisyphus, the cunning king who repeatedly deceived the gods? As punishment, Zeus had condemned Sisyphus to push a massive boulder up a hill, only for it to roll back down every time he neared the top, forcing him to begin again for all eternity.

What had Sebastian done to deserve such a fate? Caught between the woman he had once loved and the brother he had once looked up to. How was it possible that, at thirty years of age, to still be engaging in this same endless quarrel? Yet … he was not attempting to court Harriet now, so this was a pointless battle to revisit.

Philip huffed in rejection. "Not an angel? London has no shortage of tales about her exploits. That apple did not fall far from the tree."

"And you never gave her the benefit of the doubt, so we will never know what might have happened if she had married me instead of that … that wrinkled old goat, Horace Slight!"

For the second time that day, Sebastian turned on his heel and departed without a farewell.

Seething, he stalked out the front door, ignoring the footman on duty, and grunted in relief when he saw the Scott carriage at the end of the street, moving at a slow, deliberate pace and awaiting his departure, as they had anticipated this would be a short meeting.

He stormed toward it, eager to be free of his past.

What a wretched day this had been.

CHAPTER 3

Within my heart, a flame doth glow,
Yet words unspoken leave it so;
Through glances soft, I seek to share,
The secret love I humbly bear.

The New Ladies' Valentine Writer (1821)

* * *

DECEMBER 10, 1821

*H*arriet gripped the letter from her Mentor, her emotions a tangle of trepidation and excitement.

Covering her mouth with her fingers, she exhaled in relief.

From her seat near the fireplace, where the cheerful flames warmed the painted room, Evaline looked up from her needlework.

"You have received good news?"

Harriet nodded. "Rumors of an altercation with Belinda Cooper at Lord Stewart's card party. It would appear that her new benefactor is Lord Lowe. He was quite soused and handled her a bit roughly in front of the other men."

Evaline's delicate features pinched, and Harriet immediately felt like an insensitive lummox for not softening her words, especially given her friend's own painful past.

"Oh, my. Miss Cooper's prospects are bleak if she is with Lowe."

Harriet nodded again, distracted by the realization of how much effort it took to think of others' troubles when one had never been taught to do so. Her parents had never bothered with such considerations, but Harriet had decided she must. She needed to be more mindful of her friend's suffering before carelessly sharing such news.

"That part is not encouraging. However, it means we now know where to look for her. I might know her new address as soon as dinnertime."

"That is excellent news. What will you say to her when you meet with her?"

Harriet hesitated, tracing the edge of the letter with her forefinger and thumb.

"I do not know. I hope to think of something when I eventually face her. It is beyond the pale what my father has done. Thirteen years, and he threw her out without a farthing?"

A pang of guilt tightened her stomach. She thought of how she had treated Brendan Ridley when he had been accused of murder. Would helping Belinda be enough to atone for that betrayal?

Brendan no longer needed anything from her. He was happily married now. But Belinda had been wronged by her own father. Surely helping her would serve as a fair substitute for the amends Harriet could not make to Brendan. At least, that was the hypothesis she and her Mentor had arrived at.

But until she succeeded in meeting with her father's former mistress, she could only hope that helping Belinda might ease the shame she carried.

Nevertheless, the missive brought welcome tidings. She was one step closer to her discussion with the mistreated former mistress of Bertram Hargreaves. While she could not save every woman in such a predicament, this one was personal. Her father was a cruel lord, and Harriet had allowed him far too much influence over her life. This was an opportunity to reclaim her soul, and it could not be wasted. With one act of charity, she could set things right for Belinda while also taking a stand against her father—rejecting the example he had set along with his callous treatment of those within his sphere. Somehow, Belinda had become the symbol of her quest to purge her conscience.

Across the room, Evaline returned to her needlework, her face relaxing into contented lines. She appeared fragile in the sunlight streaming through the window, but Harriet was pleased to see her friend at peace. After all she had endured these past few years, Evaline deserved some measure of tranquility. And Harriet was grateful beyond words that they had struck their bargain for Evaline to move in, which had yielded unexpected benefits. Evaline had taken charge of their hodgepodge household that Harriet had put together these past months, allowing Harriet the freedom to pursue her quest.

Just then, Harriet's musings were interrupted by a cool draft that chilled her hands and lips.

Turning toward the door, she found it standing open, and there, framed within it, stood the object of her fitful dreams.

Rising swiftly to her feet, she set the letter aside and turned to face her visitor.

"Sebastian?"

His expression was severe, a far cry from the carefree young man she had once known. But then, Harriet supposed, she had given him no reason to greet her with the affinity he had once displayed in Wiltshire all those years ago.

Her stomach tightened as she recalled the egregious lie she had told him the day before—a man who had never wronged her. A lie that had left her staring at the sought-after painting half the night, endlessly debating the ethics of her deceit and the burden of her guilt until she had fallen asleep in her chair. She lifted a hand to rub discreetly at her stiff neck, still protesting such ill-advised sleeping habits.

"That girl, Jem, told me to show myself in," he said, his tone flat and unyielding. It took all the dignity Harriet possessed not to cringe at Sebastian's skeptical announcement. Her little staff were hardworking, but unaccustomed to the ways of aristocratic households. Until now, it had seemed somewhat irrelevant to address Mrs. Finch's or Jem's lack of etiquette. She had simply been trying to pull a new staff together. After all, she had not received any callers at her townhouse since—Harriet paused to calculate—late August. Perhaps it was time to have a word with Mrs. Finch about the formalities of receiving callers.

From across the room, Evaline cleared her throat, setting her needlework aside as she rose gracefully to her feet.

"I shall organize some tea, shall I?"

It was, of course, a rhetorical question.

Evaline could have easily rung the nearby bell, yet instead, she swept from the room with elegant composure, leaving Harriet and Sebastian in private as he stepped out of her way. Harriet fortified her nerves as she and Sebastian both watched her graceful departure, he having stepped fully into the painted room to clear the exit.

Swallowing hard, Harriet pinned a friendly smile to her face, though her instinct was to run after Evaline and avoid this encounter entirely. Her heart pounded in her chest at the sight of his grim—but beloved—countenance.

"Will we get tea?"

Sebastian's voice held a glimmer of humor, his facial features softening slightly as he turned back to her.

"I would not count on it," Harriet replied, allowing a twist of her lips that might pass for a smile. "I believe Lady Wood is allowing us our privacy."

He gave a brief smile of acknowledgment, as if she had confirmed his suspicions. "Is Lady Wood in residence?"

Harriet bobbed her head in affirmation. "She is a permanent houseguest. Her presence has been quite a boon to me. I … recently made some changes, and Evaline has been assisting me with the repercussions."

Sebastian's brows drew together, a flicker of curiosity crossing his features. Yet he did not comment on her strange declaration. Instead, he stepped farther into the room and, with a subtle gesture toward an armchair, asked, "May I?"

Harriet nodded before lowering herself onto her gilt-framed settee. She knew the seat highlighted her to the best advantage—the light from the window illuminating her to perfection, while the luxurious backdrop of the painted room framed her with fine art. It should have made her feel confident to be viewed in this exact spot. But instead, she felt frivolous for having designed a room for such a purpose. Sebastian was far too intuitive—both about her character and artistry in general—to miss the intention behind her placement.

Quelling the urge to fidget, she waited with the air of someone who had all the time in the world, though her racing pulse betrayed her carefully constructed composure. But then, he caught her attention, and her own vanities were forgotten.

His blond hair fell loosely around his face, like the mane of a proud jungle cat. His square face, bronzed by foreign suns, seemed somehow harsher than she remembered. The slash of a smile revealed white teeth as he contemplated her with an expression of mild fondness—a look that unsettled her far more than a glare would have.

His long, hard frame remained in excellent condition after all these years—broad shoulders tapering to narrow hips—yet there were differences now. His legs were more muscular, hugged by form-fitting buckskins. And his style of dress had shifted. Gone were the rigid restraints of English nobility. Instead, his white linen shirt billowed slightly, his cravat loosely tied in a knot she did not recognize. Overall, he had the appearance of a man who had pursued the Grand Masters of the Continent—and been changed by them.

"It occurred to me that I was not particularly friendly when I called on you yesterday." Sebastian's deep voice was softer now, though it conveyed an intensity that made Harriet's breath catch. "Seeing you after all these years … It took all my nerve to visit the girl I admired so ardently as a young man."

The admission did unexpected things to Harriet's equilibrium. Her stomach tightened; her hands grew restless in her lap. But most troubling was the sharp spike of guilt, a reminder of the lie she had told him. That wretched painting. Those planks of wood covered in oil paint, the brushstrokes of a skilled artist—they meant more to her than she cared to admit to anyone. Even Sebastian. Especially Sebastian.

"It … was unnerving for me too," she finally managed, offering a peaceable response after her dismissive words the day before. "I was quite alarmed when Evaline told me of your visit. The … timing of it was …" Harriet's mind wandered to the strange events of the past few months and to the sudden reappearance of the only person she had truly held dear.

If only she had realized the mistake she had been making all those years ago. If only she had eloped with him to Calais. Surely, she would not now be seeking redemption for the past five years. Years spent in the high-society prison of her own making. Her soul would still be intact, not broken into so many pieces that she no longer knew if they could ever be gathered again.

"… serendipitous," she finished weakly, realizing that Sebastian had raised a quizzical eyebrow when she had failed to complete the sentence.

What would it be like to turn back the clock?

To be married now to the handsome gentleman seated across from her. Would they have had babes of their own by now? The mere thought of it made her eyes burn with unshed tears.

His arrival felt like fate toying with her for its own secretive amusements. Six months ago, she might have laughed it off, reaching for a bottle of wine to dull the ache. But now—now, when she was attempting to change the course of her life, when her emotions lay raw and her sobriety was so vital … It seemed as though the gods themselves had chosen to mock her, presenting her with a tantalizing glimpse of what could have been. She could almost hear them sneering from their lofty perch: *See here, Harriet! See what you missed out on, you foolish girl!*

Sebastian's face broke into a devastating grin, and Harriet had to fight the urge to clap a hand over her heart, which had lurched painfully in her chest.

"Serendipitous?" His voice held a teasing note. "You

mean, of things that are serendipity? You still remember that?"

Harriet blinked, struggling to recover her wits as she considered what he had just asked. "The anecdote you told ... of the writer Horace Walpole?" Her voice remained steady, though it took all the courage she possessed to continue. "That he shared his coined word with his cronies at his literary clubs, your great-uncle included, in reference to the Persian tale, *The Three Princes of Serendip*? There is little I have forgotten of our time together."

It cost her dearly to make such an admission. After so many years of glib nonchalance, it was almost painful to allow even a hint of her younger, more candid self to resurface. But she supposed she owed him at least a modicum of honesty, especially after pretending his gift had been of so little import just the day before.

"Serendipitous," Sebastian repeated the word, his tone thoughtful, as if experimenting with its new form. "Walpole himself would be envious he did not think to use it in that manner."

There it was—a hint of appreciation in his expression.

Harriet watched him carefully and guessed the hurt she had inflicted yesterday had now been undone. A relief, because there was no possibility she would relinquish her most prized possession, not even to make amends.

If she gave up the painting, she feared the last splinters of her soul would be scattered beyond redemption. Anything good she had done in the past five years—every sign she still possessed a heart—had been because of that painting. It represented reflection, remorse, and an iota of hope that she was not entirely lost, arriving during her darkest hours after she had wed a man as old as time himself, and it had served as salvation from the endless despair of not having accompanied the man she loved.

The mere knowledge that he still existed somewhere out in the world, that he still thought of her with any fondness after all that had transpired, meant more than she could ever confess to another living soul. It was all she had left of … them.

Her lips curled in response, though she struggled between joy and melancholy at being near him after so long apart.

"The thing is, Harry, it turns out the painting was done by my partner's ancestor. The only painting we know of by Matteo di Bianchi, and Lorenzo is quite frantic to obtain it," Sebastian declared.

But Harriet barely heard him. Her attention was fixed—utterly and completely—on a single word. *Harry.* No one had called her that since him. Surely it meant that he still held some fondness for their shared youth?

She was overpowered by memories. Walking through the woods at Avonmead. Exploring the great library within its walls. Routing through the treasure trove of art stored within the attics—paintings of far-off places, dreams captured in oil and canvas.

Spending time with Sebastian had been the happiest moments of her youth. Of her entire life. Why were the gods so cruel as to visit him upon her now?

And then it struck her—an overwhelming desire to experience it all again. To recapture even a moment of the girl she had been, racing about Wiltshire with Sebastian at her side. A time when she had truly believed that one day they would marry and then every moment would be the happiest of her life.

Sebastian rolled his shoulders, his expression clouded with concern, as though he were waiting for her to speak. When Harriet continued to stare back at him, caught in the maelstrom of her memories, he pressed on.

"Could you tell me whom you gave the painting to?"

Harriet tilted her head, the question pulling her back from the past. She went over his last words in her mind, gathering the threads of their conversation once more: *"... Harry ... the painting was done by my partner's ancestor ... only painting we know of ... quite frantic to obtain it."*

The implication struck her. The painting must hold great value. He was determined to reclaim it.

And now—now, Harriet found herself equally determined. Determined to grasp even a glimmer of the joy she had once felt in his company.

"Do you recall whom you gave it to?"

Her scattered thoughts coalesced into a single, bright, resolute purpose. A decision. There would be hell to pay when her Mentor learned of her manipulations, but she could not allow this opportunity to slip through her fingers.

"I do."

Sebastian leaned forward, his movement drawing the navy wool of his coat taut over his broad shoulders. The motion caught Harriet's gaze, as she drank in the masculine form that made all other men seem pale by comparison.

"Who is it, then?"

Harriet's mind raced, calculating how best to present her proposal. Bluntness, she decided. It would have to be bluntness.

* * *

HE WAITED for her to speak, watching as her expression shifted, her face settling into soft, resolute lines.

A premonition stirred within him, as though destiny itself was striking, poised to alter the course of both their lives.

"I will tell you where the painting is—if you court me for the holidays."

Sebastian jerked back in surprise, the back of his skull knocking against the padded chair.

For a moment, he was painfully aware that his jaw hung open, yet he could not recall how to close it.

"Wh … I … you …"

He drew a deep breath, gathering his scattered wits. "I cannot wed you for a painting."

Harriet broke into a giggle, the sound so light and unexpected that it left him more unmoored than her proposal.

"A wedding? For a painting?" she echoed, her lips curling in amusement. "No. I only wish for a courtship. Just a couple of weeks."

She paused, her tongue flicking out to wet her lips, a gesture that drew his gaze before he dragged it back to her face. As though she needed a moment to gather her thoughts, she finally continued. "I am staying in Town for the holidays, and it is all rather depressing, would you not know it? I thought … perhaps I would like to recapture the magic of our youth." Her voice softened, tinged with vulnerability. "Before you return to Italy. You are returning to Italy, are you not?"

Sebastian nodded. "I am." He wondered if he should pinch himself to confirm whether he was truly awake or trapped in some impossible dream.

"Right." Harriet's voice was steady now, her posture poised, and there was a determined tilt to her chin that made him sit up a little straighter. "So, court me until Christmas Day, and I will inform you who currently possesses the painting."

He sat back, stunned by the request. Court her? The thought echoed in his mind, refusing to settle.

Harriet—Harry—had drawn herself up, shoulders back, her expression fixed with a familiar stubbornness that he remembered all too well. She was prepared to be obstinate, and when Harriet made up her mind, she was a force no man could easily redirect. Still … she wished him to court her?

This was an unexpected revelation. He supposed he should feel vindicated, learning that she regretted the past as much as he did. That she, too, had wondered, as often and as painfully, what might have been if things had turned out differently.

But why now?

Pondering, he searched for any ulterior motive behind such a request. Could it be that she was simply bored? Or perhaps despondent during the holidays and wished for a bit of diversion? Perhaps she had no current paramour to liven up the season? The mere notion of her with a lover troubled him more than he cared to admit.

"I am not willing to conduct an affair, Harry."

Her face fell slightly, her light dimming to be replaced by an emotion he could not quite place.

"Have you not heard?" A faint smile touched her lips, though it lacked warmth. "Lady Slight no longer has affairs, darling. She has become quite a bore in recent months."

Sebastian lifted a hand, rubbing it across his face as he tried to make sense of it all.

No longer has affairs?

He remembered her mention of recent changes, but he had not grasped what she meant. Had she truly dismissed her paramours?

By choice? Or necessity?

His thoughts drifted briefly to the odd collection of servants he had encountered in her home. Could it be that she had lost favor with the *ton*? Perhaps her servants had deserted her, eager to avoid being tarnished by the same brush of mysterious scandal that now plagued their mistress.

But no, Sebastian had maintained correspondence with

numerous members of the *beau monde*, and no whispers of scandal had reached him.

Then what has changed?

The question gnawed at him as he collected his thoughts.

"You wish me to … what? Share the holidays with you until Christmas, and then you will tell me where the painting is?"

Harriet's smile widened once more, and for a moment, Sebastian felt a quiver of relief at seeing her good spirits return.

"Precisely."

Yet even as the word left her lips, Sebastian sensed something was off. Beneath the sparkling facade, Harry was hiding something. He recognized the signs—the same air of pretense she had worn the last time they had met. That last time together when, she had pretended she would leave for Italy with him.

But after so many years apart, he no longer knew her well enough to discern what she was truly about. So, perhaps the best method of uncovering the truth was to spend time in her company in order to ferret out her secrets.

And retrieve the painting on Lorenzo's behalf.

Yet another thought tickled the edges of his mind. Perhaps the best way to close the book on their past was to spend these weeks together before bidding her a proper farewell.

What was it Marco had said at the breakfast table? *"We cannot give up on the future when it has so much more to offer than the past."*

Perhaps a couple of weeks in her company would be enough. Enough to lay the past to rest. Enough to finally let the memories go.

"All right. What does it entail?"

Sebastian left Harriet's townhouse with plans arranged

for the morning. Despite the bizarre nature of their agreement, he found—much to his surprise—that he felt lighter than he had since first reading Matteo's letter to his sister so many months ago.

Progress.

Lorenzo would be pleased that progress had been made. And Sebastian would observe Harriet—see her as she was now. And he would come to understand that it had been preordained they remain apart. Even grow relieved, perhaps, that he had never tied the knot with the young Harry who was now the Widow Slight. When he witnessed her perfidious nature firsthand, not through the letters of friends, but from his own vantage, his heart would mend, and he would be free to build a new future of his own choosing.

Yet as he climbed into the waiting carriage, settling into the squabs, a thought came unbidden: *What if she is not the woman they say she is? What if she never was?*

When the carriage finally came to a stop in front of the Scotts' small Town estate, Sebastian was no more settled on the bargain he had struck or Harriet's true nature. Despite her naysayers, Sebastian had always seen her potential. Seen into the heart of her. But perhaps he had been a besotted youth, too blinded by passion to see clearly. Or perhaps it was as he had told his brother—Harriet had never had the opportunity to prove she could reject her father's influence to carve her own path.

Shaking his head to clear his conflicting thoughts, he entered the house and made for the library where Lorenzo was certain to be awaiting his arrival.

His friend was at a library table with a stack of history books about the Tudor period. Lorenzo had been combing through them for days in an attempt to understand the British world of three hundred years ago. He looked up, his lean face strained as he greeted Sebastian.

"Did the widow tell you where the painting is?"

A twinge of worry pestered Sebastian as he tried to calculate the best way to answer. Lorenzo had grown ever more frantic regarding his quest to carve out a name for the unrecognized Matteo as a great Master of the Renaissance, and Sebastian was not sure how he would take the news that there was yet another delay.

"Lady Slight knows who has it, but she will not inform me until I fulfill a request."

Lorenzo frowned, pushing back a lock of jet-black hair as he slumped back in his seat. "A request?"

Sebastian cleared his throat, feeling deuced uncomfortable as he tried to think how to explain his unusual bargain with Harriet.

"I am to spend time in her company until Christmas."

Lorenzo's face fell, unexpectedly sympathetic. The Italian was single-minded in his quest, not often taking the time to notice what troubles others were contending with.

"I am sorry, Sebastian. I know you are reluctant to revisit the past."

Sebastian nearly burst out laughing. "You assume I agreed."

Lorenzo straightened in alarm. "Did you not?"

"Of course I agreed."

His friend exhaled in relief. "Just so. I knew you would not let me down."

Sebastian crossed the room, taking a seat across the table to wave at the books.

"Did you find anything illuminating?"

"I found your British history is bloody and complicated," Lorenzo replied in a frustrated tone. "Other than that, tell me about the painting again."

Sebastian leaned back to think, as if they had not discussed this a thousand times. Lorenzo's mission to uncover Matteo's body of work was why they were in England.

"It references an Arthurian legend."

"And your King Henry believed he was somehow linked to this King Arthur?"

"Yes, but the subject must be symbolic," Sebastian began. "Matteo worked in the workshops of Botticelli, so he would have had a rich understanding of metaphor. When Botticelli wished to depict the enlightenment of the Renaissance, he chose to paint Spring—a celebration of rebirth, knowledge, and beauty. At the center stands Venus, the goddess of love and harmony, but he was a religious man who did not believe in Roman gods, so she represented not mere romantic love, but the elevation of the soul through reason and beauty— hallmarks of Renaissance ideals."

Pausing, Sebastian allowed a smile to curl at the edge of his mouth as he recalled the beauty of the piece. "It is a scene rich in allegory. Botticelli did not simply paint springtime. He painted the awakening of man's spirit, the harmonious blending of earthly pleasures with intellectual pursuits. *La Primavera* is not only a tribute to nature's renewal but to the rebirth of thought, art, and philosophy that defined the Renaissance. Which to my mind means that Matteo's choice of Arthurian mythology had little to do with his message, if there was any message at all and he was not just pursuing a whimsy."

Lorenzo straightened in protest, his face contorting in the stubborn lines he was infamous for.

"There is a message," he insisted, his voice taut with conviction. "You always dismiss this too easily, Sebastian. But you forget, Matteo worked with da Vinci after Botticelli closed his workshop. And da Vinci was fanatical about secrets."

Sebastian studied Lorenzo with a faint smile. "Ah, yes.

The ever-elusive da Vinci. Genius, certainly, but prone to seeing mysteries where none were intended."

"You underestimate him. He hid knowledge—scientific, political, personal—because he understood its power. You really think Matteo spent time in da Vinci's workshop without learning how to bury meaning beneath the obvious?"

"He learned symbolism from Botticelli," Sebastian replied evenly. "Take *La Primavera*, a painting steeped in allegory, representing enlightenment and humanist ideals. Matteo would have understood the art of metaphor well enough. But that does not mean that this painting hides some grand secret."

Lorenzo gave a sharp laugh, without mirth. "But this is not Florence, Sebastian. It is England. And Matteo painted it after his time with da Vinci—after he came here, of all places, with this British society as his patrons." He leaned forward, eyes glinting with the familiar intensity that had dragged them both across half of Europe. "England, under Henry the Eighth. A king obsessed with Arthurian legend. Henry believed he was Arthur reborn—the destined ruler to unite Britain and restore a golden age. The Winchester Round Table, repainted with Henry's own face at its head. Everything Henry did dripped with Arthurian symbolism."

"Coincidence," Sebastian said, but his tone lacked its usual certainty.

"Coincidence?" Lorenzo scoffed. "Arthurian legend, secrecy, da Vinci's influence—do you truly believe Matteo would paint such things without purpose? He came to England for a reason. And that reason is tied to Henry's obsession. This painting references Arthur, which must mean the *Regis Aeterni* was linked to your monarch. Perhaps they even instigated or encouraged his obsession so he would ascend to religious leader of England. You know it."

Sebastian glanced back at the pile of books, his brow furrowed. "And you truly believe Matteo buried a clue?"

"I think he wrote to his sister and mentioned that painting as a signal. This secret society, *Regis Aeterni*, brought him to England, for whom he painted for decades, yet he left not a single known work of art until you found your painting in the attic of your ducal home. Matteo wrote of the painting and the duke to point the way to his body of work, and when we finally find that body of work, we will claim Matteo's rightful place in history as one of the greatest artists to ever live!"

Sebastian admired the tenacious nature of his friend. He did not know what they would find when they finally retrieved the painting, but he hoped that one way or the other, finding it would bring peace to Lorenzo and his family who had pursued this mystery for three centuries.

The painting in question had moved Sebastian, made him feel things that no other art had done until he had reached Florence and beheld the work of Botticelli, da Vinci, Michelangelo, and the other Masters. If he had not witnessed the splendor of Matteo's work firsthand, he might dissuade Lorenzo from his crusade with more persistence.

However, having seen the delicate brushstrokes himself, Sebastian knew it could be argued that Matteo was indeed fitting company for the most talented artists to have walked the earth. He owed it to his friend to help solve the mystery of Matteo's journey to England and his subsequent disappearance.

CHAPTER 4

Two brilliant sapphires are your eyes,
Reflecting light from azure skies;
No gem on earth can e'er outshine
The radiant glow that in them lies.

The New Ladies' Valentine Writer (1821)

* * *

DECEMBER 11, 1821

*T*he cold air bit at Sebastian's face as he stepped down, the sleek black carriage bearing the Scott family's crest gleaming in the pale winter sun as he came to a stop in front of Harriet's door. Her townhouse stood dignified and immaculate, though he wondered if its façade masked deeper unrest. Her cryptic remarks about changes she had wrought remained unexplained, but he did not know how to ask her about them. He adjusted his gloves, pausing to steel his expression, uncertain what the day would bring.

A couple of weeks in her company.

Then the painting.

Then closure.

The door swung open before he could knock. Mrs. Finch, the housekeeper, barely spared him a glance.

"Lord Sebastian."

"Mrs. Finch." He inclined his head.

The painted room remained as he remembered—elegant, curated, designed to highlight Harriet's beauty. His fingers brushed the back of a gilt chair that made him think of a similar one at Avonmead she had liked to pose on—laughing, confident, always the center of attention. Yet when she entered the room at last, Sebastian's breath caught.

Harriet entered with regal poise, draped in a deep blue pelisse trimmed with white fur, a matching bonnet framing her silky auburn hair. Her gloved hand rested lightly on the doorframe as she beamed with restrained joy. Harriet was a woman in her prime, possessing the confidence of a viscountess who had ascended the ranks of the noble classes to carve out her niche as a well-admired beauty, and Sebastian had never seen her more ravishing than this.

"Good morning," she greeted.

"You look well."

The words escaped before he could stop them, and his cheeks spread in a grin wider than was proper, but he was not of the stilted upper classes any longer. He was struck by how fetching she was in the colors that accentuated her curvaceous form. Even in her youth, she had an impressive bosom that had caused many a sweat-soaked dream for Sebastian in his youth.

But Sebastian fixed on her face, quelling any urge to caress her with his passionate gaze. The throbbing wounds of the past receded in the presence of such feminine perfection to leave him wondering … if he had not been a spare all those years ago —but a man in his own right as he was now, a man who had made his own fortune—how different would their circumstances be? Would she have had the courage to walk away from society's expectations? From her father's expectations?

"Do I?" Her brow arched. Playful, but cautious.

Before the tension could thicken further, Lady Evaline Wood appeared, swathed in dove-gray wool. "I believe we are ready?"

Sebastian escorted them to the vehicle, handing Harriet into the carriage with practiced ease, with Lady Wood following close behind. Taking his place across from Harriet, he found his gaze resting on her as she peered out the window at the world passing by. As the wheels rolled toward the museum, he could not help but wonder—was this truly just a courtship of convenience, or had fate offered them a final chance at something far more dangerous?

He could feel the risk even now, the urge to forget everything that had happened and discover if they were still as compatible as they had been back then.

Be careful, Sebastian. You have been misled before.

It was a much-needed reminder as the carriage wheels rumbled over stone-paved streets.

Harriet's gaze remained on the window. "It feels an age since I last visited the British Museum."

Sebastian observed her profile. "You enjoyed it once. I recollect an enthusiastic dissertation when you regaled me about your visit."

A faint smile. "I enjoyed many things once."

A pause. The atmosphere thickened with unspoken memories—walks at Avonmead, shared dreams of travel, whispers in candlelit libraries.

"Perhaps you will enjoy it again," he said softly.

Her gaze met his, sharp and searching. "Perhaps."

Soon the British Museum loomed, a temple of knowledge, its imposing facade softened by the low winter sun. Sebastian experienced a stirring of his first visit, how exciting it had been to enter its doors.

Inside, the air smelled of old parchment, polished wood, and the faint chill of stone floors. The soft murmur of scholars and curious visitors echoed through the halls, and Harriet's face brightened with genuine interest, Sebastian noticed, when they came to a stop within its hallowed halls.

"Shall we begin with the Egyptian Room?" he suggested.

"Naturally," Harriet replied. "Mysteries awaiting discovery … how appropriate."

The Egyptian Room greeted them with rows of ancient statues, stone tablets adorned with symbols, and intricately carved amulets. The air was tinged with dust and age. Harriet stopped before the Rosetta Stone, her gloved fingers hovering just above the glass case. Sebastian himself was awestruck to behold it once more; arguably the most famous artifact in the entire building, it had drawn crowds for two decades.

"The key to an entire civilization." Her voice softened. "One stone, unlocking so many secrets."

She inspected it closely, and Sebastian was reminded of the discernment of her painted room. Harriet had always been a connoisseur of art, it being one of the many interests they had in common. If only he had such a key to decipher this woman of secrets who had entangled his thoughts these many years.

Sebastian stepped beside her. "Do you believe some mysteries should remain unsolved?"

Harriet turned to him, lips curving into a knowing smile.

"No. Not anymore. Understanding the truth, even when uncomfortable, has value."

Their gazes held.

Was she speaking of more than hieroglyphs?

Sebastian felt the familiar tug of longing. As he had feared, proximity to Harriet could lead to fresh wounds if he did not practice caution. He might have the experience of more years, but the truth was that Harriet seemed more compelling than ever.

"Perhaps," he murmured, "we are not always prepared for what we discover."

The Mummies Room was quieter. Heavy sarcophagi lay open, revealing linen-wrapped remains. The scent of resins and faded incense lingered. Harriet approached a glass case where a mummy's delicate fingers peeked from its wrappings. She leaned closer. Sebastian stepped beside her, barely inches away. Their shoulders brushed.

"Do you suppose they feared being forgotten?" Harriet asked.

"Perhaps," he said, his voice low. "But they ensured they would be remembered. Even in death."

Their closeness did not escape him. Propriety be damned, this moment felt intimate in a way no ballroom ever had. One thing was certain—Harriet need never fear being forgotten. Not by him. The scent of her fragranced hair spread upon his sheets haunted him to this day. Those stolen moments on that fateful Valentine's Day had been the sweetest he had ever grasped. But followed by the worst, he reminded himself sternly, when she had failed to arrive the next morning at their designated point.

It took resolve to remind himself because it was difficult to think of anything but how heavenly the scent of her hair was even now, as he caught just a trace of it in the muted air when she turned away to smile at their chaperon.

Next, they visited the Greek and Roman collections where the Townley Venus stood tall in the Sculpture Room, marble pale and gleaming beneath the filtered daylight. Harriet once again took the lead, approaching slowly. Her gown hugged the sweet curves of her womanly form as she strolled ahead of him, stopping to tilt her head back and revealing the creamy column of her slender neck.

"Venus, the goddess of love. Yet, her face is inscrutable."

Sebastian stood beside her, his focus on the statue. "Perhaps she trusts few with her secrets."

Harriet turned to him, contemplating him for several seconds before she finally responded. "Do you believe trust is given or earned?"

Sebastian's gaze did not waver. "I believe it is broken far too easily."

The unspoken words—the past betrayal—hung between them. Harriet looked away first, and Sebastian was unsure if he should be relieved or ashamed of the bitter reference to the day she had left him waiting like a fool. It was disorienting to have his thoughts swivel back and forth between what could have been, what could be, and the proven hazards of allowing his guard to drop.

The sound of their footfalls echoed through mostly empty halls as they reached the fragments of the Elgin Marbles. Grand and stark, its horsemen, gods, and mortals were frozen in stone.

Sebastian gestured toward a frieze of horsemen. "The power captured here—it is almost alive."

Harriet stood beside him, her gloved hand brushing the display's edge. "The riders trust their horses completely. A partnership without words."

Sebastian looked at her. "Do you still believe such bonds are possible?"

Her lashes fluttered. "I want to."

The simplicity of her words shook him more than any argument. It made him think again of her cryptic remarks. What changes had she made these past few months? Was she being honest when she said she no longer entertained men, or had she said what she thought he wanted to hear? The problem in dealing with Harriet, even in their youth, had been the Hargreaves's malleable sense of truth that made it difficult to assess any member of the illustrious but warped family. It was one of the reasons he could not convince Philip to wield his power as duke so that Sebastian might have courted her.

And, for a second, Sebastian froze—much as the subjects depicted in the Marbles—when he was struck with a revelation. He was glad he had left British high society behind!

In Florence, he had found an entirely new life, a fulfilling one in the pursuit of art. If Philip had helped him formally court Harriet all those years ago, he would never have left on his Grand Tour. Never have met Lorenzo or Marco and Angelo Scott or any of his friends back in Italy. Nor built his thriving business with Lorenzo.

It was regrettable that Harriet had not the courage to accompany him, but perhaps his continued anger at his older brother was something to let go. Perhaps his grievance with Harriet was theirs alone, and it was time to stop blaming the duke for his unwillingness to assist. Sebastian exhaled, releasing much of his pent-up resentments. Marco had been correct—facing the past would allow him to build a better future.

As he came back to the present, he found Harriet with an eyebrow arched as if she was awaiting a reply. Running a hand through his mane of hair, Sebastian smiled politely, still shaken by the understanding that he had to leave Britain when he had. Had to explore the exotic locations that had beckoned. Had to arrive in Italy. It had all been a vital part of his journey.

"I beg your pardon, what did you say?"

"Shall we go to the Reading Room?" she repeated, her expression curious.

He gave a quick bow in agreement, offering her his arm while Lady Wood returned from where she had been examining the truncated carving of a goddess in motion.

The Reading Room was hushed, winter light shining through tall windows. The scent of old paper and wax filled the air. Harriet trailed her fingers along the spines of leather-bound books, her tone wistful when she eventually spoke.

"Do you remember Avonmead's library?"

Sebastian followed her. "I do. You always wanted to read everything."

Harriet smiled faintly. "Because you promised we would see the world."

Sebastian licked his lips. He did not wish to say it, but it hovered on the tip of his tongue until he could no longer stop himself.

"And yet, you did not come." The words slipped from him, sharper than intended.

Harriet turned, her countenance clouding with regret and things unsaid. She hesitated, then made a confession he was not expecting to hear her say aloud. "Because I was afraid."

The silence pressed in.

"Of what?" he asked.

"Of losing everything I thought I wanted." She exhaled shakily. "I did not understand then what truly mattered."

Sebastian stepped closer. "And now?"

Their gazes locked, so close, but Lady Wood's polite cough from the doorway reminded them of the world beyond their moment.

And when he looked back, he knew that moment had passed. Harriet's shields were back, the enigma of her a puzzle without a solution, and Sebastian knew it was safer for him to step back from the yawning abyss of what could have been if only she had had the courage to trust him so many years ago.

As the museum visit drew to a close, they strolled out to wait for his carriage to be brought around. Standing in an amicable silence, Sebastian looked about and thought how fortuitous it was that most of polite society had left Town for the holidays. A chance encounter would have interrupted what had been a very pleasant time, even started tongues wagging. Sometime in the near future he would leave, and being the subject of gossip would not signify then, but it was better to just savor this rite of passage without distraction.

These two weeks would serve as the farewell he had never had with the girl he had loved. So that when he left these English shores, he would finally leave the past behind, free to explore new avenues.

They drove through London, briefly making plans for their next outing, until reaching her street. Sebastian helped the ladies out and escorted them to the front door. Harriet turned as she reached it, glancing back at him with an expression of gratitude. The first of such that he could recollect.

"Thank you for today. It was … enlightening."

Sebastian smiled faintly. "Sometimes, the past has lessons for the present."

Harriet stepped inside, her gaze lingering on him. "And sometimes the present offers a chance to rewrite the past."

The door closed, leaving Sebastian with her words echoing in his mind.

* * *

"IF THE *TON* could see me now."

Harriet surveyed the basement-level dressing room, resisting the urge to groan aloud. Dimly lit by a single high-set window, the room bore no resemblance to the elegant chambers she commanded abovestairs. The walls of the hitherto unused closet, once cream, were now faded and blotched, and the air carried a faint scent of damp stone.

A copper tub, recently dragged down from her bedchambers, occupied a corner, its once-bright surface dulled in the muted light. Against the far wall, a clothing rack sagged under the weight of carefully chosen garments, mostly gowns and petticoats, a far cry from the extensive wardrobe Harriet should be enjoying upstairs. It was a mere two stories away, but due to the limited space, she had had to select what came belowstairs with careful thought.

Evaline, perched on a narrow bench, lifted a brow. "You look as though you mean to storm the battlefield, not change for an outing."

"Battlefield, indeed." Harriet gestured broadly. "Behold, my war room: a tub I cannot fill, a wardrobe I cannot manage, and not a single competent lady's maid in sight."

The copper tub, Harriet noted sourly, had become a mockery of her situation.

"Do you know," she began, waving a hand at the tub, "it took Mrs. Finch and poor Jem nearly an hour to drag this monstrosity down here? All because I have no footmen to haul hot water up two flights of stairs quickly enough before it cools down. A lady of my standing, forced to bathe like a scullery maid!"

Evaline gave her a sympathetic glance. "Well, it is a fine tub. Stately, almost. Like its owner."

"Ha! Stately? It mocked me daily. Sitting there, empty and gleaming, reminding me that I cannot even summon enough hot water for a proper soak."

"Perhaps you might consider cold baths?"

"Cold? Have you lost your mind? I would sooner spend time with the Boyles."

Harriet shook her head in disgust at the mere thought of the silly noble family on the next street. She had recently been stuck in a dinner seated next to Lord Boyle who liked to woefully whine about trivial matters. Not that he was as trying as his bacon-brained wife who perpetually spouted vulgar tongue she confused for fashionable colloquialisms— much to the lip-quivering amusement of the other dinner guests.

What was it Lady Boyle had said?

Something about how the Boyles had recently held a dinner with several bachelors, so she supposed they had provided bachelor fare. Everyone present, other than the Boyles themselves, had experienced a sudden need to dab their mouths with their napkins lest they burst into gales of incredulous laughter. One had to assume Lady Boyle was unaware of the true meaning of her words because mentioning doxies in polite company was simply not the done thing.

Harriet turned her attention to the clothing rack, which sagged under a small selection of gowns—muted greens, dark blues, and ivory. Her silks and satins looked dreary in the terrible light. The bright colors of her former wardrobe had been packed away, cut too low for her current require-ments, replaced by more elegant tones better suited for her new life.

"Do you see this?" Harriet pointed at the rack. "Reduced to appropriate clothing. How far I have fallen."

"It is practical for visiting Miss Cooper." Evaline's tone was mild. "And you did say you wished for new beginnings."

"New beginnings, yes. But must they be so missish?"

Harriet lifted a gown of powder-blue muslin. "This has all the excitement of tepid tea."

"You chose it."

"Under duress."

Evaline tilted her head. "I prefer this new you. I think you look lovely, and it puts focus on your personality rather than … than …" Evaline's fair face turned scarlet as she painted herself into a corner.

Harriet chuckled at her friend's mortification. "My diddeys?"

Her friend blushed anew, her creamy skin turning to blazing red at Harriet's crude choice of words.

"Just so."

They both giggled.

Then Harriet spun on her heel, stalking the two steps needed to cross the room and flopping down onto the bench. She gestured dramatically at the copper tub.

"Bah! I have not had a proper bath in weeks. Weeks! Do you know why?"

"The lack of footmen, I presume?"

"Precisely. How am I expected to maintain the refinement of an important viscountess when I am forced to wash in the basement like a maid?"

"You did decide to move it here so that you could access your hot baths once more," Evaline said with a pointed look. "And you could hire footmen."

"Ah, yes. Footmen. I suppose that it is time to reintroduce men into the household, but I think that any of the male persuasion who are hired must be mild-mannered enough not to frighten our delicate staff."

Evaline huffed in humor. "Given their fragile dispositions, we shall need footmen with the temperament of lambs."

"And the strength of dockworkers so that I may return to dressing in my own bedchambers." Harriet sighed. "I shall summon Mr. Benton tomorrow. A lady's maid and at least one suitably meek footman. I refuse to live like this any longer."

She peered down at the prison of her pelisse. Life had been much simpler with a full complement of staff. But back in August, when she had begun to make changes to her life, it had quickly become clear that her father had corrupted too many of her servants into reporting back to him. Fearing his interference, Harriet had been forced to release them all—with references.

All except Cook, who was trustworthy, or at least she hoped so. Cook was her last remaining luxury until she finished rebuilding her household, and Harriet was not letting the old woman go. Cook was all that stood between her and a digestive complaint.

"I swear, I shall never wear this blasted pelisse again. It has a thousand tiny, cloth-covered buttons."

Evaline removed her gloves with practiced ease before setting them aside on a washstand. "It did not look so troublesome when you put it on."

"Because I had the illusion of purpose then," Harriet groaned, tugging at the fitted pelisse that clung to her shoulders. "Now, it is a cage. Help me out of it before I lose what little patience I have left."

"Arms up."

"They are up," Harriet snapped. "The pelisse is simply refusing to yield."

Evaline tugged. The garment, snug-fitting and stubborn, refused to budge.

"You must relax your shoulders."

"I am relaxed. You are pulling like you intend to detach my arms entirely!"

"It is caught on the back seams. Hold still."

With a sharp yank, the pelisse gave way, sending Evaline stumbling backward and Harriet spinning to grip the bench for balance.

"Victory," Evaline declared, holding the garment aloft like a prize.

"Victory?" Harriet gasped. "I nearly perished in the attempt!"

Sitting down, she began to tug on the next resistive item.

"These cursed boots," Harriet muttered, propping one leg onto the bench. "Evaline, you must pull."

"I should never have agreed to this."

"And yet you did. Now pull!"

With a great heave, the boot came free, sending Evaline toppling backward into the copper tub with a resounding clang.

"Oh, heavens!" Harriet cried, covering her mouth. "Evaline, are you well?"

Evaline sat in the tub, hair askew, an expression of calm resignation on her face. "Remind me again why we have no lady's maid to do for us?"

Harriet sank onto the bench, laughing until tears welled.

"Because I am a fool. A complete and utter fool." Then she sobered, rising to go stand beside the tub. "But mostly, because I must make sure it is a woman whom Bertram Hargreaves cannot persuade to spy on me. My father is a snake, but he can be most seductive when he wishes to be."

"Then we shall struggle on, doing for each other," Evaline replied as she climbed back out of the tub with Harriet's assistance. "I, of course, am in no position to make demands when you have done so much for me, but I hate to see you frustrated with my novice skills." Evaline lifted the dark blue walking gown from the rack—simple but elegant, with a high bodice, long sleeves, and modest embroidery at the cuffs.

Harriet turned around to contemplate her friend. "You are a valued friend, Evaline. Having you as a guest helps me just as much as it helps you. You need not feel timid about making demands."

Evaline smiled, returning to her side. "Thank you … for everything."

Harriet reached out, wrapping her arms around her guest's delicate frame. "You are most welcome. I am pleased to offer you my address on a prestigious street and access to my motley crew of servants, for what they are worth. It is not right that your late husband's family is withholding your stipend."

"My solicitors assure me it will be resolved soon, but you bought me much-needed time to sort it out."

"Not at all … I hope you will remain in residence even then. I need the company, and this house is far too large for one lonely widow. Your funds will stretch further without the cost of high rent and a staff."

Evaline dropped her head in affection against Harriet's shoulder, being inches shorter. "Thank you."

Her voice was suspiciously thick, and Harriet had to discreetly lift a hand to swipe at her own moistened lashes. Stepping back, Harriet turned around again to finish the torture of changing. Next came the petticoats, two lighter layers more suited for the walking gown, and then it was time for the gown itself.

"Arms up," Evaline instructed.

"We shall see if I survive this round."

The gown proved uncooperative, catching first on Harriet's elbows, then refusing to slide over the structured stays.

"It is stuck again!" Harriet's voice emerged muffled from under the fabric. "I swear this dress despises me."

"Lower your arms a little. No—slowly!"

With a final, ungraceful tug, the gown settled into place.

"I feel like a trussed goose."

"A very fashionable goose," Evaline said, adjusting the sleeves. "Now for the fastenings."

Harriet balanced herself on the bench as Evaline worked the back closures.

"Honestly, Evaline. Why must gowns fasten in the back? It is as though fashion is deliberately cruel."

"It is to ensure you need a maid," Evaline replied. "Keeps the classes in order."

"Ha! The classes. I would trade my title for one competent lady's maid right now."

"You say that, but you would not part with your jewelry collection."

"You wound me, madam."

Harriet had wanted to look her best for Sebastian, wanting him to think well of her. And, if she were honest, wanting to draw his admiring glances while she had the chance. No one had ever made her feel as important as he had done.

These past few months had been a reengagement of her intellect, which had been dormant for too long. It was easy to be glib. Practically a necessity to quiet a noisy conscience. Imbibing in wine and attending endless social events had dulled her dark thoughts until she had become a gleeful lackwit.

Spending the afternoon with Sebastian after these trying months of sobriety and moderation had reminded her of the girl she had been, the one who had been excited by art and culture, wishing to see the world with him at her side. Who had been buoyed by the possibilities.

Of course, she still had the pesky problem that she had lied to him about the painting upstairs.

Eventually, I will tell him the truth.

Despite the reassurance, she still felt guilty about deceiving him. But now that she planned to call on Belinda, she needed to avoid attracting any undue attention, which meant suffering the trials of changing her attire. She and Evaline did not even try to change into evening wear for dinner when it was just the two of them. With their inept skills, it would take all day to make that many wardrobe changes.

"Lift your skirts," Evaline said.

"I cannot believe I am reduced to this." Harriet complied with a theatrical sigh. "Just months ago, there were three maids for such tasks."

"Yes, well, months ago you also had footmen. We have Finch, Jem, the belowstairs staff, and some questionable tea."

"Hardly adequate for two respectable widows of the *ton*! I must summon Mr. Benton. If I must dress myself again, I shall expire."

Evaline smiled, smoothing Harriet's skirts.

"You are still standing. A triumph, truly."

Harriet laughed at the ridiculous situation, but as she pulled on her slippers and gloves, her smile faded.

"Belinda Cooper may not be aware, but she awaits me," she said quietly. "I owe her something. I do not yet know what, but I shall make it right."

Evaline stepped forward, resting a hand on Harriet's arm.

"You will do it. You always do. Beneath the theatrics, you are far more capable than you admit."

"That may be the kindest lie ever told."

"Not a lie," Evaline replied. "Not from me."

A final glance in the cracked mirror showed Harriet transformed—no longer a widow being courted by a handsome gentleman to the museum, but a woman with purpose, dressed in muted tones for a quiet mission.

"Well," Harriet said, standing tall. "Let us see what the day brings."

"With luck," Evaline replied, "it will not bring any more stays."

They shared a laugh, stepping out of the dim basement room, ready for the afternoon ahead.

CHAPTER 5

Your vows, like gold, so pure and true,
Inspire my heart with faith anew;
No doubt shall dim the love we share,
For in your words, I place my care.

The New Ladies' Valentine Writer (1821)

* * *

Sebastian sat motionless in the dim interior of his borrowed carriage, the leather seat cool beneath him despite the faint warmth of the afternoon sun that filtered through the drawn curtains. His gloved fingers drummed a slow rhythm on his thigh, betraying the tumult within him.

The visit to the British Museum with Harriet had unsettled him far more than he had anticipated. He had expected polite conversation, perhaps some lingering awkwardness after all these years. Instead, he had found himself treading perilous ground, where glances held too much meaning and silences whispered of unspoken truths.

He shifted, glancing out the slit of the carriage window toward Harriet's townhouse. The street was quiet, the distant clatter of hooves and wheels a reminder of life continuing elsewhere. Yet he remained, his carriage parked discreetly down the street, as if he were some lovesick youth loitering in hopes of a glimpse.

Ridiculous.

He ran a hand through his unruly hair and exhaled slowly. He should have left by now. The rational part of him, carefully cultivated over years abroad, urged him to return to the Scotts' townhouse. To forget the afternoon entirely. But his heart—damn it—his heart was refusing to obey.

The museum visit had started simply enough. Conversation about the exhibits, light recollections of shared memories. Yet with each step, each quiet room, he had felt the old pull, the dangerous familiarity that Harriet still possessed in abundance. The gleam in her eye when she had spoken of the Rosetta Stone, the subtle curve of her smile when discussing ancient secrets—it had all reminded him of the girl he had once loved.

But was that still who she was now?

Sebastian leaned back, recalling the years he had spent hearing whispers of Lady Slight's exploits. The rumors had been plentiful and pernicious. Tales of lovers taken and discarded, of reckless wagers and scandalous behavior. Harriet had become known for her beauty and her disregard for society's expectations while upholding just enough respectability to maintain her status in polite society.

Had any of it been true?

This afternoon, he had caught glimpses of the Harriet he remembered—intelligent, curious, with a quick wit that could disarm even the most rigid members of society. Yet the rumors gnawed at him. They clashed violently with the woman who had gazed at ancient statues with such appreciation. Was she simply playing a role for his benefit?

Sebastian cursed softly under his breath. He hated uncertainty. And Harriet Hargreaves—no, Lady Harriet Slight—was an enigma he could no longer ignore.

The rational course would be to walk away. To leave England as soon as Lorenzo's business was concluded and return to Florence, where life was simpler, where art was the enigma to be solved rather than the clutter of actual people. Yet here he sat, unable to bring himself to order his coachman onward.

His gaze drifted once more to Harriet's townhouse. A home of luxury that he could not have provided her with when he had left for Florence. Fortunately, these days, his circumstances were vastly different from that time. The door remained firmly closed as he considered their day together. Was she inside, reflecting on their day as he did now? Or had she already dismissed him from her mind, her attention captured by another?

The thought twisted unpleasantly in his chest.

He had almost convinced himself to depart when movement caught his eye. His posture straightened instantly, every sense sharpened.

An unmarked carriage—a sleek black one without any identifiable crest—rolled to a stop before Harriet's residence. The door opened smoothly, and his breath caught when Harriet stepped out the front door.

But she had just returned not an hour past. Where could she be going now?

Sebastian leaned forward, narrowing his gaze.

Harriet's appearance had changed. Gone was the elegant pelisse and bonnet she had worn to the museum. Now, she was dressed in a demure dark blue walking gown with a matching cloak draped over her slender shoulders. Her distinctive hair was pinned up higher, concealed by a large but unassuming bonnet. She was dressed for a private visit, not a public outing, and Sebastian got the sense she was hiding her identity. That notwithstanding, he would recognize those lush curves even if he were drunk to the point of blindness—as he had been when he first reached Florence and made a laudable attempt to drown his memories of the female now stepping into the discreet vehicle.

He stretched his neck in frustration as he considered the reasons that she would own a carriage that was impossible to identify, and the answers he found made his nerves ferment with jealousy. He felt like a cad for being suspicious, but his instincts stirred. He rapped twice on the roof of his carriage, signaling his coachman.

"Follow that carriage," he ordered as his own vehicle pulled into a slow roll behind Harriet's.

As the two carriages wound their way through the quieter streets of Mayfair, the streetlamps hissed softly as they flickered to life, casting a pale glow over the refined streets of the prestigious neighborhood. The early twilight of winter draped the district in a silvery veil, the grand townhouses standing in elegant rows, their symmetrical facades framed by wrought-iron balconies and tall sash windows. The faint scent of coal smoke from drawing-room fires mingled with the sharper tang of the winter air. From behind silk curtains, the muted notes of a harpsichord drifted into the street—preparations for an evening soirée in full swing.

Sebastian's carriage followed Harriet's unmarked vehicle at a cautious distance, the steady clatter of hooves on cobbles echoing between quiet streets. Gas lamps glowed before exclusive clubs and well-tended gardens, casting long shadows where liveried footmen waited at imposing doorways. This was Mayfair—respectable, dignified, a bastion of wealth and decorum.

But as the carriages turned onto narrower lanes, the atmosphere shifted. The houses grew less grand, their facades touched by soot. St. James's Market loomed ahead, where gambling hells, taverns, and houses of ill repute thrived. Sebastian leaned forward, unease tightening his chest.

What in the deuce is Harriet doing here?

As they passed St. James's Square and edged closer to St. James's Market, Sebastian felt his frown deepen. This neighborhood was not where a respectable viscountess would be expected. The area had a reputation— the realm of degenerate gamblers, fortune-seekers, and those with secrets best kept in shadows.

The black carriage ahead slowed, preparing to turn, but just at that moment, a cluster of vehicles clogged the narrow street. Sebastian's coachman exclaimed as a delivery cart overturned some barrels. Sebastian thrust open the carriage door and leaned out.

"Can you get us through?" he demanded.

"I will try, m'lord," the coachman replied, tugging the reins.

But it was too late.

By the time Sebastian's carriage cleared the congestion, Harriet's vehicle was gone.

He stepped down from the carriage, scanning the street intently. The black coach had vanished, swallowed by the warren of streets near the market.

"Damn it," Sebastian muttered, glancing up and down the road.

The area was alive with noise now—hawkers calling out, the raucous laughter from nearby establishments, and the clatter of passing carts. But Harriet was nowhere to be seen.

Sebastian raked a hand through his hair again, frustration prickling at his skin. He had come so close. He turned in a slow circle, considering the possible destinations.

Why here? Was she meeting someone? An old lover, perhaps? The thought sent a sharp pang through him, though he immediately cursed his own foolishness for caring.

He had to be careful. He had heard too many stories over the years—rumors of Lady Slight's indiscretions, of her ability to ensnare hearts, only to discard them when they ceased to amuse her. His own heart had paid the price once. He would not be a fool a second time.

And yet …

She had seemed so different at the museum. For a fleeting moment, she had appeared like the Harriet he had once known. But what was truth? What was performance?

Sebastian exhaled slowly, forcing his racing thoughts to settle. He would discover what she was about. He had not returned from Florence to be ensnared by the same troubles that had driven him away years ago. No, this time he would be careful.

But even as he climbed back into his carriage, instructing the coachman to head for home, Sebastian could not shake the unease gnawing at him.

What in the bloody hell was Harriet Slight doing near St. James's Market?

And why did he care so damned much?

* * *

HARRIET PAUSED before the narrow entrance of a weathered building—Belinda Cooper's address above a shop in St. James's Market. The streets here bore little resemblance to the refined lanes of Mayfair. Stalls crowded the thorough-fare, peddling everything from silk scraps to tarnished silver spoons, and the scent of roasted chestnuts mingled with the less savory odors of the market. The raucous voices of merchants hawking wares filled the air. This was no place for a viscountess.

Glancing back at her coachman, he and her grooms being the only men remaining in her employ, she was relieved to see he had stepped down and taken up the position of a sentry, his stout figure looming beside the carriage with an air of quiet authority.

Jonas Fletcher had been with Harriet's household for several years—long enough to have seen her at both the pinnacle of her social triumphs and through her most recent trials. A man of perhaps five and forty, he bore the rugged features of someone who had spent his life exposed to the elements. His weathered skin hinted at years on the box, driving through both the misty mornings of the countryside and the crowded streets of London. His dark hair, streaked with silver at the temples, was tied neatly at the nape of his neck in the fashion of an earlier era, a quiet rebellion against more modern styles. A faint scar curved along his left cheekbone, though he never spoke of how he came by it. His blue eyes were sharp—ever watchful—and Harriet took comfort in the steady gaze that missed nothing.

Fletcher wore his livery with easy confidence; the deep navy coat, though a few years old, was immaculately kept, brass buttons gleaming in the fading light. The faint scent of leather and horses clung to him, along with a quiet competence that set him apart.

Like many coachmen of his age, Fletcher had grown stout from long hours on the box, but he had yet an air of discipline. He carried himself with the posture of a soldier, which some whispered he might have once been. Harriet had never pressed him on the matter. His loyalty had been proved when most of her household had scattered, and that was all that mattered.

For all his quiet reserve, her retainer had a way of putting the grooms in their place with a single look, and the horses responded to his steady hands like obedient children. He rarely spoke unless spoken to, but when he did, his voice was low and steady, with the faintest trace of a rural accent—Devonshire, perhaps.

Now, he stood watch, arms folded behind his back, scanning the street with a narrowed focus. No gambler, hawker, or street urchin would dare approach the carriage under his watchful gaze. Fletcher might not speak much, but his presence said everything: *I am here. I am watching. And I will protect what is mine.*

And knowing Fletcher kept a pistol in the box beneath the seat certainly eased her worries. St. James's Market could be a dangerous place, and despite the early hour, darkness had fallen to usher in a chilly evening.

Harriet gave a subtle nod of appreciation before turning back toward the staircase that led to the rooms above the shop. With Jonas Fletcher standing guard below, she could face whatever waited for her within.

She took a steadying breath and climbed the narrow steps. The faded door at the top creaked as she rapped sharply. For a moment, there was only silence. Harriet raised her hand again, but the door opened abruptly.

Belinda Cooper stood framed in the doorway, dressed immaculately in a deep plum gown that accentuated her average height and slender frame. Her hazel eyes, sharp and intelligent, widened slightly at the sight of Harriet, though she masked her surprise with admirable speed. Her dark brown hair was styled flawlessly, and despite her surroundings, she looked as elegant as ever.

But Harriet noticed it immediately. The redness on Belinda's right cheek. As if someone—Lord Lowe, no doubt—had struck her. What a despicable toad he was, frequently soused and always inappropriate.

"Miss Cooper," Harriet said softly, stepping forward. "May I come in?"

Belinda hesitated, her shoulders stiffening. "Of course, my lady."

The room was small but tidy, with two armchairs positioned around a threadbare rug covering the floor, and the scent of lavender soap lingered in the air. Belinda had arranged the limited furnishings with care, though Harriet's gaze kept returning to the flush of red on her cheek, recalling the rumor that had helped her find Belinda. That Lowe had lost his temper and manhandled her in the presence of others.

"You should not be here, Lady Slight," Belinda said, her tone anxious. "This is hardly a neighborhood for someone of your standing."

"And yet here I am," Harriet replied, removing her gloves. "Because you should not be here either."

Belinda's lips tightened. "Not all of us have a choice."

Harriet's gaze sharpened. "Lowe? He did that?" She gestured subtly to Belinda's cheek.

Belinda turned away. "It is nothing."

"Nothing?" Harriet's voice rose. "A man lays his hands on you, and you call it nothing? You, of all people, Miss Cooper. You are too proud to suffer fools like Lowe."

The other woman turned back, her expression hard. "Pride? Pride will not keep me fed, my lady. Or would you prefer I take a position in a bawdy house? Because that was the other option."

Harriet flinched. "No. Of course not."

The tension between them crackled. Harriet studied Belinda carefully. The woman's appearance remained flawless, despite her circumstances. Her hair gleamed, her gown was pressed, and her posture impeccable.

"You look as though you have not suffered a day in your life," Harriet murmured. "Who is doing for you? Did Lowe hire you a lady's maid?"

Belinda laughed bitterly. "Lowe? Ha! The man is too cheap to provide more than a maid and an old woman who comes in to cook. He only does that to keep my hands soft. I do for myself. Lowe has no interest in keeping me comfortable. Only convenient."

Harriet's fingers curled around her gloves. "Belinda, you cannot live like this."

Belinda's expression softened, and for the first time, Harriet saw the exhaustion there. "Do you think I don't know that? But what choice do I have? I am nearly forty years of age, my lady. Forty! My beauty fading, my reputation tarnished."

Seething, Harriet clenched her fists and turned away. "My father is such a bastard!"

There was no response. When she turned back, she found Belinda dabbing at her damp lashes with a lace handkerchief, and her heart broke all over again.

"Not to me. Not until … now."

"You cared for him?"

Belinda's face contorted with grief, and she quickly turned away in a bid to salvage her dignity. "Aren't I ridiculous? The oldest story in the book. A respectable woman in service seduced by a viscount. So foolish as to believe it was love until I grew too old for his tastes."

Harriet stared at her back—how on earth had Belinda done up the buttons on the back of the bodice alone?—and tried to think what to say. What would help. It was still a novel experience trying to find the words to lift the spirits of another person, not being a skill she had developed.

"Perhaps it was."

The other woman turned back in surprise, her face carefully dabbed but shocked.

"Perhaps ... he did once care. The thing is, some men do not take aging well. It is possible that as he saw you age, the young woman he seduced so many years ago, perhaps it made him aware of his mortality. Perhaps that is why he felt the need for ... a younger paramour. So he could pretend he was younger, too."

Belinda tilted her head, musing this notion with a flutter of eyelashes.

"That does sound like Bertram," she eventually remarked.

Harriet nodded. "My father does not have well-matured morals. He is rather single-minded about maintaining his vanities. A more desirable paramour reflects better on him."

"It is just that ... taking back the gifts and refusing to pay the settlement—" Belinda lifted a trembling hand to fidget with her hair. "Never mind that. Can I offer you some tea?"

"I shall not stay that long."

Harriet tried to think what to do next. She had assured Evaline that when she met with Belinda, she would know what to say, but she found her mind a blank at this crucial time. "How is it? Here?"

Belinda sighed sadly. "Dull. I used to maintain a household for your father. He visited often, and we went frequently to social events together. Lowe mostly drinks and gambles, while I spend most of my time in these two rooms. Venturing out into the neighborhood is ... daunting. I find myself regretting my choices that led me here."

Harriet thought about how reassuring it was to have Fletcher waiting for her downstairs and nodded in understanding.

"You mentioned you were in service when Father—"

Harriet hesitated, trying to find a kinder word than seduced. "—met you. What did you do?"

Belinda smiled. "I was a lady's maid for two young ladies making their debut. I sometimes accompanied them as a second chaperon."

"So that is how you met my father." Then she experienced a flash of inspiration. Harriet was still awestruck how the woman had dressed herself. Even with Evaline's help, she dreaded dressing in the mornings, or changing her clothes. This was ... serendipitous!

"You should take a position as a lady's maid. Your skills are exemplary."

Belinda's eyebrows flew up to meet her hairline in utter amazement at Harriet's bold declaration. "That is a lovely idea. It would certainly solve my current predicament. The only thing is ... who would hire me?"

Harriet lifted her chin, casting her fears aside to reach a decision. It would certainly send a message to her father. She was rejecting his corruption. She was standing on her own two feet. His reign of influence was over. "I would."

Belinda blinked. "You?"

"Yes. You could be my lady's maid."

A brittle laugh escaped Belinda. "Do not mock me."

"I am not." Harriet stepped closer. "You would have a respectable position. A roof over your head. Safety. And I will advance you a loan to put legal pressure on my father. You should hold him accountable."

Belinda's mouth parted in disbelief. "You are serious."

"Entirely."

Belinda shook her head. "I will not take your money."

"What is this? Pride?" Harriet's voice sharpened. "Pride did not stop Lowe's hand, Belinda. Pride will not protect you when you are destitute."

Belinda turned away, silent.

"We both know my father's promises were worth less than the paper they were written on," Harriet pressed. "But you do not have to let him desert you like this. You deserve more than this."

Belinda's shoulders rose and fell with a deep breath. "A lady's maid," she repeated softly. "After everything."

"Would it be so terrible?" Harriet asked gently. "You were a lady's maid before Bertram Hargreaves noticed you. Before he seduced you with his false promises. I am offering you a chance to step back into that role, with dignity. It is just me and Lady Wood, and we are far less demanding than two silly chits coming out for their first Season."

Belinda turned slowly, searching Harriet's face. "And you think society would accept it? That I could simply become your maid after all these years?"

Harriet smiled, a flash of the impudent woman she had been when she still ruled London's ballrooms before eschewing such. But this time for something that mattered. This time to do good. "I am very pleased with my new lady's maid, Miss Bélise Coupier. Elegant. Discreet. A woman of impeccable taste."

Belinda stared at her.

"I shall tell them you are French. Parisian, perhaps. Newly arrived in England. Who will question it? Society turns a blind eye when it chooses. Why, Lord Fenwick has his mistress living openly as his children's governess. Everyone knows it, yet no one speaks of it."

Belinda's lips twitched, despite herself. "Bélise Coupier?"

Harriet gave a little shrug of nonchalance. "A touch dramatic? Perhaps. But French names are all the rage, and high society is far more forgiving when scandal hides behind a fashionable accent. Besides, it suits you."

Belinda gazed around the small room. The faint redness on her cheek, though partially concealed with careful powder, remained a silent testament to Lord Lowe's temper. She drew her shoulders back with practiced poise, though Harriet noted how tightly her fingers clasped together.

"And what of Bertram?" Belinda asked at last, voice even, but Harriet could detect the worried undertone.

Harriet smiled—cool, confident. "Knowing his only daughter has hired his former mistress will keep him silent. It would be far too embarrassing for him to point it out. No, it is likely he will stifle any whispers, lest his own credibility suffer. He would not want his peers to think he cannot control his own kin." Harriet stepped forward, lowering her voice. "Belinda, take this chance. Let us both turn the page."

Silence stretched between them. The sounds of the street below—vendors calling out wares, the distant clatter of carriage wheels—filtered through the windows that faced a busy street. At Harriet's home, Belinda would have her own room in a prestigious house. Peace. Quiet. Prospects. Perhaps even squeeze her settlement from Bertram's icy fingers.

Harriet resisted the urge to press her case further, knowing the nature of human desires well enough to let her sit with the offer. Finally, Belinda's lips twitched in the faintest ghost of a smile, and Harriet perceived the woman relax as if she had put down a great burden.

"Very well, Lady Slight. Let us see if society will believe in Miss Bélise Coupier."

Harriet exhaled, the tightness in her chest easing. For the first time in a long while, she felt as though she had done something right. This was another secret, yes, but one that might lead to redemption rather than regret.

She smiled, genuine this time. "Excellent. How long will it take to pack your trunks?"

Belinda gave a short, dry laugh.

"Trunks? You flatter me. What little your father allowed

me to keep fits in two modest valises. It is mostly just my clothes."

Harriet paused. She had wondered at how perfectly put together Belinda appeared despite her circumstances—her hair styled elegantly, her gown simple but perfectly fitted. It appeared she had found an eminently competent addition to their eclectic household. Now all Harriet needed was a couple of footmen so she could take a proper bath.

And, perhaps if she kept this do-gooding up, she herself would one day be worthy of love. And find a gentleman like Sebastian to give it to her. While she was still young enough to consider having children.

Her own hopes for the future notwithstanding, it certainly eased her mind in the present to know Belinda would be taken care of.

CHAPTER 6

With gentle words and glances sweet,
Our lips in tender union meet;
A kiss bestowed with love's pure art,
A silent vow from heart to heart.

The New Ladies' Valentine Writer (1821)

* * *

DECEMBER 12, 1821

*H*arriet sat at the breakfast table, stirring her tea with slow, thoughtful movements. The house felt different this morning—subtly, but undeniably so. Belinda was in residence. As a result, some of Harriet's conscience had eased as she had hoped it would.

The older woman had returned with her the night before, slipping into the townhouse under the cover of darkness. No grand announcements, no fuss, just a woman reclaiming a measure of dignity after weeks of precarious survival.

Harriet had instructed Mrs. Finch to prepare a small room for her on the upper floor. Finch, ever the model of discretion, had made no remark about the late-hour arrival, though her sharp eyes had taken in Belinda's elegant appearance with a wary glance.

Now, in the light of morning, Harriet could not help but feel a quiet sense of satisfaction. She had done good—twice over, in fact.

Because the letter had already been sent.

A simple request to a veterans' charity, inquiring about honorable men seeking respectable work. The idea had come to her the moment she had looked at Fletcher, standing sentry outside Belinda's lodgings, ever watchful and steady. She needed footmen—strong men, but moderate ones. And who better than those who had served their country?

She had felt strangely light after writing the letter, as if she had taken one step further away from the selfish girl she had once been. Fletcher was to help her interview the prospects, being experienced at hiring men for the stables. A reliable man of vast experience, he would know how to read the character of those who applied.

"You look quite pleased with yourself," Evaline remarked from across the table, cutting into a warm roll with practiced precision.

"I am." Harriet sipped her tea, then set the cup down with a decisive nod. "Two problems solved in one day. A rather productive stretch, if I do say so myself."

Evaline dabbed at her lips with her napkin. "I assume one of those problems was Miss Cooper?"

"Miss Bélise Coupier now. We have a French lady's maid to do for us," Harriet corrected with a playful smirk.

Evaline blinked, then let out a small, surprised laugh. "You are serious?"

Harriet spread her hands. "It is the done thing, is it not? If one must assume a new position in society, one must have a suitably mysterious name."

Evaline shook her head in amused disbelief. "I can only imagine what she thought of that particular notion."

"She found it ridiculous," Harriet admitted, "but I think she rather likes it."

"Then I suppose that is one matter handled. And the other?"

"The grooms are moving the tub back to my rooms. Fletcher assures me he can keep them in line, so they will help with hauling hot water for us, but I have a more permanent solution." Harriet sat back in her chair, proud of her ingenuity. "I have sent word to the veterans' charity I have been supporting recently, requesting recommendations for footmen."

Evaline's brows lifted slightly. "That is an excellent idea."

Harriet nodded. "I thought so, too. Our coachman, Fletcher, was my inspiration. There are so many honorable men who have returned from war with no place to go. I requested men of good character, strong enough for their duties but not so severe as to frighten our staff. I stipulated that injuries or appearance were not a disqualification, thinking there might be some excellent candidates who would not usually be considered for footmen."

Evaline's gaze softened. "That is rather inspired."

Harriet gave a small shrug, trying to appear unaffected. "It is practical. And it is only fair, given what they have sacrificed."

Before Evaline could respond, the front door knocker sounded down the hall, the loud rap startling in the quiet of the morning. Someone knew about her shortage of staff, and that they needed to be heavy-handed with the brass ring if they wished to be attended to.

Harriet straightened instinctively. A moment later, Mrs. Finch entered, her ever-stern expression in place. "Lord Sebastian's 'ere."

Harriet's heart gave a small, unwelcome flutter. She had not expected him so soon. She and Evaline rose, dabbing their napkins to their mouths before making their way to where Sebastian waited in the entrance hall.

Impeccably dressed as ever, his navy coat fit snugly over broad shoulders, his snowy cravat in the same loose knot that she assumed must be a style from Florence. His gray eyes flicked to hers immediately, scanning her face in that way he always had, as if she were a puzzle he could solve, if only he studied the pieces long enough.

He bowed slightly. "Good morning, ladies."

"Good morning, my lord," Harriet replied smoothly.

A pause. A hesitation, almost imperceptible, but there nonetheless. Then, his voice dropped to a quieter register.

"And how did you spend your evening?"

Harriet's stomach tightened. She had no intention of telling him about Belinda. The last thing she needed was Sebastian prying into her affairs, casting judgment where it was not wanted about her goings-on. So she smiled—a slow, practiced smile—and said, "Oh, I spent a quiet evening at home."

Sebastian's expression darkened. Something passed through his gaze, something sharp.

"You did not go out at all?"

"No," Harriet said lightly, forcing a casual shrug. "I was rather tired after our visit to the museum."

His jaw ticked. She had not expected him to look so dissatisfied.

Evaline cleared her throat delicately, cutting through the tension. "I believe we are ready?"

"Of course."

Sebastian's gaze lingered on Harriet for a beat longer before he nodded once, curtly. Harriet and Evaline donned their overcoats, gloves, and bonnets. When she had assembled herself, Sebastian offered her his arm and she took it, even as she wondered why he seemed so very displeased.

* * *

SEBASTIAN SAT STIFFLY in the carriage, his arms crossed as he studied Harriet from the corner of his eye.

She had lied to him. The way she had smiled—too poised, too smooth—when she told him she had spent a quiet evening at home. The slight hesitation before she answered. The way her chin lifted ever so slightly in defiance, as if daring him to challenge her.

He had spent years navigating the cunning twists and turns of art dealings, spotting forgeries at a glance, reading the nuances of deceit in a seller's tone. Not to mention he had stooped to the ignoble behavior of following her to St. James's Market. Which meant he knew Harriet was lying.

About what, precisely, he could not yet say.

But it bothered him. Far more than it ought.

Sebastian exhaled through his nose, staring out at the streets of Mayfair as the carriage rocked forward. He had no claim on her whereabouts, nor any right to expect the truth. She was no longer the girl who had once promised him everything, only to leave him waiting.

And yet …

He turned his attention back toward her.

Harriet was sitting beside Lady Wood, her gloved fingers tracing a pattern over the top of her reticule as she stared out the window, her auburn lashes casting delicate shadows on her cheeks. He could not interpret her expression, but her lips—damnable lips, still as lush as he remembered them—curved in a faint smile.

A woman with secrets.

But was she the same woman he had known all those years ago? Or was she someone entirely different now?

Sebastian clenched his jaw. He had vowed to keep his heart guarded this time. He had vowed not to be lured in again. But then she spoke, and the irritation faded—just a little.

"I have neglected my reading these past years," she murmured, almost as if to herself. "It is time to fill my library again."

Sebastian arched a brow. "Was it ever empty?"

She tilted her head, giving him a sidelong glance. "Not empty, no. But neglected. A library is a living thing, is it not? It must be tended, refreshed, filled with new voices. Otherwise, it becomes little more than a mausoleum for old words."

Sebastian smirked. "You always did enjoy dramatic declarations."

"And you always did enjoy needling me about them," she shot back, but there was no bite to her words. Only warmth.

He leaned back slightly, tapping a gloved finger against his knee. "What sorts of books do you intend to buy?"

Harriet sighed, her breath fogging lightly against the cool carriage window. "I do not know yet. Writings to stimulate the mind, perhaps."

"No scandalous novels?" Sebastian teased.

She grinned. "I have read my share, of course. But it would not do for Miss Bélise Coupier to find such stories beside my bed, would it?"

Sebastian blinked, momentarily thrown. "Miss who?"

Lady Wood, who had been quietly reading, glanced up in faint amusement.

Harriet's eyes glittered with mischief. "My new lady's maid."

Sebastian frowned, the name sparking a distant memory, but before he could question her, Harriet waved a hand.

"Never mind that. Back to books—what do you recommend, my lord?"

He studied her for a moment, then decided to let it go. For now.

"Well," he said at last, settling deeper into his seat. "If you truly wish to exercise your mind, I suppose I should steer you toward histories."

Harriet made a mocking grimace. "Must I?"

Sebastian chuckled. "If only for balance. What was it you told me once? 'All knowledge is worth having'?"

Harriet sighed dramatically. "Did I? How insufferable I must have been."

"I shall not argue that."

She gasped in mock outrage and leaned over to swat at his arm. Sebastian laughed, and for a moment, it was as though no time had passed at all—as though they were still young, still carefree, still standing in Avonmead's library making lists of all the places they would go, all the books they would read. The thought made his chest tighten.

But then the carriage slowed, and the spell was broken.

"We have arrived," Lady Wood murmured, tucking away her book.

Sebastian reached for the door and stepped out first, turning to offer his arm to Harriet. Her gloved fingers, soft and warm, slipped around his elbow, and for the briefest moment, he felt something old and familiar stir in his chest. Then she was stepping down, and he let go an instant too quickly.

Inside Hatchards, the air smelled of leather, paper, and burning oil. Harriet lit up at once, surveying the towering bookshelves like a conqueror surveying her new domain.

Sebastian peered down at her, dismayed at how familiar this felt. "Shall we make a list first or dive in blindly?"

Harriet tilted her head. "Where is the adventure in making lists?"

He chuckled. "Where is the sense in wandering aimlessly?"

Harriet sighed. "Very well. A brief list, then."

She led them toward a quiet corner, where she and Lady Wood scribbled down titles and subjects while Sebastian leaned against a nearby shelf, watching her.

Harriet had changed. She was more guarded. More careful. But then she would smile—truly smile—and she was the girl he had once known again. Which one was real? And which one would break his heart if he let himself believe in her again?

"Sebastian?"

He blinked. Harriet was watching him, her head tilted in curiosity. "You looked lost in thought," she murmured.

He straightened. "Just wondering how long I shall be made to carry your selections."

She laughed and turned away, moving toward a tall shelf. Sebastian followed at a leisurely pace, watching as she scanned the spines, her fingers trailing over the leather bindings. Then she spotted something.

Without hesitation, she grasped the ladder and began to climb. Sebastian felt his pulse kick up unexpectedly.

She moved with ease, the hem of her skirts lifting slightly as she reached for a book. And then he saw it. A flash of stocking. Not wool for the chilly weather, but silk. A glimpse of delicate slipper. A small, utterly indecent peek of trim ankle.

Sebastian swallowed hard, tearing his gaze away. But it was too late. The damage was done. Then—

A gasp.

A slip.

Harriet's foot missed the rung.

Sebastian lunged forward without thinking. She spun around as she fell against him, her momentum knocking them both back slightly before he caught them both steady. And then, silence.

Harriet froze in his arms. Sebastian's heart pounded violently as he realized how close she was. Her face was mere inches from his, her breath warm against his cheek. His hands were firm around her waist, holding her close. Slowly, she tilted her head up, her lips parted ever so slightly.

Sebastian's grip tightened. And then he realized—they were alone. No one in sight. He dampened his lips.

Harriet's eyes dropped to his mouth. And Sebastian—God help him—he closed the distance.

The kiss was soft at first, tentative, as if testing a memory. But then it deepened, intensified, an ache twisting through his chest as something wild and long-buried roared to life when their lips fused together. It was as though no time had passed at all. As though they were still young, still foolish, still tangled in each other's arms beneath the stars at Avonmead.

Sebastian's tongue slipped into her mouth to find hers, silky and hot, melting together as if both starved for human contact, and they surrendered to their fervor.

Footsteps in the next aisle brought him back to his senses. Time had passed. They were no longer a couple. And Sebastian was no longer the boy who had loved her so recklessly.

He pulled back, breathing hard, his hands still curled around her waist. Harriet stared at him, her lips still slightly parted, her eyes dark with an emotion he could not yet name. He tasted honey on his tongue.

And Sebastian knew, with absolute certainty—

I am in danger. So much danger.

* * *

HARRIET'S BREATH caught in her throat, her heart slamming against her ribs like a wild bird desperate for escape.

Sebastian's lips had been warm against hers, firm yet searching, as if he, too, had not anticipated this moment but was helpless to stop it. The scent of him—sandalwood, winter air, and something undeniably male—invaded her senses, leaving her drowning in memories of what could have been, what should have been.

For a single, heart-stopping moment, she had let herself feel it. The tenderness of his mouth, the way his hands settled so surely at her waist, the tingling awareness crackling between them. It was unlike any kiss she had ever experienced—searing, consuming, a whisper of all they had lost and all they might still find if only she had the courage to reach for it.

Italy. The thought had snuck in, unbidden. What if she went with him?

What if, just this once, she leapt without hesitation, without calculation, without the endless weighing of risk and ruin? What would it be like to walk the narrow streets of Florence with her hand tucked in his, to drink coffee beneath a painted ceiling, to wake each morning knowing she had chosen passion over status?

But then a footstep creaked nearby, and the moment had fractured.

She pulled away abruptly, pulse thudding, barely

managing to stifle a gasp. Sebastian's hands fell from her waist as they both turned sharply toward the sound.

Evaline.

Dear, observant Evaline, moving through the next aisle with unhurried grace, utterly unaware of the tempest raging between them.

Harriet's body tensed, her mind racing for escape. She could not let Evaline see. Could not let Sebastian see. The vulnerability of the moment had been too raw, too revealing, and she would be damned before she let either of them glimpse the depths of her turmoil. With a practiced tilt of her chin, she turned back toward the ladder, climbing the rungs with knees that trembled only slightly.

"Blast it," she murmured, feigning distraction. "I nearly forgot my book."

She climbed, hand over hand, forcing her breath back into normalcy. Above, the leather-bound volume sat waiting, the object of her supposed pursuit. A moment to compose herself. That was all she needed. Her grip tightened on the shelf as she stared blindly at the spines before her, blinking hard against the prickling sensation in her eyes.

Harriet had not felt anything like this since the morning she had chosen to stay at home, knowing Sebastian would leave without her. She had taken lovers over the years, and she had not been untouched by passion. Yet none of them had ever unraveled her like this. None had made her feel as if she stood at the precipice of something vast and unknowable, something terrifying and intoxicating all at once. And none had ever made her want to weep for what she had lost. And for how she had betrayed him. For everything she had thrown away.

She swallowed hard, reaching for the book with fingers that still tingled from the sensation of pressing them to

Sebastian's solid frame. When she climbed down, Evaline was already at the counter, speaking with the bookseller.

Harriet turned, glancing once at Sebastian. He had not moved. He stood precisely where she had left him, his hands curled into fists at his sides, and his eyes—those storm-gray eyes—were locked on her, as if trying to decipher what had just happened between them.

She forced herself to smile. Lightly. Carelessly.

"You ought not distract a lady when she is mid-climb," she teased, infusing her tone with as much levity as she could muster. "I might have tumbled."

He exhaled sharply, a combination of a chuckle and a scoff, but he did not respond. Instead, he offered his arm, leading her to the counter where Evaline was inspecting a selection of bindings.

Harriet focused on the books, grateful for something—anything—to anchor her thoughts. She ran her fingers along the spines, considering.

"Morocco leather," she said at last, tracing the smooth crimson cover of a volume. "Durable, elegant, and soft to the touch. Yes, this will do."

"Calfskin has a finer grain," Evaline pointed out, turning one of the books over in her hands. "And ages beautifully."

"True," Harriet mused. "But I want these to be read, not simply displayed."

Sebastian, standing at her side, reached past her to lift a navy-bound edition of Ovid's *Metamorphoses*. "Gilded edges," he noted. "Very fine."

Harriet glanced up at him, forcing her voice to remain steady. "It will catch the candlelight beautifully in my library."

Sebastian said nothing, but something was evident in his gaze—something knowing, something that told her he was still thinking of the kiss. She turned away quickly, reaching for another volume.

"I am excited to order some excellent books. It has been an age since I read."

Evaline gave her a soft smile. "Then let us do so."

Together, they completed their selections, noting her choice of binding, which would be embossed with her initials and could be delivered within the week. Harriet focused on the details, on the business of purchasing books, on the texture of paper and leather. Anything to keep her thoughts from wandering back to Sebastian.

Once the transaction was complete, they stepped out into the cool winter air.

Harriet inhaled sharply, the world outside suddenly overwhelming. The streets bustled with life—carriages rolling past, street vendors calling out their wares, gentlemen tipping their hats to passing ladies. It was familiar, all of it, but in this moment, she felt unmoored. As if she had stepped out of time itself.

She had been a girl again just moments ago, her heart light with possibility, the future sprawling before her like an open road. Now, she was a woman grown, a woman who had made mistakes, who had burned bridges, who had lied.

The scope of her mistakes pressed against her chest.

She had lied. Again. What a terrible decision that had been. She had told Sebastian she did not have the painting. And because of her past betrayal, only compounded by her recent lie, this—whatever this was—could go no further. Because no matter how much he might still feel for her, no matter how much she might still long for him, the moment he learned the truth, it would be over. She had done this to herself, ensuring her own heartbreak by breaking trust with him a second time.

Swallowing hard, she let Evaline take her arm, guiding her toward the waiting carriage. She would enjoy this charade while it lasted. Pretend, for a little while longer, that she had not already ruined everything.

CHAPTER 7

That heart appealing word, "Obey,"
Drives half thy loveliness away;
Turns thy warm heart as cold as clay.

The New Ladies' Valentine Writer (1821)

* * *

*T*he carriage rattled over the cobbled streets of Mayfair, its interior warm and quiet, yet Harriet could not summon any sense of comfort. She sat with her hands folded primly in her lap, but her mind raced like a horse bolting toward a precipice.

Sebastian sat opposite, speaking with Evaline, and Harriet did her best to focus on their conversation, but her thoughts would not still. Every time she dared glance at him, at the strong lines of his face, the way his cravat was slightly loosened as if he had already run a hand over his throat in exasperation, the memory of his kiss burned through her like a brand.

A kiss like that should not have happened.

Not after everything. Not after she had deceived him.

Her fingers curled into her skirts, and she turned to look out the carriage window, the passing townhouses blurring together. How had she let it come to this? She had told herself that she had only meant to indulge in a sliver of nostalgia, to recapture a fragment of the past, and yet her heart beat like a drummer marching into battle.

Foolish. It was all so foolish.

She had spent the last few months trying to be someone else, trying to be stronger, wiser, and better than the idiotic girl who had let him go. And yet, the moment he had touched her, she had felt undone, unmoored, as though no time had passed at all.

And the worst of it? Her fresh falsehood stood between them.

If it had only been the past to contend with, she might have dared to hope. But she had committed an act so inexcusable that there could never be anything real between them. Not now.

The painting.

Her throat tightened. He trusted her, even now. Despite everything, he trusted her enough to enter this strange courtship with her. And she—wretched fool that she was—had looked him in the eyes and told him a lie. An untruth she could not undo.

She forced herself to listen to the conversation between Sebastian and Evaline, desperate for a distraction.

"… your husband died?" Sebastian was asking.

"He did," Evaline answered, her voice light despite the morbid subject. "Shot in a drunken brawl with his own pistol."

"My condolences, Lady Wood. Your husband was …" Sebastian stopped as if he were struggling to find pleasant sentiments about the brutish Lord Wood, infamous for solving his arguments with his very large fists. "Excellent at pugilism."

Evaline let out a small breath, her lips quirking. "A diplomatic phrasing."

Harriet finally turned her head, grateful for something else to focus on. Presumably, he had heard something of the matter, considering his family connections, but he had been in Florence at the time so perhaps did not know the full story. That Evaline mentioned the scandal at all meant that she had decided to relax the proprieties with Harriet's lofty suitor—a high compliment from such a proper woman.

"Sebastian has only heard whispers, I imagine. He does not know the full tale."

Evaline hesitated, then set aside her embroidery and met Sebastian's gaze with a wry quirk of her lips. "Well, my husband—rest his soul—was a proud man, but not a wise one. He had a rather spectacular gift for making enemies."

Sebastian arched a brow. "I gathered as much."

"One evening, he found himself in a dispute over a game of cards," Evaline continued. "A dispute which, in his drunkenness, he decided to settle with a pistol."

Sebastian's expression did not change, but Harriet saw a knowing air settle as if he recalled whatever story had made it to him on the Continent. "Ah."

"Yes. He stormed into the home of another lord, pistol in hand, and demanded retribution for his supposed slight."

"I assume the other lord was not particularly receptive to such demands?"

Evaline let out a dry chuckle. "No, he was not. They struggled over the pistol, and it went off."

Harriet sighed, shaking her head. "The gossip was tremendous."

Evaline gave a small shrug, as though it were nothing

more than an amusing anecdote rather than the defining moment that had left her reliant on the charity of others. "It was a relief, in some ways. I was finally free of him. He was not a pleasant man, nor his family with whom I had to stay after his death."

When Evaline then explained how much worse it might have been if not for the mercy of his death, Harriet reached for her hand in sympathy. And her heart squeezed at Evaline's subsequent words of gratitude for Harriet's generosity.

Sebastian looked between them both before murmuring, "So you came to live with Harriet."

Evaline inclined her head. "A few months ago, she was kind enough to offer me refuge, and I was wise enough to accept."

Harriet smiled at her friend, some of the guilt that had been clawing at her chest receding. At least she had done some good things to atone for her ugly past. At least she had provided Evaline with a safe haven when she needed it most.

Sebastian's gaze flicked to Harriet, as if assessing her. "And you? Did you find it easy to take in a houseguest?"

She met his eyes, summoning a semblance of lightness.

"Would you believe it was rather an easy transition? Evaline has excellent taste and took charge of my household in a way that I never had patience for."

Sebastian hummed, clearly unconvinced, but before he could say more, the carriage rolled to a stop. Harriet exhaled, relieved. The coachman opened the door, and Sebastian descended first, offering his hand to help Evaline and Harriet down. The moment her feet touched the ground, she squared her shoulders.

Home. Safe ground.

She stepped forward, only for the door to swing open

before she reached it. Mrs. Finch stood at the threshold, her usual look of stern competence fixed firmly in place.

"Tea, if you please, Finch," Harriet said as she removed her gloves. "I could use a warm cup after all that shopping."

Finch did not move. "Ye've got a visitor, m'lady."

Harriet's fingers stilled. Something about the way Finch said it, the clipped tone, the lack of elaboration, sent a prickle of unease down her spine. She swallowed. "Who?"

Finch did not answer. She merely stepped aside with a grim expression that told Harriet all she needed to know. Harriet turned to Sebastian and Evaline. "Well, come in, then. No use lingering in the cold."

She swept past Finch into the painted room, her heart thudding, and the moment she entered, she saw him.

Bertram Hargreaves stood by the window, hands clasped behind his back, his stiff posture signaling his bristling displeasure.

Harriet stopped just inside the doorway. How? How had he found out so soon?

She barely kept her expression schooled as Sebastian and Evaline entered behind her. Sebastian's presence gave her strength. She lifted her chin, ignored her father entirely, and turned to her guests.

"Please, sit," she said, gesturing toward the elegant chairs near the hearth.

Sebastian hesitated only a fraction of a second before he moved to take his place, his gray gaze flicking between Harriet and her father as he lowered himself into the chair opposite her. Evaline, less affected by the tension, followed suit.

Harriet turned to Finch. "You may bring the tea now."

Finch hesitated, as if she, too, expected some sort of explosion to occur at any moment, but when Harriet arched a brow in silent command, the housekeeper gave a short nod and disappeared down the hall.

Harriet finally turned to her father. "You need not loom like a specter, Father," she said smoothly. "Do take a seat."

Lord Hargreaves did not move. He merely turned his head, his sharp gaze piercing her like a blade.

"I am comfortable where I am," he said, his voice deceptively mild.

Harriet tilted her head, meeting his stare without flinching. "Suit yourself."

She crossed the room and lowered herself onto the settee, arranging her skirts with deliberate elegance. Sebastian's attention never left her. Her father had come here in anger, that much was clear. But Harriet had learned long ago that anger was a tool—one men wielded to make others flinch.

She would not flinch.

And besides, she had Sebastian sitting just across from her, watching everything, weighing everything. A part of her —the girl she had been, the one who had once believed Sebastian could be her escape—wanted to turn to him and say, *See?* See what she had endured. See what she had been raised beneath.

But she said nothing. Instead, she folded her hands in her lap, fixed a pleasant smile upon her face, and waited. Her father wanted something. She would find out what it was soon enough.

* * *

THE RIDE back to Harriet's townhouse had been suitably agreeable, though Sebastian remained keenly aware of the way she carefully sidestepped any mention of her evening the night before. He had asked again, rather casually, whether she had spent a quiet night at home, and she had responded with an easy smile and a vague confirmation that she had.

But he did not believe her.

Not for a moment.

It was the manner in which she said it—too smooth, too well-practiced. And it gnawed at him, because if Harriet had learned to lie so well, what else had she mastered hiding over the years?

Yet, despite the lingering irritation, he could not deny the satisfaction that came from spending the morning in her company. The familiar lilt of her voice, the quick wit that had once enthralled him so effortlessly—it was all too easy to forget the years that lay between them. Too easy to remember what it had been like when he had thought she would be his.

Sebastian had exhaled and forced his thoughts elsewhere, settling in with Harriet and Lady Wood to discuss the books they had ordered at Hatchards. He learned, in the course of their conversation, that Lady Wood's late husband had met his end in a most spectacularly foolish way—breaking into another lord's home over a card game dispute, pistol in hand, only to be shot for his trouble.

Sebastian had to admire Lady Wood's composure as she had spoken of it, her voice light, as though she were discussing the weather. "It was a mercy, in truth. I would not have relished the alternative—him being hanged for trespass and attempted murder."

Harriet had reached over to squeeze her friend's hand in support. "You deserved better," she had said quietly.

"And I have found better. A peaceful home. Good company. What more could I ask?"

The conversation had turned lighter after that, and soon, they arrived at Harriet's townhouse.

As the footman opened the carriage door, Sebastian had

stepped down first, offering his hand to Harriet, then to Lady Wood. Harriet's fingers were steady in his grasp, but he could not help but remember how they had trembled, just slightly, when she had slipped from the ladder in Hatchards, right before he had kissed her.

The memory sent a rush of warmth through him, quickly followed by irritation at his own foolhardy weakness.

The door to the townhouse had opened before they reached it. Mrs. Finch, the formidable housekeeper, stood at the threshold, her expression as impassive as ever.

Harriet ordered tea, and Finch replied that a guest was waiting for her. Sebastian did not miss the way Harriet's posture stiffened ever so slightly before she stepped inside. She had turned back to them and, with a smile too serene to be genuine, gestured toward the drawing room.

"Well, come in, then. No use lingering in the cold."

Sebastian had followed, noting the slight tension in her shoulders as they entered the painted room.

And then he understood—Harriet's father was in the room. Bertram Hargreaves stood at the window, his hands clasped behind his back, staring out at the street with the rigid air of a man who disapproved of everything he saw. He turned only when Harriet stepped inside, his cold blue eyes raking over her before flicking to Sebastian.

Harriet took a seat and invited her father to join them for tea.

"Well," Hargreaves eventually declared after staring at Sebastian for several icy seconds, his voice as smooth as silk, the menacing tone insidious. "Lady Slight, I see you are still keeping questionable company."

Lady Wood, the viscount ignored completely; presumably, a lowly widow was too below his station to acknowledge even with a sneering insult.

Sebastian smiled, unruffled. "A pleasure as always, Lord Hargreaves."

The older man ignored him, his gaze settling on Lady Wood next, and though his expression did not change, Sebastian sensed the slight curl of disdain that lingered beneath the surface. Hargreaves considered a spare to a duke beneath his notice. To make matters worse, Sebastian was no longer even the spare. His brother had sired his heir.

Harriet did not acknowledge her father's comment. "You must have urgent business with me if you have taken the trouble to visit," she said lightly.

Hargreaves gave a faint smile and turned fully toward them. "I am merely paying a visit to my only child. Is that so unusual?"

"It is," Harriet returned. "Unless you are here to harass my staff again. But let us not waste time pretending. What is it you really want?"

Sebastian observed with mild fascination as she held her father's gaze without the slightest hesitation. The flinty viscount was not a man easily ignored—his presence compelling, the kind that made lesser men quail. Yet Harriet faced him with the same effortless poise she had always possessed, as though he were nothing more than an inconvenience she meant to endure.

Sebastian was impressed. Harriet had always quavered in her father's presence, so this was an invigorating evolution to witness.

Hargreaves sighed, as if disappointed by her lack of pretense. "Very well. I came to inquire about a certain … absence."

The viscount's attention shifted to Lady Wood and Sebastian briefly, and Sebastian guessed the wintry lord was being vague intentionally. Perhaps he had not expected the audience for this discussion, but Harriet was obviously unwilling to make allowances for privacy. It was an astute maneuver to gain the upper hand, and Sebastian was impressed to see it. As a girl, Harriet had always been petrified of disappointing her disapproving parent.

Harriet arched an auburn brow. "Whose absence?"

A thin smile. "Cooper."

Sebastian sat straighter. The name tickled the edge of his memory, but he could not immediately place it. But then, it was a common name. Perhaps it was nothing.

Harriet, for her part, did not react—at least, not visibly. "And why, pray, would I know anything about that?" she asked smoothly.

Her father's freezing stare sharpened. "Because Cooper vanished last night, and we discussed this matter just days ago."

Sebastian stilled. Harriet had lied about spending last evening at home. The reminder left a sour taste in his mouth. Had she met with this Cooper? But he said nothing. He merely sat, watchful and silent, as Harriet's expression remained calm.

"I have no knowledge to share," she stated evenly.

Hargreaves chuckled, but there was no humor in it. "Cooper could not leave without a ... benefactor."

Sebastian watched Harriet closely, waiting for some sign of unease. But she only tilted her head. "Perhaps. Or perhaps Cooper simply decided to forge a new path."

Her father's gaze did not waver. "Such an endeavor will not last long without protection."

Harriet's smile was saccharine. "I shall be sure to keep that in mind, should I ever have an opportunity to discuss it with ... Cooper."

It was clear father and daughter were being enigmatic on purpose.

Sebastian glanced toward the doorway then, drawn by

the suggestion of movement beyond the threshold. The young waif stood just beyond the painted room, her wide, anxious eyes peeking in before she darted back out of sight like a frightened rabbit.

Jem.

Sebastian frowned, unsettled by the unease in her posture, but then Mrs. Finch entered, carrying the tea tray, and the moment passed.

Harriet poured the tea herself, her movements graceful and deliberate. "Will you take tea, Father?" she asked sweetly.

Hargreaves's mouth thinned. "No."

She handed a cup to Lady Wood before turning her attention back to him. "Then I suppose this discussion has run its course."

Sebastian did not miss the suggestion of irritation in the viscount's expression. Harriet had dismissed him. Neatly, efficiently.

And Bertram Hargreaves knew it. He glanced toward Sebastian then, his lips curling. "I am sure, Lord Sebastian, that you have no interest in such sordid matters of discarded affairs."

Affairs? Was Hargreaves alluding to Harriet having an affair with this Cooper fellow? To what end would Hargreaves do so? To frighten Sebastian off as a suitor?

Sebastian lifted his cup. Uncertain of the game Hargreaves was playing, Sebastian decided to lay a safe card upon the table, neither a gamble nor a concession. Hargreaves had a terrible reputation as a landlord back in Wiltshire. Several of his tenants had been accommodated by the duke at Avonmead over the years after Hargreaves failed to resolve their complaints. So Sebastian chose to prod at this sore point, rather than reveal he was in the dark about their cryptic quarrel.

"Indeed. Though I do find discussions of integrity in land stewardship quite fascinating."

Harriet's lips twitched. Hargreaves's gaze turned from ice to freezing. And then, with a dangerous growl—a warning, perhaps—Hargreaves turned toward the door.

"Good day, Harriet."

She sipped her tea. "Good day, Father."

The viscount left without another word.

Sebastian leaned back, studying Harriet over the rim of his cup. "You handled that well."

She lifted a shoulder in an elegant shrug, but did not meet his gaze. "I have had months of practice."

His brow tightened. Again the mention of these past few months. And Lady Wood had mentioned she had been staying with Harriet for the same time period. What did it all mean?

Harriet was hiding something.

But what?

CHAPTER 8

Beneath the ancient oak's embrace,
We wander'd slow, in gentle pace;
Your hand in mine, a perfect fit,
As evening's glow in silence lit.

The New Ladies' Valentine Writer (1821)

* * *

DECEMBER 13, 1821

Sebastian woke with a start, the cold light of dawn spilling through the curtains of his guest bedroom. He exhaled sharply, rubbing a hand over his face as if to wipe away the remnants of his restless sleep. The sheets were tangled around his legs, the warmth of slumber long gone, replaced by a familiar, gnawing disquiet.

It had been years since he had allowed himself to dwell on that last day with Harriet—years since he had permitted the memory to rise from where he had buried it. And yet, ever since seeing her again, the past clawed its way to the surface, dragging him back to a time when he had been young and foolish enough to believe in forever.

He swung his long legs over the side of the bed, bracing his elbows on his knees. The embers of a fire from the night before still smoldered in the grate, casting flickering shadows against the paneled walls.

That St. Valentine's Day. It had been the day before they were supposed to flee.

The fevered whispers in the half-light, the weight of her body pressed against his, the unshakable conviction that she was his and he was hers. He had touched her with reverence, with the certainty of a man who believed he would spend his life by her side. She had whispered promises against his skin, her voice hushed but fierce with belief.

Then morning had come, and she had not.

Sebastian sucked in a breath, his hands clenching into fists. The betrayal had carved into him deeper than he had ever admitted. Even now, with years between them, he could not entirely banish the sting of it.

He pushed himself to his feet, crossing the room to splash cold water onto his face. It did little to clear his thoughts.

She had changed. That was what unsettled him most.

The Harriet he had known had been flirtatious, beguiling, always laughing, always seeking the admiration of those around her. The woman he had met again was different. Still sharp, still beautiful, but there was something guarded in her now, something almost wary.

And she was keeping something from him.

Dressing quickly, he donned a dark waistcoat and coat, shrugging into them with an impatient tug. He had no desire to pick at old wounds, but neither could he ignore the strange puzzle she had become. By the time he descended to breakfast, Lorenzo was already seated at the table, a cup of coffee in hand, his sharp black eyes assessing Sebastian the moment he stepped into the room.

"Another late morning, *amico?*" Lorenzo smirked, his Italian accent giving the words an easy lilt.

Sebastian grunted, pouring himself coffee. "I did not realize I had a nursemaid now."

Lorenzo chuckled, setting down his cup. "A nursemaid? No. A friend who happens to be deeply invested in retrieving a certain painting? Absolutely." He leaned forward. "Tell me, how does your charming courtship progress?"

Sebastian exhaled slowly, stirring his coffee with more force than necessary. "It progresses as one would expect of a staged courtship."

Lorenzo was unimpressed. "Which means?"

"She plays her part well."

"Ah." Lorenzo took another sip of coffee, watching him over the rim of his cup. "And yet you are brooding over your morning meal like a man who has spent the night wrestling with ghosts."

Sebastian shot him a warning glance. "I am merely considering our next steps."

Lorenzo hummed in disbelief. "You spoke of her past yesterday, of what she once was to you. But you have not yet told me if you learned anything about our true purpose." He tapped a finger against the table. "Matteo's painting."

Sebastian had known this was coming.

He set down his cup carefully. "I did not mention it."

Lorenzo's brows lifted. "Not at all?"

"No."

His friend tilted his head. "And why is that, I wonder?"

Because speaking of paintings and business felt utterly inconsequential when faced with the reality of Harriet in front of him, standing in the soft glow of the British

Museum, her lips curving in a knowing smile, thinking thoughts he could not yet name. Or the press of her mouth against his in that stolen moment at Hatchards when passion had overtaken him, and only the risk of being caught had made him push away. Or watching her put her father in his place, an unexpected development that had made his heart swell with pride for the strong, independent woman she had become.

The instant he had seen her again, his carefully laid plans had begun to unravel. Because some foolish, reckless part of him still wanted to believe she was more than a means to an end.

He did not say any of that.

Instead, he leaned back in his chair, meeting Lorenzo's gaze evenly. "Harriet has always been adept at keeping her secrets. I will learn what I need to in time."

Lorenzo studied him, his expression shrewd. "See that you do, *amico*. You and I both know why we are in England, and we have obligations to see to in Florence."

Sebastian said nothing, merely raising his cup once more, hiding his expression behind the rim as he swallowed down the bitter taste of coffee and something far more dangerous —his own uncertainty.

He arrived at Harriet's residence just as a fresh gust of December wind howled through the streets, whipping stray flakes of snow from rooftops and scattering them like powdered sugar over the cobbles. The morning was crisp, the sky a pale and frigid blue, the kind that promised a day without further snowfall but no relief from the biting cold. He flexed his fingers in his gloves, rolling his shoulders beneath his heavy greatcoat as he stepped down from the carriage, a faint grimace curling at the corner of his lips.

London in December was a paradox, bustling and yet subdued, lively but weighed down by the gray pallor of winter. The Season was mostly concluded, the brightest lights of the *ton* having long since retired to their country estates for Christmastide, leaving the city a quieter, less gilded version of itself. The once-crowded avenues were less frenetic, the grand houses draped in a more somber dignity without the constant flux of carriages and visiting callers. Even so, the heart of the city still pulsed with life, particularly in the commercial districts where merchants peddled holiday goods and street vendors huddled over steaming carts of roasted chestnuts and hot meat pies. The chill did little to deter the scent of fresh bread from wafting from the bakeries, mingling with the sharper tang of horsehair and damp wool.

Sebastian took in a long draught of morning air, ignoring the way the cold burned his lungs. It was an odd thing to be back here, walking familiar streets as though he had never left. But the longer he stayed in London, the more he realized that the city had moved on without him.

When the door opened, he was greeted by Harriet's odd housekeeper. Finch was a squat, no-nonsense woman with an assessing gaze that reminded him of a drill sergeant inspecting the troops. She barely blinked at his presence, nor did she bother with unnecessary formalities before stepping aside to let him in.

"Lady Slight and Lady Wood will be down presently," she announced before disappearing down the hall.

Sebastian removed his hat and gloves, handing them off to a new footman who looked as though he had been recently pressed into service—older than most and slightly too eager, not yet possessing the polished indifference of a seasoned servant.

Sebastian was still adjusting to Harriet's peculiar household. Everything about it was unexpected, from the lack of traditional footmen to the unorthodox servants who seemed more like strays taken in than proper domestics. He had not yet made up his mind whether to admire Harriet for it or worry over what it meant.

A moment later, the rustle of skirts signaled their arrival, and he turned to find Harriet descending the stairs, Lady Wood just behind her. Both were bundled in thick cloaks, layers of wool and fur carefully arranged to ward off the chill. Harriet's deep green pelisse was lined with sable, the color striking against the rich auburn of her hair, which was neatly tucked beneath a bonnet of the same green shade. Lady Wood, by contrast, wore a more subdued ensemble of dove-gray, her gloved hands primly clasped before her as she stepped down with quiet grace.

"You are well prepared for the elements," Sebastian observed, his gaze lingering on Harriet.

She arched a brow. "London in December is hardly forgiving. I do not intend to spend the day as an icicle."

He grinned, offering his arm as he escorted them to the waiting carriage. He helped Lady Wood in first, then turned to Harriet. As she placed her gloved hand in his, he felt the briefest hesitation—an unspoken awareness sparking between them as they both remembered the stolen kiss in the bookshop. Then she was inside, settling into the squabs, and the moment passed.

As the carriage lurched forward, they fell into easy conversation.

"I enjoyed our book shopping," Harriet remarked as she adjusted the folds of her cloak.

"Then Hatchards was the right place for such an endeavor," Sebastian replied. "Have you thought of any more titles?"

"I will need novels, of course, but also travelogues. I should like to read of faraway places. Perhaps it will inspire me to venture beyond England's shores one day."

Sebastian's lips quirked. "Ah, so you will take to

wandering at last? I seem to recall someone invested in my enthusiasm for the Grand Tour in our youth."

Harriet's expression softened and grew wistful. "I was terribly envious of your freedoms as a young man."

"That is one way to describe it," he teased. "If I recall, you once declared in a fit of pique that anything beyond the borders of England was bound to be dreadfully inconvenient and full of strange customs."

She huffed a small laugh. "I was young and foolish."

"Young, certainly," he conceded. "But never foolish."

A pause. A moment of quiet understanding.

Across from them, Lady Wood continued with her novel, choosing not to interrupt their exchange.

The journey continued with pleasant conversation, their discussion drifting through old memories and musings about what additional books ought to be deemed essential for a proper library. The warmth of the carriage made the outside world seem distant, a fleeting unreality beyond the frosty windows.

Before long, the carriage slowed, and Sebastian glanced out to see that they had reached their destination.

The Royal Menagerie at the Tower of London had long been a fascination for the curious-minded. Though its heyday as a grand attraction had somewhat faded, it still held an air of mystique—particularly in winter, when fewer visitors braved the cold.

Inside, the space smelled of straw and damp stone, with the occasional sharp tang of animal musk. The echoes of distant growls and calls reverberated through the corridors, punctuated by the occasional rustle of unseen movement.

Sebastian watched as Harriet moved through the exhibits, alight with curiosity. There was something fierce about her, something untamed beneath the polished veneer of her societal role. He had always known her to be a woman of intelligence and boldness, but this Harriet—this woman who had shed some of her former coquettish airs—intrigued him in a way he had not expected.

They paused before the lion's enclosure, where a great beast lounged upon a raised platform, watching them with lazy indifference.

Harriet tilted her head, studying it. "Magnificent, is he not?"

"Indeed," Sebastian murmured. "Proud. Regal. But dangerous, if one does not understand its nature."

Her lips curved slightly. "Are we speaking of the lion, my lord, or something else entirely?"

He met her gaze, his expression carefully composed. "Perhaps both."

She did not look away. The moment stretched between them, taut with things unsaid.

Then Lady Wood cleared her throat, breaking the spell. Harriet turned back to the lion, her demeanor shifting into something more contemplative while Sebastian let out a slow breath, adjusting his gloves.

Perhaps it was the atmosphere of the menagerie—the lingering scent of the wild, the way the air seemed thick with an ancient, primal energy—but for the first time in years, he felt as though he was standing at the edge of something unknown. Something that, despite his better judgment, he wanted to explore.

* * *

As the carriage rolled away from the Tower, the imposing stone fortress receding behind them, Harriet pressed her gloved hands against her lap, willing her emotions to settle. The Royal Menagerie had been an interesting distraction, but Sebastian's lingering presence beside her, so close and so warm in the winter chill, unsettled her more than the sight of the great beasts pacing behind their iron bars.

She had expected this courtship—this playacting—to be a simple matter. A few outings, a few stolen glances, and then a graceful parting when Christmas arrived, as if they had never been more than polite acquaintances.

But Sebastian had kissed her. And the memory of it burned through her like mulled wine, warm and heady.

He sat opposite her now, the winter sunlight filtering through the glass of the carriage, catching on the clean, striking lines of his face. He appeared pensive, as if he, too, was troubled. Evaline sat beside her, blissfully unaware of the silent war raging within Harriet's chest.

Their destination was Hyde Park, a perfect place for a gentleman to promenade with a lady on his arm. Harriet had walked there many times, but not like this. Not with Sebastian.

Not with her heart in shambles.

London bustled outside the carriage, the streets teeming with life as the city prepared for the afternoon's business. The wintry air carried the scent of roasting chestnuts from a street cart, mingling with the ever-present tang of soot from chimneys.

Sebastian broke the silence first. "Did you enjoy the menagerie?"

"I did," she admitted, "though I confess, I have always found something rather sad about wild creatures in cages."

He nodded slowly. "They are trapped, yes. But in a way, they are safer than they would be in the wild. Some of those animals would never survive beyond those bars."

Harriet turned her gaze to him, studying the thoughtful set of his mouth. "Is that what you believe? That captivity is preferable to danger?"

Sebastian looked at her then, really looked, and for a

moment she thought he might respond with truths too raw, too real. But instead, he only offered a faint smile. "It depends on the creature, I suppose."

The carriage came to a halt, jolting them slightly. Harriet glanced out the window and saw the familiar wrought-iron gates of Hyde Park.

"We are here," Evaline announced cheerfully, adjusting her gloves.

Sebastian stepped out first, turning to offer his hand. When Harriet placed her fingers in his, a shiver that had nothing to do with the cold ran up her arm.

They entered the park, the gravel path crunching beneath their boots. The air was crisp, and though the trees had long since shed their autumn foliage, Hyde Park was still lively. Children bundled in coats and scarves ran ahead of their governesses, laughing as they kicked up the last remnants of frost-covered leaves. A young couple strolled arm in arm, their heads bent together in quiet conversation. A gentleman cantered past on a fine black gelding, his breath clouding in the cold air.

Evaline, ever the sociable one, soon spotted an acquaintance—a matronly woman in a fur-trimmed pelisse, accompanied by a daughter of marriageable age. She paused to greet them, offering Harriet and Sebastian a polite smile before turning away to engage in conversation.

And then, quite suddenly, Sebastian took Harriet's hand. She barely had time to register the sensation of his fingers curling around hers before he was leading her away, stepping behind the thick trunk of an ancient oak.

"Sebastian—"

And then his firm, warm lips were on hers.

The world tilted.

She gasped, her fingers gripping the lapels of his coat as all sense of cold vanished. This kiss was different from the one at Hatchards—where that one had been impulsive, this one was deliberate, searing, demanding. He pressed her against the rough bark of the tree, his gloved hand cradling her cheek, tilting her face up to him as if he could not bear even a whisper of distance between them.

It was madness.

But Harriet had never felt so alive.

She melted into him, letting herself drown in the taste of him, the feel of his body against hers. The years between them, the regrets, the lies—none of it existed in that moment. There was only this, only him.

When they finally broke apart, she was breathless.

Sebastian's forehead rested against hers, his breath warm against her chilled skin.

"This is a mistake," she whispered.

He exhaled, his fingers still tangled in her hair where her bonnet had slipped. "Then why does it feel so right?"

Harriet closed her eyes, her heart pounding like a wild stallion bucking against its master.

If she were another woman, if she had made different choices, she would go with him to Italy. She would leave all of this behind, abandon the burden of her mistakes, and become his.

But she was not that woman.

And she had lied.

The thought sliced through her like a blade, sharp and merciless.

She wrenched herself away, wrapping her arms around herself as if to hold in the ache that threatened to spill over.

"I cannot continue," she said, her voice unsteady. "Knowing it is a pretense is breaking my heart."

Sebastian stared down at her for the longest time. Then he said the one thing she had not dared to allow herself to hope for. "What if it is not a pretense?"

Harriet's head snapped up.

He was watching her with an intensity that sent her pulse into a wild, desperate rhythm.

For one glorious, reckless moment, hope blossomed in her chest.

But then, reality returned like a bitter wind.

She had lied about the painting. Then there was her shameful behavior these past years for which she was attempting to make amends. If Sebastian knew the half of it, he would be repulsed by her base nature and desert her.

He was a foolish dream, a glimpse of the life she could have led if she had been a better person. And after all she had done to him in the past, he could never be so forgiving as to allow her another deception. Whatever spark had rekindled between them would be extinguished the moment he discovered the truth.

She forced a smile, though it felt brittle on her lips. "I think," she said carefully, "we should return to Lady Wood before she notices we have gone."

Sebastian studied her. "And I think we should make this courtship a genuine exploration of a shared future."

Harriet stared up at him, searching for any sign he was funning her, but he seemed sincere. Her breath caught, and she nervously licked her lips. She wanted so badly to say—

"Yes."

She blinked, uncertain if she had truly consented. Then, in affirmation that she had indeed spoken out loud, Sebastian gave a slow nod and offered his arm. She hesitated for only a moment before taking it.

As they stepped back onto the path, Harriet forced herself to do what she had done for years. She buried the ache, smothered the longing, and vowed to enjoy the courtship as long as it lasted. Because once Sebastian learned the truth— about the painting, about her repellant entanglement with his cousin Perry last year, about her disloyalty with the duke's brother-in-law Brendan earlier this very year—there would be no more kisses beneath the trees, no more glances filled with unspoken promises.

And she had no one to blame but herself.

But for now, every impossible dream had come true until brooding reality inevitably returned. The only man she had ever loved was courting her!

CHAPTER 9

In silence, I adore your grace,
Afraid to speak or show my face;
Yet through this verse, my heart's revealed,
A love that's deep and long concealed.

The New Ladies' Valentine Writer (1821)

* * *

DECEMBER 18, 1821

"*T*his is a terrible idea."

Harriet sat rigid before the dressing table, watching her reflection as Belinda twisted her hair into an elegant coil. The candlelight flickered against the mirror's surface, but no amount of flattering glow could soften the worry etched between her brows.

The last few days in Sebastian's company had been blissful, their courtship progressing to the natural next stage—dinner with his family!

"Nonsense," Evaline said from the nearby settee, where she lounged with a cup of chocolate in hand. "It is an inevitable idea."

"I prefer terrible."

"Then terrible it shall be," Evaline said dryly. "Yet we are still attending."

Harriet groaned, gripping the arms of the chair. "It has been years since I have dined at Markham House. *Years*, Evaline. And now I am to eat my supper, all smiles and good cheer, as if they have not all spent half a decade *despising* me?"

"Not all of them," Evaline countered. "Sebastian does not despise you."

No, he did not. But his brother, the Duke of Halmesbury, certainly did. And she did not know what to expect from the others—Lord and Lady Saunton were likely to be the peacemakers, but Brendan Ridley would be there. And Lily Ridley.

It was Lily's curse that had set this current quest for redemption in motion. Harriet let out a slow breath, the name alone making her chest tighten when she recalled that moment when Lily had uttered those damnable words and shattered Harriet's glib shell that had protected her from confronting the consequences of her selfish behavior.

"I should feign illness," she mused aloud.

Belinda snorted. "And have Lord Sebastian fetch a physician? I daresay he would see through that ruse."

Harriet caught Belinda's smirk in the mirror. "You are enjoying this too much."

"A little," Belinda admitted, securing a pin before stepping back to admire her work. "There. Now you look like a woman perfectly suited for the Duke of Halmesbury's dinner table."

Harriet studied herself. The intricate ivory gown of velvet complemented her complexion, and the sapphires at her throat were understated but elegant. A picture of composed grace.

A lie.

Belinda's expression softened as she rested a hand on Harriet's shoulder. "It is not just the duke that worries you."

Harriet hesitated. It was not often that someone saw past her outward bravado, but Belinda was no fool.

"I hear you had an affair with Lord Saunton's brother," Belinda prompted.

Harriet let out a short laugh. "Oh yes. We were … acquainted … last year, briefly."

Belinda's fingers tightened on her shoulder. "Acquainted?"

"For a matter of weeks," Harriet admitted. "Until he met Miss Emma Davis of Somerset and married her. It was a fortunate escape, truly."

Belinda arched a brow. "And Lord Brendan Ridley?"

Harriet's stomach knotted. She looked down, fingers tracing the embroidery on her gown.

"That was … different."

"Different how?"

Harriet swallowed, meeting Belinda's gaze in the mirror. "Because I betrayed him."

Belinda studied her intently, but Harriet had no desire to explain further. She turned her attention back to her gloves, slipping them on with deliberate precision. The silence deepened, until Evaline finally spoke from across the room.

"I can explain it, if you wish?"

Harriet gave a curt nod, a blush of shame washing across her skin as she fiddled with her evening gloves. Belinda and she had become fast friends in the few days since joining their household, the older woman being both elegant and pragmatic about the ways of high society.

"Brendan Ridley was accused of patricide. At the time of the murder, he was here at Harriet's, but she would not provide him an alibi, so a young debutante provided it in her place."

Belinda gasped. "Miss Lily Abbott! That makes much more sense than those bizarre rumors that an innocent young miss had an affair with him!"

Harriet flinched. Rescuing Belinda from her father's faithlessness was meant to help make up for that repugnant misstep. Which it had, but having dinner with both Brendan and Lily Ridley was not a hill she was ready to climb quite yet.

"It does not matter now," Harriet said. "This dinner will be a disaster regardless of past sins. His Grace despises me. I … have given him cause."

"Perhaps," Evaline murmured. "Or perhaps this dinner will be a chance to mend what has been broken."

Harriet forced a smile. "Optimism is exhausting."

Evaline set down her cup with a soft clink. "Then let us simply endure. You are not alone in this, Harriet."

No, she was not.

But as she rose and took a final look at her reflection, Harriet could not shake the feeling that she was walking into a den of wolves. Or rather, a den of her past mistakes with important peers to witness the reckoning. Each one of them had an axe to grind, and surely her and Sebastian's fledgling courtship would not survive such revelations if they should come to pass.

Or did he already know what she had done to members of his circle?

That thought made her hunch her shoulders in abashed despair. Then she felt Evaline's hand on her shoulder.

"I will be there to support you. You are not alone."

Tears sprang into her eyes, and Harriet raised a hand to

cover that of her friend in relieved gratitude. Thank heavens Evaline was attending as her companion.

* * *

SEBASTIAN STOOD in the grand foyer of Markham House, adjusting the cuffs of his coat as he listened to the measured tick of the tall case clock against the far wall. The scent of fresh pine lingered in the air, mingling with the faint aroma of roasted meats drifting from the dining room beyond.

Despite the festive garlands draped along the banister and the holly-adorned chandeliers, the atmosphere was anything but warm.

The butler, Clinton, had barely concealed his disapproval when he had announced Lady Slight's arrival, and Sebastian had been quick to come meet her in the entrance hall, unwilling to leave her at the mercy of disapproving stares.

Curiously, she had not yet entered the house, so he awaited her with some concern. He did not, however, expect her hesitation as she finally stepped inside, nor the way she briefly squeezed his offered arm before schooling her features into polite serenity.

Harriet was not a woman who hesitated.

The murmur of voices in the drawing room hushed at their entrance, resuming only in stilted bursts as the assembled guests took in the sight of her.

His cousin, Richard, and his wife, Sophia, were the first to recover. The earl inclined his head with his customary easy charm, while the countess stepped forward with a warm, if slightly cautious, smile.

It was still startling to witness the earl settled in marriage. His cousin had been a charming but notorious rake, chasing skirts across the length and breadth of England, and Sebastian was unaccustomed to Richard taking the time to attend family dinners. He had always expected the earl would wed some mouse of a girl and leave her to rusticate in the country while he continued his hedonistic pursuits, much like Bertram Hargreaves had eventually done with Harriet's mother.

"Lady Slight," Sophia said. "How lovely to see you."

Harriet matched her smile, though Sebastian could feel the faint tension in her arm beneath his touch. "Lady Saunton, the pleasure is mine."

Across the room, Brendan Ridley toyed with the stem of his wineglass, barely looking at Harriet. His wife, Lily, however, was not nearly so composed.

"Oh, what a surprise!" Lily's voice was too bright, too forced, as she adjusted the lace of her sleeve with nervous fingers. "How unexpected to see you here, Lady Slight."

"It is not unexpected," the duke said flatly. "Lord Sebastian was invited."

The words were cool, aloof. His brother had not moved from his place near the hearth, his stormy gaze assessing Harriet with quiet scrutiny. Beside him, the duchess—resplendent in deep burgundy—rested a gloved hand over the curve of her very rounded belly, and she smiled politely.

Sebastian's jaw tensed. He had known Philip would be displeased, but there was a severity to his brother's somber regard that set him on edge. Harriet, however, remained composed. If the duke's coldness bothered her, she did not show it.

"The weather has turned bitter," the earl said into the silence, as though determined to stir warmth back into the room. Sebastian appreciated Richard's efforts. "Did you have a comfortable drive?"

"Yes," Harriet said simply, offering no further elaboration.

The countess smiled tightly before shifting to Lady

Wood, who had entered just behind them. "And you, Lady Wood?"

Lady Wood, ever unflappable, inclined her head. "Quite comfortable, thank you. Markham House is as lovely as I remember."

Philip said nothing but smiled tightly at the widow.

"Shall we go in to dinner?" the duchess suggested after a beat, her voice soft.

The butler appeared in the doorway, bowing slightly. "Your Grace, dinner is served."

The guests filed into the dining room, where a long, elegantly set table gleamed beneath a cascade of candlelight. The silver shone, polished to perfection, and a towering arrangement of evergreen and red berries stretched the length of the center. The footmen, dressed in rich navy livery with gold-trimmed epaulets, moved with silent efficiency as they pulled out chairs and poured wine.

Harriet took her seat beside Sebastian, across from Lily and Brendan. At the far end, the duchess presided, serene and elegant, while the duke sat at the opposite head of the table. Richard and his countess were seated in places of honor nearest their host.

Sebastian did not miss the way Harriet's fingers curled against the edge of her napkin, nor the slight tension in her shoulders as the first course was served—oysters on the half shell, their briny scent mingling with the fragrant warmth of fresh-baked bread.

"A fine selection," Richard remarked, breaking a piece of bread and spreading it with butter. "Nothing heralds the Christmas season quite like a proper feast."

"Indeed," his countess agreed. "Though I find I am most looking forward to the plum pudding. My cook has been soaking ours in brandy for weeks."

"The best way," Sebastian said, taking a sip of his wine. "It would not be Christmas without a proper pudding."

"And the Yule log," Lily added, dabbing her lips with her napkin. "Was that not a lark, Brendan? We made a dreadful mess of the kitchen trying to help with the sugared holly leaves."

Brendan merely nodded, still avoiding Harriet's gaze.

Sebastian glanced at Harriet, who had barely touched her oysters. Her expression remained serene, but there was something distant in her demeanor.

"Have you any particular traditions, Lady Slight?" Richard's wife prompted gently, clearly trying to draw Harriet into the conversation.

Harriet smiled, though it did not quite reach her eyes. "Nothing so grand as a proper Yule log."

Lily bit her lip, shifting in her chair. "I … I remember your mother hosted lovely Christmas gatherings," she said quickly, as though the words had escaped before she could stop them. "When we were girls. Sophia—I mean, Lady Saunton—and I loved to dress in velvet for the holidays."

There was a pause, barely a heartbeat long, but heavy with unspoken history.

Harriet's fingers stilled on her napkin. "Yes," she said softly. "She did. But these days my mother does not leave Wiltshire."

Philip's gaze flickered with distaste. Sebastian set down his glass, glancing between his brother and Harriet. He did not understand the entirety of what had passed between them in the past, but he knew Harriet had once been welcome at this table and he had believed she would join this family.

And yet here she sat, poised and lovely, but a stranger nonetheless.

The footmen cleared the first course and replaced it with

roasted venison, fragrant with rosemary and juniper. Golden roasted potatoes gleamed alongside it, with bowls of buttered parsnips and stewed apples set at intervals down the table.

The conversation continued—of holiday gatherings, of the earl's plans to host a Twelfth Night ball, of Brendan and Lily's plans to spend Christmas in the countryside.

Harriet spoke when addressed but offered nothing more. Her silence was not cold, nor resentful, but it was measured.

Sebastian wondered if she, like him, was remembering what it had once been like—when her laughter had filled these halls, when she had belonged.

When she had been all but his.

Dinner continued in a similar vein, with Lily's nervous chatter providing a distraction from the terse interactions with the duke. Richard and the countess made considerable efforts to keep the conversation going, and Sebastian noted that Lady Wood frequently spoke up to cover for Harriet, who maintained her quiet composure but he could see the strain was wearing on her. Perhaps it had been a mistake to force an intimate family dinner on her, but it was an inevitable step if their courtship were to proceed.

He did wonder about Brendan Ridley, the duchess's brother, who barely spoke the entire meal. But, finally, it was over and Harriet and Lady Wood made a quick escape with excuses about an early morning.

The scent of strong coffee curled through the air as the four men gathered in the duke's study, the fire casting shadows across the dark-paneled walls. Sebastian wrapped his hands around his cup, its warmth doing little to ease the simmering frustration tightening his shoulders.

Philip, seated behind his mahogany desk, was as composed as ever, his cold scrutiny resting briefly on Sebastian before he took a brief sip of his coffee.

"I am surprised you brought her here," he said at last.

Sebastian set down his cup with deliberate care. "You made it clear you disapproved." He met his brother's gaze, unflinching. "Yet she came. I thought it was rather brave, considering she knew she was unwelcome."

Brendan and Richard exchanged glances. The duke exhaled slowly, setting his own cup aside. "There are good reasons for her to be wary of attending. You do not know everything."

Sebastian's jaw tensed. "I know enough."

Philip's expression remained stern. "She was—"

In his peripheral vision, Sebastian saw Brendan straighten in alarm, as if eager to cut the duke off. Curious. What was Brendan worried about? Richard was fidgeting with his cravat—a tell that he was nervous—before speaking up in a hesitant tone.

"Ah … Philip, I do not think it is fair to discuss—"

Harriet was not the only one keeping secrets from him, it would seem. His own brother, cousin, and the duke's brother-in-law all appeared to be privy to some shared mystery.

"If Harriet wishes me to know, she will tell me herself."

Sebastian's voice was firm, though inside, he burned to demand answers. But not like this. Not behind her back. Whatever truths she held would be meaningless unless she chose to reveal them herself.

Philip's expression hardened. Darting a glance at Richard, he inclined his head. "As you wish. But I will repeat my warning—the apple does not fall far from the Hargreaves tree."

Their cousin leaned forward, his tone conciliatory. "And sometimes a person defies expectations by rejecting the example their parents have set."

Sebastian examined Richard, surprised by the unexpected

defense of Harriet. Had the earl truly reformed so thoroughly? Even worse than Richard had been his late father, unfondly referred to as the Earl of Satan in reference to the Saunton title.

Since returning to England, Sebastian had been told about Richard's conversion to honorable conduct. How was it that Philip could remain close friends with Richard these many years during his licentious activities, but the duke would make no concessions that Harriet might, too, have redeemable qualities?

The earl stood up after his remark, proposing a game of billiards in an obvious ploy to lighten the tension, but the other men declined. The earl had had quite a change in character in the years Sebastian had resided in Italy, acting as peacemaker the entire evening, and raising Sebastian's suspicions of what his cousin was about. Was he merely trying to ease tensions?

In Sebastian's experience, Richard was rather self-absorbed with his own pleasures, so it was still startling to see him making an effort to mediate in this manner. Even the lack of a fine French brandy in his cousin's hand after such a lavish dinner was an unexpected development. What did Richard stand to gain from all this?

Sebastian regretted maneuvering Harriet into attending this dinner in the first place. Everyone had been on tenterhooks, and despite their foreknowledge of her attendance, they had seemed taken aback when she was actually announced. There had been so many undercurrents at dinner, he had worried that Harriet would be pulled into a whirlpool and swept away before he could grasp hold of her.

He took another sip of coffee, but it tasted bitter now.

CHAPTER 10

Beneath the moon's soft silver light,
We wandered through the tranquil night;
Your hand in mine, our hearts entwined,
In love's sweet dance, our souls aligned.

The New Ladies' Valentine Writer (1821)

* * *

*H*arriet wrapped her hands around the porcelain cup, letting the warmth seep into her fingers as she stared into the fire. The painted room was a sanctuary, but tonight, even its familiar elegance did little to soothe the constriction in her chest. The events of the evening had left her raw, her composure stretched too thin. She had sat through dinner with people who despised her—people who had every right to.

She had smiled, spoken when spoken to, and kept her back straight, but now that she was alone, her past sins crashed down upon her. The guilt was a noxious thing, curling in her belly like smoke from a dying candle. Sebastian. Perry. Brendan. Her cowardice.

Even now, she writhed with remorse over the afternoon she had drunk far too much wine, protesting the loss of another lover to a less sophisticated woman, and had tried to seduce Brendan in his own home. Until his wife had walked in and caught her embracing the panicked baron who had been trying to tear himself away.

How could Sebastian forgive her when he learned the truth? How could anyone forgive her? She had been a terrible person. Now she could only claim to be a regretful person. It was surely premature to claim she had the right to be considered good after all her sins.

A quiet knock at the door startled her. Jem's small freckled face appeared in the dim candlelight.

"M'lady," she whispered. "You have a visitor."

Harriet frowned. "At this hour?"

The girl hesitated. "It is Lord Sebastian."

Her stomach dropped. Light played over her silk-wrapped knees as she set her chocolate aside, forcing her voice into calmness. "Send him in."

Jem disappeared, and a moment later, Sebastian stepped inside, closing the door behind him with quiet precision. He was still dressed in his evening clothes, though he had loosened his cravat. His gaze swept over her, from her loose hair to the Parisian negligée peeking from beneath her thick wool wrapper, the lacy garment being one of the indulgences of her old life that she still clung to.

"You should not be here," she murmured.

"And yet, here I am."

Harriet tilted her head, studying Sebastian in the glow of the fire in the hearth. He seemed unsettled, his usually sharp gaze unfocused, as if he were warring with thoughts he had no wish to voice. His lips were pressed into a firm line, his hands clenched at his sides, and though he was standing mere feet away from her, he looked as if he were caught in the grips of something far away—something painful.

"Sebastian?" she asked softly, rising to her feet.

He did not answer.

Instead, in two swift strides, he closed the distance between them, his hands framing her face before she could react. His lips claimed hers in a kiss that stole the breath from her lungs, deep and unhurried, as if learning the taste of her, memorizing the feel of her beneath his hands.

Harriet shuddered, sinking into him, unable to stop the way her fingers curled into the fabric of his coat. It was intoxicating, this feeling of being consumed by him. How many times had she imagined this very moment, alone in the dark with nothing but regret and longing to keep her company?

But this was no dream. This was Sebastian. And he was here, kissing her as if the years apart had never been.

When he finally lifted his head, his breathing was uneven, and she saw the glint of raw emotion.

"How many have you invited to your bed, Harry?"

The question was a blade, slipping between her ribs and lodging itself in her heart.

She stiffened, but she did not look away.

"Too many. Less than people think."

Sebastian's jaw tensed. "How many?"

"Why does it matter?" she whispered.

"How many, Harry?" he repeated, his voice low, unrelenting.

She hesitated, but then, what was the point of lying? Here was a small truth she could give him when there were so many secrets to hide.

"Seven or eight," she admitted, her voice barely audible. "I always imagined they were you."

A muscle tightened in his jaw. The grip he still had on her loosened, his thumb stroking idly over her cheekbone.

"Does that include Horace?"

She snorted inelegantly, some of the tension in her chest easing. "My late husband could not remember his own name, never mind that he had a bride lurking in his halls. I stayed out of his way until he departed."

"Ruthless."

"It was," she admitted, her voice quieter now. "But I am no longer proud of that. I should have taken a chance on you. On us."

Sebastian's expression darkened.

"What about you?" she asked, the words leaving her before she could stop them.

He exhaled, stepping back slightly, as if putting space between them would soften the blow of whatever he was about to say. "It is hard to tell. Fifteen? Twenty, perhaps? I was foxed most of the time until Lorenzo convinced me it was time to stop."

Harriet swallowed against the jealousy that surged within her, unwelcome but undeniable. She had no right to it—after all, she had tried to drown her own pain in the arms of others after a healthy dose of alcohol to make her forget the one she truly loved. But hearing him say it made it real in a way she had never allowed herself to think about before.

She had spent so many years trying to forget him, numbing herself with wine and empty affections. But he had done the same, had tried just as hard to erase the past with women who would never mean anything.

"We were a world apart, yet we spent our time doing the same thing," she murmured, half to herself. "Trying to forget."

Sebastian reached out, tucking a loose curl behind her ear. "Spirits and bed sport do not heal a broken heart."

"No," she agreed, voice thick with regret. "They do not."

For a long moment, they simply stood there, the fire crackling in the hearth the only sound in the stillness between them. Harriet felt raw, exposed, as if the small part of her burden had been lifted but there were so many more parts to contend with.

And, in that moment, she did not feel entirely alone. Sebastian had carried his own burdens. Perhaps, just perhaps, they could find a way to set them down. Together.

Sebastian's gaze darkened as he watched her, golden light casting against his sharp cheekbones and firm mouth. He reached for her, his hands steady yet urgent, settling on her waist with a possessive familiarity that sent a shiver of anticipation skittering down her spine. Even through the thick layer of wool and the thin silk beneath, his warmth seeped into her, setting every inch of her skin alight.

He drew her close, and she swayed into him, her body responding with a will of its own. His hands slid lower, over the curve of her hips, down to cup the soft swell of her derriere. Harriet gasped at the intimate caress, her fingers tangling in his hair, tugging as if to anchor herself against the storm of sensation rising within her.

Her stomach tightened, desire pulsing low and insistent in her belly. The scent of him—clean linen, a hint of sandalwood, a thread of musk purely masculine and uniquely Sebastian—wrapped around her, stirring memories she had long since buried.

"You are playing with fire," she whispered against his lips, but she made no effort to pull away.

"I have been burning for years," he murmured in return, and then his mouth was on hers again, deep and searching, coaxing her lips apart until she trembled against him.

She scarcely noticed when he began to untie the belt of her wool robe, only realizing its absence when cool air licked against the thin silk of her negligée. He spread his hands over her back, his touch gentle, molding her to him as his fingers traced the delicate curve of her spine. She gasped as he reached the small of her back, then lower, until his palms pressed against the flare of her hips, drawing her closer until there was no space left between them and she could feel the hard length of his arousal against her quivering belly.

Sebastian's lips abandoned hers, traveling downward, pressing open-mouthed kisses along the column of her throat, his tongue searing heat against her chilled skin. She arched, a moan slipping from her lips, granting him better access. He lathed the sensitive skin of her neck, his breath hot against her ear as she shuddered in surrender.

He stepped her back and then lowered her down onto the rug in front of the fire, stretching her out beneath him before leaning back to shrug out of his winter overcoat and his evening coat beneath until he was down to his linen shirt and waistcoat. His hands splayed over the delicate silk covering her body. Harriet felt his ravenous gaze as he took in the sight of her, almost laid bare, her chest rising and falling with each breath.

His fingers skimmed her shoulder, slipping beneath the delicate strap of her negligée. Slowly, excruciatingly, he eased the fabric downward, baring one shoulder, then the other, until the silk pooled around her waist. The air kissed her skin, sending a fresh shiver through her even as his gaze burned over her exposed flesh.

"You are magnificent," he said hoarsely, his voice thick with interest far deeper than desire.

His hands followed the path of his eyes, cupping her breasts, his palms warm against her skin. Harriet gasped as his thumb brushed over the tight peak, sensation shooting straight through her. Her body responded instinctively, arching toward him, seeking the heat of his touch.

Sebastian lowered his head, his lips replacing his fingers, his tongue teasing over the puckered tip. A soft cry escaped her, her fingers digging into the muscles of his back as pleasure coiled low in her belly.

His body was hard and unyielding above her, a contrast to the patient worship of his mouth. He kissed a slow, searing path down the length of her torso, his breath warm against her skin, nuzzling every inch of her until Harriet thought she would go mad with need.

She pressed closer, seeking him, feeling the unmistakable heat of his arousal straining against the fine wool of his trousers. Her heart pounded wildly, a desperate rhythm that matched the fire coursing through her veins. But despite her urgency, Sebastian's hands mapped the curves of her body with aching precision, his touch lingering at the swell of her hips before dipping lower. His mouth followed, his lips grazing her lower belly.

She could scarcely think, could scarcely breathe beneath the onslaught of sensation. She had taken lovers before, but this was different. This was not the pursuit of pleasure or distraction. This was a synchronism that stripped her bare, left her vulnerable in a way she had never allowed herself to be.

It was as if she were awakening from a deep slumber, rediscovering the magic of true affinity. As if, for the first time in years, she was truly alive.

Rising up to his knees, he quickly unbuttoned his waistcoat and tossed it aside before grabbing at his linen shirt, yanking it free of his trousers, and whipping it off in one fluid motion.

The firelight cast a golden glow over his bare skin, illuminating the lean, hard planes of his torso. The years had honed him—sculpting the smooth expanse of his chest and the taut ridges of his abdomen into pure masculinity, undeniably powerful. Fine blond hairs dusted his chest, a faint trail leading downward over the firm muscles of his stomach before disappearing into the waistband of his trousers. His shoulders were broad, his arms strong, corded with sinew that flexed as he braced himself above her.

Harriet had seen beautiful men before, but Sebastian was different. He was a study in contrasts—elegance and raw strength, refinement and untamed desire. She reached up, her fingers gliding over the warmth of his skin, tracing the lines of muscle and the faint scars earned through years of travel and adventure. He was perfect, a veritable warrior descended from the halls of Valhalla.

And for this night, he was hers.

Her fingers trailed downward to the waistband of his trousers. His breath hitched, his muscles tightening beneath her touch.

Her gaze met his, and for a moment, the world held still.

No past regrets. No lies. No future uncertainties.

Just this.

Just them.

Sebastian's fingers found the delicate edge of her night-dress, inching it down over her trembling legs with aching slowness as if unwrapping something rare and precious. Harriet's breath caught as he slipped it over her extended legs in a whisper of silk. A shiver stole over her skin, though she did not feel the chill. It was not cold that made her tremble but the sheer intensity of Sebastian's gaze as it roamed over her naked body.

His knuckles brushed over her stomach, tracing the fragile musculature as if reverently inspecting a sculpture for its veracity. "You are exquisite," he murmured, his voice hushed with awe. He lifted his hands, gliding over the swell of her breasts and the curve of her waist, caressing her inch by inch.

Harriet could scarcely breathe, her body caught between instinct and restraint. She had never felt so exposed, so utterly vulnerable with no wine to mask the truth, yet she did not move to cover herself. She wanted this—wanted him. And she could see in his eyes that he wanted her just as desperately.

Sebastian let out a slow breath, as if steadying himself, before his hands traced down the column of her throat, along her collarbones, lower, exploring every dip and hollow of her body. His fingers skimmed down her arms before settling at her waist, spanning the curve of her hips.

His lips followed the path of his hands, pressing a trail of slow, lingering kisses down the slope of her shoulder, across her collarbone, over the aching, sensitive skin of her ribs as she reclined on the rug. Every touch left a burning imprint, every caress unraveling her bit by bit.

"Mine," he whispered against her skin, his voice thick with longing.

Harriet exhaled a shuddering breath, threading her fingers through his hair, pulling him closer, drowning in the exquisite torment of his mouth as he devoted himself to her, inch by inch. His lips found the dip of her navel, his tongue flicking softly against the sensitive skin there, drawing a gasp from her throat.

Every touch, every murmur against her skin, sent liquid heat pulsing between her thighs.

"Sebastian," she breathed, his name a plea, a surrender, as his hands continued their slow, deliberate exploration.

He lifted his head then, his gray eyes burning into hers, searching. "Say it again," he murmured.

Her fingers tightened in his hair. "Sebastian."

A slow, wicked smile curved his lips before he lowered his mouth once more, pressing a lingering kiss to the inside of her thigh, his voice a husky promise against her skin.

"Good girl."

Indulging in fleeting moments of passion had never been like this. Never included this bone-deep awareness, this sense of being seen—truly seen—by the one man who had always mattered. It was overwhelming, intoxicating, terrifying.

He lifted his head, his gaze locking onto hers, and for a moment, the air between them pulsed with something unsaid, something fragile and raw.

"This is not a dream, Harry," he murmured, his voice rough with restraint.

She swallowed hard, her fingers tightening against his skin. "It feels like one."

His lips curved faintly, but there was no amusement in his expression—only a hunger that mirrored her own. "Then let me make it real."

And he did.

His hands and mouth worshipped her, learning her anew, as though they had all the time in the world. Harriet shivered beneath his touch, arching into his warmth, pressing herself against him as though she could fuse them together and never let go.

"Sebastian," she whispered, her voice a breathless entreaty, a plea she did not know how to voice, as his hot mouth slid over to the soft auburn curls that shielded her womanhood. His breath teased her senses more than any before him, or after him, and when she felt the first languid stroke of his tongue against her slick crease, she nearly swooned from the heady delight. Sebastian had learned things about lovemaking since that fateful St. Valentine's Day, and he took his time revealing his newfound experience one sensual lick at a time, as he explored the tender folds of her sex with the tip of his knowledgeable tongue.

Harriet's passion mounted as she writhed and squirmed,

arching her hips up in supplication until he centered his attentions on the sensitive nub at the apex of her seam. Searing, endless waves of sensation hit her as she pushed up against his questing mouth, a muffled shriek of fulfillment escaping her lips as she found the heights of paradise.

Gasping, heaving with the force of her unanticipated pleasure, Harriet slowly returned to the moment to find Sebastian leaning over her with masculine smugness. He licked his lips as he stared deep into her eyes, waiting for her to find her breath.

Eventually, she was able to get the words out of her mouth. "Take me," was all she said.

His response was silent but powerful—his arms tightening around her, his body pressing closer, the heat between them spiraling into irresistible heights. He kissed her then, slow and deep, tasting her, savoring her, drawing her back into the present when her mind threatened to fracture beneath the awareness of all she had lost, all she had ruined.

It was as if he were rewriting their history with every caress, erasing the years of longing and regret, making her believe, for this one fleeting moment, that they had never been apart.

She wanted to cling to that illusion. Wanted to hold onto it with everything she had.

But the truth lurked in the back of her mind, whispering its cruel reminder. She had lied to him. And when he found out, this would all come crashing down.

So she surrendered herself to him, drowning in his touch, knowing that come morning, the fantasy would shatter.

But for tonight, she was his. And that would have to be enough.

Sebastian rose onto his knees, his breathing uneven as he gazed down at her, his eyes molten with a hunger that sent a shiver through her body.

Harriet could only watch, spellbound, as he reached down, unsteady fingers working the buttons of his falls. The soft rasp of fabric, the quiet catch of his breath—every sound seemed heightened, every movement deliberate.

He stood, his tall, powerful frame looming over her, and to her surprise, he toed off his fine leather shoes first, the gentle thump of them landing on the rug strangely intimate.

Then, without hesitation, he pushed his trousers and small clothes over his hips, the heavy fabric slipping to the floor. His stockings followed, rolled down his calves and cast aside, revealing long, muscled legs dusted with fine golden hair, Harriet's breath catching in her throat.

He was beautiful. The refinement of an English gentleman and the untamed rawness of a man who had forged his own destiny beyond these shores. The planes of his body were honed from travel, his skin kissed by foreign suns, his strength evident in every flex of sinew and muscle.

He stood before her unabashed, the heat in his gaze searing through her very soul.

Harriet swallowed hard, her heart pounding like a trapped bird. Never had she felt this way. Shy. Never had she trembled, not from fear, but from the sheer anticipation. But, then, she was sober and experiencing this moment in the now, not imagining her last time in his arms.

Sebastian reached for her then, drawing her forward, his hands firm yet reverent as he guided her up onto her knees, their bodies flush against one another.

"Harry," he murmured, his lips brushing the shell of her ear, his voice a low, rough caress. "Tell me to stop, and I will."

But she did not.

She could not.

Instead, she lifted her face to his, her fingers splaying against the hard planes of his chest.

"I do not want you to stop," she whispered.

A muscle ticked in his jaw, as though he were barely holding back.

Then, with a soft curse, he captured her lips once more, and the world fell away.

Their mouths met in a heated clash, their bodies pressed flush against each other, skin against skin. Harriet clutched at his shoulders, nails digging lightly into the taut muscle beneath, overwhelmed by the strength coiled in his frame, the unyielding warmth of him.

Sebastian deepened the kiss, his tongue sweeping along hers with a slow, devastating thoroughness, as if he were committing every taste and sigh to memory. She gasped into his mouth as his hands traveled over her, tracing the delicate slope of her waist, the curve of her hip, pulling her against his naked body as though he could imprint her onto his very being.

His skin was a furnace against hers, as he lowered her onto the thick rug, and Harriet felt as though she were being laid upon an altar. Revered. Worshipped.

Her breath came in shallow gasps as he loomed over her, propped on his elbows, bracing his weight so that he did not crush her, though she almost wished for it—to be utterly consumed by him. He brushed a strand of hair from her cheek, his fingers warm and gentle, in stark contrast to the fierce hunger in his eyes.

"You are …" He exhaled roughly, as though words failed him, and instead, he lowered his head to taste the delicate skin just below her ear, his lips branding a path down her throat. Harriet arched into him, tilting her chin back to grant him better access, her fingers sliding into his thick golden hair.

Sebastian groaned against her skin, the sound reverberating through her as he pressed kisses along her collarbone, then lower, following the curve of her body as if he sought to map every inch of her with his lips. One of his hands drifted down, skimming the length of her thigh before hitching it over his hip, pressing her open beneath him.

Harriet gasped at the contact, at the sheer intimacy of it, heat pooling low and insistent as Sebastian's grip tightened on her leg. His forehead came to rest against hers for a moment, grounding himself.

"I have dreamed of this," he admitted, his voice rough with need.

Her heart twisted. "So have I."

For a brief moment, he stilled, his breathing heavy, his body pressing into her deliciously.

Then, with a raw, whispered curse, he shifted, preparing to claim her fully. Harriet felt the blunt tip of his hard length nudging against her dripping womanhood, slickened with her desperate need to feel him enter her, to fill the aching void.

Then he nudged forward, before thrusting in one powerful stroke to seat himself inside her, and Harriet gasped with the overwhelming sensation, bucking against him in a plea for more. Sebastian took his time, measured and patient, although his jaw was firm and his face strained to reveal the depths of control he was mustering.

He rode her, thrusting in and out until Harriet was overwhelmed once more, arching beneath him in mindless pleasure. And as she neared her peak, she felt the instant Sebastian lost control, his thrusting more frantic as he sought his own release.

They reached it together, his deep groan mingling with the muted shriek she pressed into his muscled shoulder as they rode the waves of passion to its final destination, before collapsing together in a panting heap of tangled limbs and sweat-soaked tendrils of hair.

CHAPTER 11

As morning light doth chase the night away,
Your love dispels the darkness from my day;
With every dawn, my heart anew doth sing,
For you, my love, are life's eternal spring.

The New Ladies' Valentine Writer (1821)

* * *

DECEMBER 19, 1821

*H*arriet awakened as the pale light of morning filtered through the curtains, casting a soft glow over her bedchamber. A deep warmth curled through her limbs, the lingering sensation of last night's intimacy wrapping around her like the heavy coverlet. She turned, reaching out instinctively, eager for the solid warmth of Sebastian beside her. But her searching fingers found only cool, empty sheets.

Blinking, she propped herself up on one elbow, pushing her tousled hair from her face. The remnants of the candle they had burned low the night before sat in a pool of hardened wax, its feeble light having long since extinguished.

The fire had burned to embers, leaving only a faint glow in the grate. The air in the room was thick with the mingling scents of spent wax, lingering smoke, and something more intimate—the musk of their passion still clung to the sheets.

A thrill of memory coursed through her. She had brought him up to her rooms—heedless of consequence, heedless of everything but the aching need to be close to him. They had undressed each other again by candlelight, their fingers exploring, their movements slow and deliberate. Even now, the ghost of his touch lingered on her skin, as if his hands had left invisible brands upon her.

But the warmth of recollection faded the moment she spotted him. Sebastian stood near the fireplace, fully dressed save for his coat, his arms crossed over his chest, his expression carved from stone. His piercing gray eyes, always so full of depth and hidden emotion, were overtly ambivalent as they bored into her.

"You lied to me."

The words landed like a slap, striking her deeper than she thought possible. Harriet's lips parted, but no sound came. Her body, languid and content just moments ago, stiffened in alarm. His gaze shifted past her, toward the wall behind her head. A slow, dreadful realization curled in her gut.

No.

Whipping around, she followed his gaze.

And there it was. The painting.

Matteo di Bianchi's lost work, the one she had sworn to him she no longer possessed, hung in plain sight above her bed. A cruel, damning revelation framed in gilt and shadow that in the low glow of a single candle and the heat of passion might as well have been invisible last night.

Her breath caught. How could she have been so careless? When she had led him upstairs, her mind had been a whirl-wind of desire, of yearning. She had thought of nothing but him—never once considering that her newest deception loomed over them as they tangled in the sheets.

"I ... I could not let it go," she whispered.

Sebastian let out a bitter laugh, shaking his head as if the sight of it was too much to bear.

"No," he said, his voice quieter now, but no less cutting. "I suppose you could not."

She sat up fully now, clutching the sheet to her chest, shame pooling in her stomach like lead. "Sebastian, please, let me explain—"

"Explain?" He scoffed, pacing away only to whirl back to face her. "Do you think there is anything you could say that would undo this? That would make me believe you meant anything you have said these past couple of weeks?"

His anger, sharp as a blade, sliced through her, and Harriet flinched.

"It was never about the painting," she said desperately. "Not truly."

"Then why lie?" His voice was raw now, stripped of the patience he had once offered her so freely. "Why deceive me, Harriet? Have you no faith in me at all?"

Tears burned at the backs of her eyes, but she refused to let them fall.

"I was afraid," she admitted. "Afraid that if I told you the truth, you would take it from me. And I could not bear to lose it."

"Not even for me?" His voice was quieter now, but there was no mistaking the bleakness beneath the question.

Harriet swallowed past the ache in her throat.

"I have lost everything before," she whispered. "This was all I had left."

Sebastian's lips pressed into a hard line before he gave a single shake of his head. "You could have had *me*."

And then, without another word, he turned on his heel and strode toward the bedchamber door.

Panic seized her, the significance of her choices crashing down upon her like an unforgiving tide.

"Sebastian, wait— Once we made our arrangement, I planned to give it to you on Christmas Day."

Sebastian stopped, his hand hovering over the door handle. His shoulders were rigid, the taut lines of his back betraying the effort it took to contain his temper.

Slowly, he turned, his expression unreadable. "Planned to?" he echoed.

Harriet nodded, swallowing hard. "Yes. That was always my intention. I only wanted—" She hesitated, her hands gripping the sheets as though they were the only thing keeping her from unraveling. "I only wanted a little more time."

His mouth twisted. "Time for what?"

"For us," she whispered.

Silence hung between them, heavy with things unspoken. The dying embers in the grate crackled, as if to punctuate their conversation.

Sebastian exhaled sharply and ran a hand through his hair, his movements tight with frustration. "Damn it, Harriet," he ground out. "You speak of time as if it were something we could steal back. But time was stolen from us long ago— by *you*. And now, once again, you have chosen secrets over trust."

She flinched at the accusation, her pulse hammering against her ribs. "I was going to tell you," she insisted. "I never meant to deceive you, not like this."

Sebastian's laugh was low and humorless. "Not like this?

Then how, exactly?" He gestured toward the painting. "You let me believe it was gone. You lied to my face. How am I supposed to believe anything you say now?"

Harriet's fingers curled into the sheets, nails pressing into her palms. "I never wanted to hurt you."

"And yet, you have."

His voice was quiet, but there was an emotion far worse than anger in his tone now. Disillusionment. Disappointment.

Her chest ached as she sat up straighter, pulling the sheet tighter around herself. "You think I do not regret it? That I do not hate myself for not telling you the truth sooner? You cannot imagine what it has been like—to feel as though every choice I make only drives you further away."

Sebastian shook his head. "No, Harriet. That was your own doing." His voice was hoarse with emotion, and his hands flexed at his sides. "All I ever wanted from you was honesty."

A lump formed in her throat.

"I thought if I gave you the painting too soon," she confessed, "you would leave. I thought once you had it, there would be nothing left to hold you here."

Sebastian's breath caught, old hurts flittering behind his gaze. "You truly believed that?"

She nodded, her teeth sinking into her lower lip. "Yes."

His jaw tightened, and for a long moment, he simply looked at her. The fury was still there, simmering beneath the surface, but something else lurked beneath it now—something more vulnerable.

"Do you think so little of me?" he asked finally.

Harriet's heart clenched. "No," she said fiercely. "Never."

I think so little of myself, was the errant thought she had been fighting all these months as she walked the path of sobriety and tried to find a return to the happiness she had shared with Sebastian so many years ago.

Sebastian exhaled heavily, rubbing his temples as though trying to will away his frustration. "You could have told me," he said, his voice quieter now, the edge of anger dulling. "I would have understood. But instead, you chose to deceive me—again."

Harriet's throat tightened. "I did not mean—"

"But you did," he cut her off. "You always mean to, whether you admit it or not."

She shook her head. "I was afraid."

"Afraid of what?"

"Of losing you," she admitted, voice breaking.

Sebastian let out a ragged breath, and for a moment, he looked as though he might soften. Then his expression hardened once more. "You never had me to lose, Harriet."

The words were a death knell. She sucked in a sharp breath, the pain of them cutting deeper than she could have anticipated. Sebastian turned back toward the door, his hand clenching into a fist before he let it fall open again. He hesitated for only a moment, then grasped the door handle.

"You asked for more time," he said without looking at her. "But time is the one thing I can no longer afford to give you."

With quiet finality, he strode through her private drawing room and then stepped out into the hall beyond it, closing the door behind him. Harriet sat frozen in place, the sound of his retreating footsteps echoing in her ears. She supposed she should be concerned that the other women in the house would be alarmed by his presence. About their own security if Harriet ruined her reputation. But in that moment, she could not find the will to care.

The room felt impossibly empty without him.

She turned slowly, looking over her shoulder at the painting that had betrayed her.

No. That was not right. She had betrayed herself.

And once again, there was no one to blame but her.

* * *

Sebastian stormed into the Scott residence, barely acknowledging the footman who opened the door before shrugging out of his coat and tossing it over a chair in the entryway. His boots struck hard against the polished floor as he strode down the corridor, his fury barely contained beneath the surface.

Damn her.

Damn her lies, her secrets, the way she had looked at him with those wide, pleading eyes as if she had not just shattered whatever trust had been growing between them.

He had spent the evening at his brother's house, facing the cold disapproval of Philip and the barely concealed unease of the others. He had defended her against them all, against every muttered doubt, every veiled warning. He had sat there, knowing full well that his family did not approve of his courtship, did not trust Harriet, and still, he had been determined.

Because he had believed in her. Because he had wanted a future with her.

And all the while, what had she been doing? Lying to his face. Smiling at him, allowing him to believe in a shared future that had never been real.

A deep sense of betrayal twisted in his gut. He had been a fool.

As he entered the library, he found Lorenzo lounging in one of the armchairs, a book resting open on his lap. At the sight of Sebastian's thunderous expression, Lorenzo's dark brows lifted in mild concern.

"I take it the dinner did not go well?"

Sebastian let out a harsh laugh, running a hand through his disheveled hair before crossing to the drinks cabinet. He poured himself a brandy with more force than necessary, the liquid sloshing against the sides of the glass.

"The dinner went precisely as expected," he bit out. "It was the events after that ruined everything."

Lorenzo closed his book, watching him closely. "Do I want to know?"

Sebastian downed half the glass in one swallow, the burn of the alcohol doing little to soothe the fire in his chest.

"She lied to me," he said flatly.

Lorenzo did not react, merely tilting his head in question.

Sebastian exhaled sharply. "She told me she no longer had the painting."

Lorenzo's eyes widened with understanding. "But she did."

"She did," Sebastian confirmed. His grip tightened around the glass. "It was hanging above her bed the entire time. And I—" He cut himself off, jaw clenching.

Lorenzo's lips twitched. "You were in her bed?"

Sebastian shot him a dark look, but Lorenzo only leaned back, utterly undaunted. "Well, that does complicate matters, does it not?"

Sebastian slammed his glass down on the table, pacing the room. "I defended her. I was prepared to stand against my entire family if need be. I …" He hesitated, exhaling sharply. "I wanted her, Lorenzo. Not just for now. I was ready to build something real with her."

His friend watched him carefully. "And now?"

Sebastian let out a bitter laugh. "Now I do not know what to think. Every time I begin to believe in her, she reminds me why I should not."

Lorenzo considered this for a moment before speaking. "Do you believe she meant to betray you?"

Sebastian hesitated, the question catching him off guard. Did he?

He thought of the way she had looked at him when he confronted her—the shock, the regret, the raw emotion in her eyes. She had not looked triumphant. She had not gloated in her deception.

She had looked … heartbroken.

But what did that change?

"She had a hundred opportunities to tell me the truth," Sebastian said finally. "And she chose not to."

He rubbed his jaw as he stared into the flames of the library's fireplace. His anger had cooled, but the sting of betrayal remained. He had been prepared to walk away, to leave Harriet to whatever schemes she had spun, but Lorenzo's words lingered in his mind.

Lorenzo nodded slowly. "Perhaps the question you must ask yourself is not whether she lied, but why."

Why, indeed.

Lorenzo sat forward, fixing him with a steady look. "Return to her. Borrow the painting."

Sebastian scoffed, shaking his head. "You think she will simply hand it over?"

"I think," Lorenzo said carefully, "that she has her reasons for keeping it, and if you ask the right way, she may just let it go."

Sebastian clenched his jaw. "And if she refuses?"

Lorenzo ran a finger through his thick black hair and huffed. "Then at least you will know where you stand."

Sebastian knew it was sound advice, but the idea of returning to her house, to the very place where the morning had unraveled so spectacularly, made his insides twist. He should walk away. He should let it go.

But the need for answers gnawed at him.

With a resigned sigh, he got back to his feet. "If I return with the painting, you owe me a bottle of brandy."

Lorenzo grinned. "Deal."

* * *

BY THE TIME Sebastian reached Harriet's street, the unease in his stomach had deepened. The morning's confrontation was still too raw, but as his carriage approached her townhouse, he caught sight of something that made his breath hitch.

Her carriage was already at the door. The same one from before. The one she had used the night he followed her through the streets of St. James's. His hands curled into fists at his sides.

Moments later, she emerged from the house, swathed in a discreet dark cloak, her bonnet tilted forward to obscure her features. Just as before.

A bolt of anger shot through him, tangled with feelings far more dangerous. She had said she spent her nights at home. He had caught her in that lie once before. And now, after this morning—after what they had shared—here she was again, dressed for secrecy, preparing to disappear into the city without a word.

His pulse thundered in his ears.

Had it all been a performance? Had the heartbreak in her voice, the regret in her eyes, been nothing but well-placed deception? Sebastian had not been prepared to follow her again. He had wanted to claim the painting and leave with whatever dignity he had left. But now he needed to know. Needed to see for himself whether she was slipping away to another man.

Leaning out, he gave his driver a terse command. "Follow her."

The wheels rumbled over the cobbled streets as they trailed her discreetly. The Scotts' coachman must think that he was a terrible guest, following a noblewoman like this, but he could not summon the will to care. Sebastian sat back, his fingers drumming against his knee, every nerve strung tight. And when her carriage veered toward Rotten Row, his unease deepened.

Why the devil was she going there?

The main thoroughfare of Rotten Row was bustling despite the chill of December, filled with riders in their fine riding jackets and top hats, ladies wrapped in rich velvets and furs as they guided their mounts in graceful circuits. The crisp air carried the scent of damp earth and the faintest trace of frost, while the occasional jingle of harness bells punctuated the steady rhythm of hooves on the well-maintained path.

Yet Harriet had directed her carriage away from the spectacle, toward one of the more secluded trails that wound beneath bare-branched trees, their skeletal limbs etched stark against the gray winter sky. Patches of frost still lingered where the sun had yet to touch, and the Serpentine shimmered in the distance, thin tendrils of mist curling above its surface.

Here, away from the fashionable crowd, the park was quieter, broken only by the distant sound of children's laughter as a group of governesses shepherded their charges through the crisp morning air.

Sebastian's breath left him in a harsh exhale as he watched a rider approach Harriet's carriage. Not just any rider.

Richard Balfour, Earl of Saunton. His cousin.

Sebastian stiffened, his fingers digging into the worn leather of the seat. What the devil was Richard doing here?

The answer came swiftly, and it made his stomach churn.

Richard had defended Harriet last night at dinner, trying to smooth the tensions. He had done his best to lighten the mood, carrying conversations when the duke refused to speak, when Lily was too nervous to do anything but prattle. At the time, Sebastian had thought it was just Richard's usual charm at play. That, despite his past as a notorious rake, he had softened after his marriage to Sophia.

But now, watching him ride up to Harriet's carriage in a quiet corner of Hyde Park, a sickening thought took root.

Had Richard been defending her not out of familial courtesy, but because he was involved with her? Was he one of her many secrets?

Sebastian's jaw clenched so hard it ached. It would explain too much. Why Harriet had lied about her outings. Why Richard had acted the peacemaker. And most of all, why the duke had been so cold. Was that why Philip had been trying to warn him away? Because he knew their own cousin had been carrying on with Harriet behind closed doors?

The possibility sent a fresh wave of fury surging through Sebastian. He had spent the morning tormented by what had happened between him and Harriet. He had been prepared to fight for her. To make sense of the tangled mess between them.

And yet, here she was. Meeting another man in secret. His cousin, no less.

Sebastian's vision narrowed, his blood hammering as he shoved open the carriage door.

"Wait here," he snapped at his driver, already striding toward the pair across the discreet distance where his carriage had stopped, his boots crunching against the frozen ground.

His fury propelled him forward, each step matching the

pound of his heart in his chest. Whatever lies Harriet had woven, whatever deception Richard had entangled himself in, Sebastian would have his answers. And he would have them now.

CHAPTER 12

Nay: if 'tis a crime to love thee,
Then no lot's so hard as mine.

The New Ladies' Valentine Writer (1821)

* * *

*H*arriet's hands trembled in her lap as she sat rigidly in the carriage. This time it was not passion that made them shake, but deep regret. She had ruined everything.

Sebastian had looked at her this morning as though she had shattered whatever fragile bonds had begun to form between them. And now, she was certain she had lost him forever. The burden of her poor choices pressed down upon her, suffocating and inescapable.

When Lord Saunton rode up alongside her carriage, his expression shifted immediately from casual curiosity to concern. He reined in his horse and dismounted with fluid ease before striding toward the carriage door. She barely waited for him to assist her before stepping out onto the cold ground, the air biting at her skin even beneath her gloves.

"Lady Slight?" Lord Saunton's voice was low and careful, but the keen perception in his gaze told her he had already deduced that something was amiss.

She swallowed, wrapping her arms around herself, seeking comfort where none was to be found. "I have made a terrible mistake."

Lord Saunton frowned, his gloved hands settling on his hips. "That much is clear. But which mistake in particular are we discussing?"

Harriet laughed, a sharp and humorless sound. "I trapped Sebastian into a courtship in exchange for a painting he once gave me. I told him I no longer had it, and that I would tell him who did if he pretended to court me until Christmas. But I did have it, and now he knows and I ... I spoiled everything."

The earl's brows shot up in unmistakable dismay. "You what?"

She nodded miserably. "I ... I know it was wrong. I knew it when I did it. But I thought ... I thought if I had time, I could make him see—" Her voice broke.

"That you belonged together?" he guessed, his expression sympathetic.

"Yes." The admission scorched her throat.

He ran a hand down his face, frustration plain. "And instead, he has discovered the truth, and now you are standing here like a lost child, trembling over the consequences of your choices."

She flinched. "I did not mean to hurt him."

"No, I imagine you meant to secure your own happiness first and foremost," Lord Saunton said, his voice firm.

Harriet turned away, squeezing her eyes shut. "I know I have done wrong. But you have been my Mentor these many months. Advised me on making amends for my past behavior. Until now, I did everything you told me to do, and I am terribly sorry I did not tell you what I was about. But, please, tell me how to fix this?"

The earl was silent for a long moment before he spoke again. "Lady Slight ... once one starts on the path of honesty, it is imperative not to stray from it. You cannot simply confess one truth and expect all else to be forgiven if you continue down the road of deception. I am afraid you have not heeded my advice in this regard."

She turned back to him, desperation clawing at her chest. "Tell me what I can do. You are the only one I know who managed to find your way back. You ... and Perry, whom I cannot ask to help for obvious reasons." She could hardly ask her former lover to advise her on redemption, which was why she had sought out not him, but Perry's brother back in August when she had made her decision to change her circumstances.

His jaw ticked. "You already know what must be done. This path requires commitment. You cannot mend a broken foundation by stacking more stones atop it."

Harriet nodded, barely breathing.

She knew.

She had always known.

She would have to confess all her secrets to Sebastian. Her affair last year with his cousin Perry. Her affair with the duke's brother-in-law, Brendan, earlier this year, followed by her betrayal when he was arrested. The awful facts of her attempt to seduce him as a married man, and how Lily had caught her in the act.

Was she brave enough to do it?

The admiring glances he had given her this past week would turn to condemnation, and she would lose all possibility of ever claiming her place at his side. But if she withheld the rest of her secrets, she stood no chance of winning him back. She was damned if she did and damned if she did not. A jail of her own making that she could have eased by not telling the lie about the painting he wished to acquire for his friend. Sebastian had always been loyal. And in her case, his desire to be loyal to her had been his only mistake.

* * *

SEBASTIAN SAW red as he watched from nearby. The couple were too absorbed to notice his presence a mere thirty feet away, and the winter landscape around him seemed to mirror the slow, creeping cold crystallizing in his chest.

The towering oaks and elms, stripped of their summer finery, stood desolate against the overcast sky, their barren limbs reaching toward the heavens like pleading supplicants. Frost clung stubbornly to the shaded hollows at their roots, while the brittle remnants of autumn's fallen leaves crunched underfoot when the occasional walker passed along the distant paths.

A biting wind swept through the park, rattling the bare branches, tugging at the few withered leaves that clung desperately to the trees—just as he had once clung to the illusion of Harriet's honesty. The distant surface of the Serpentine reflected the bleak sky, its edges lined with a thin crust of ice that had begun to spread overnight, a silent testament to the deepening cold.

Sebastian forced himself to breathe deeply, his gloved hands flexing at his sides. He should not feel betrayed—not after all her deceptions—but the storm inside him raged nonetheless. The cold had never bothered him before. He had spent years in Florence, under the warm Mediterranean sun, but now, standing in the heart of a London winter, he had never felt more frozen. Or hot.

177

His fury had simmered beneath the surface all morning, ever since he had stormed out of Harriet's house. He had told himself he was done with her. That he would not let himself be lured back into her tangled web.

Yet here she was—again—slinking about London in her discreet dark blue walking dress, just as she had the last time he had followed her. And this time, she was meeting his own cousin.

He still could not credit it—Richard Balfour, the Earl of Saunton. The man who had so diligently played peacemaker at the duke's dinner the night before. The man who had shielded Harriet with careful words when she had been under scrutiny in the men's gathering after dinner. And now, the man who had the audacity to meet her alone in a secluded part of the park.

Richard was betraying both his graceful wife and Sebastian. Did Philip know about this? Was this the source of his brother's disapproval?

Sebastian launched toward them, the sheer force of his rage propelling him like a cannon shot. Richard had just placed his hand on Harriet's arm in a steadying manner, and Sebastian did not stop to consider that it might have been an innocent gesture. All he saw was betrayal. Betrayal from the woman he had loved. Betrayal from his own blood.

With long, punishing strides, he closed the distance between them. Harriet gasped as she caught sight of him, but before she could say a word, Sebastian grabbed Richard by the lapels of his greatcoat and yanked him forward, bringing them nearly nose-to-nose.

The difference in their sizes was almost comical.

Sebastian towered over his cousin by a solid five inches, his broad chest and thick arms making Richard seem almost boyish in comparison. The usually unshakable earl looked genuinely alarmed, his emerald eyes going wide.

"Sebastian," Richard choked out, his hands coming up in startled protest. "This is not what it looks like."

"Not what it looks like?" Sebastian snarled. "Then do tell me, *cousin*, what exactly does it look like?"

Harriet surged forward, grasping Sebastian's arm, which, despite everything, made him want to turn and pull her into an embrace so she could comfort him and tell him that his heart was not breaking for the third time.

"Have you been following me?" she demanded, her voice sharp with disbelief.

Sebastian barely spared her a glance, his fingers tightening in the fabric of Richard's coat. "And if I have?" he snapped. "It seems I had good reason."

Harriet's cheeks flushed darkly. "You had no right—"

"I had every right," he growled, jerking his chin toward Richard. "It appears I am the only one in this situation who does not know what the hell is going on."

Richard grimaced, attempting to pry himself free. "I swear to you, this is not an assignation."

Sebastian gave him a hard shake. "Then what is it?"

"I-I cannot say," Richard stammered, looking to Harriet with desperation.

"How convenient." Sebastian's lip curled in a sneer. "The great scoundrel of London, sworn off his wicked ways, but still unable to keep his hands off my woman."

Harriet stiffened beside him. "Your woman?" she repeated, her voice quiet but vibrating with undefined emotion.

Sebastian turned on her, his fingers finally unclenching from Richard's coat. "You demand trust," he bit out. "And yet all I ever seem to find are secrets. Lies. Clandestine meetings."

Harriet's mouth tightened. "Perhaps," she shot back, "if

you had a bit more trust, I would not have to keep so many secrets."

Sebastian flinched as if struck. Something sharp and cold slid through his gut at her words. Had he prevented her from telling him the truth? Had he failed her in some way—now and ... then?

Harriet stared at him, her breath unsteady, her eyes burning with a mix of hurt and defiance. For a moment, it was just the two of them, locked in battle, standing at the edge of something neither of them knew how to navigate. Then, with a swift pivot, she turned on her heel and strode toward her carriage. Sebastian was frozen, caught between wanting to call her back and wanting to walk away from her forever.

Richard exhaled heavily, rubbing at his throat as if still feeling the imprint of Sebastian's grip. "That was not necessary."

Sebastian gave a humorless laugh. "No? Then explain."

Richard hesitated. "I cannot. Lady Slight's confidences are not mine to repeat."

Sebastian let out a sharp bark of laughter. "Of course you cannot." He cast him a scathing look. "A rake does not change, Richard. Perhaps you have reformed enough to wed, but that does not mean you have changed. You are no better than your depraved father, after all—the Earl of Satan lives on!"

Richard's jaw tightened, but he did not respond.

Sebastian clenched his fists, his rage still simmering, but what use was it? Harriet was gone. The truth—whatever it was—remained out of reach.

Sebastian walked away, his boots crunching against the frozen ground, the cold air biting at his face. He should have felt victorious—he had finally pried himself free of the spider's web Harriet had spun around him. No more half-truths. No more watching her dance around his questions with coy evasions. No more wondering if she had ever truly cared for him.

He should have felt relief. Instead, all he felt was bone-deep exhaustion.

The carriage ride back to the Scott townhouse passed in a blur of gray skies and damp streets, of fog curling around lampposts and pedestrians bundled against the frigid air. The city felt hollow, as if it reflected the emptiness yawning inside of him.

England had always felt like a place of constraints. Duty. Expectations. A cage built of propriety and familial obligations. It had taken him years to break free, to carve out a life in Italy that was his and his alone. And yet, here he was, once again shackled to the past, to a woman who had owned his heart since they were barely more than children.

Damn her.

Damn himself for loving her still.

Because despite the morning's revelations—despite the lies, the manipulations, the endless string of secrets—he knew the truth with startling, painful clarity. He would always love Harriet. And that meant he had to leave.

If he stayed in England, he would never walk away from her. He would never be free of her smile, of her maddening ability to make him feel both utterly alive and utterly destroyed in the same breath. He would never stop looking at her and thinking, *What if?*

He had spent years living with the fact she had betrayed him once before. And now, she had done it again.

His carriage pulled to a stop before the townhouse, the iron-wrought lanterns casting weak halos of light against the deepening gloom of afternoon. His decision settled over him, heavy and suffocating.

It was time to go home.

To Florence. To the life he had built for himself. To a place where Harriet did not exist in every shadowed memory and stolen dream.

He stepped down from the carriage, his movements stiff, his fingers curling into fists at his sides. Inside, he would inform Lorenzo of his decision, who would have to visit Harriet and ask to view the painting himself. Sebastian would arrange for his own passage out of England as soon as possible.

And he would never look back.

CHAPTER 13

And, in truth, if aught could banish,
From my heart thy form divine,
Then all love for worth must vanish—
Farewell every Valentine!

The New Ladies' Valentine Writer (1821)

* * *

*H*arriet's heart pounded in her chest, a relentless drumbeat of anguish and regret. The cold seeped through the windows, but she scarcely noticed, too consumed by the storm raging within her.

She had ruined everything.

The pain in Sebastian's eyes when he had stormed toward her, the fury in his voice as he had accused her—it was all seared into her memory. And now, as the carriage rattled back toward home, the enormity of her mistake dragged her down like an iron yoke.

Fool. I have been such a fool.

What had she expected? That she could manipulate fate into giving her a second chance? That she could control the outcome with a clever scheme? It was laughable, truly. Sebastian had always been an honorable man, and yet she had sought to ensnare him through trickery. She had told herself that, given time, he would remember why he had once loved her, that he would forgive the past.

But now, after this morning, that was impossible.

And worst of all, she had no one to blame but herself.

She pressed her gloved fingers to her temples, closing her eyes against the burning sting of regret. She had sought redemption, had spent months trying to be someone better, someone worthy. But what did that matter when she had undone it all with one foolish lie?

A scoundrel. That was what Sebastian had called Lord Saunton. And yet, who had been the true scoundrel here?

She should have trusted him. She should have given him the truth. Instead, she had clung to her fear, her selfishness, and now it had cost her everything.

Her hands trembled as she dropped them into her lap. What would happen now? Would Lord Saunton keep her secret? Or would he break trust and tell Sebastian everything?

And even if the earl did not speak, what did it matter? Would Sebastian leave England thinking the worst of her— that she had been carrying on an affair with his own cousin?

A bitter laugh bubbled up from her throat. Why should that even surprise her? After all, had she not already been with his other cousin?

Perry.

The thought of him struck her like a physical blow. It had been more than a year, and yet that mistake still clung to her. She had not sought out Perry, had not meant to fall into that particular ruin, but she had been weak, reckless, and in her despair, she had let herself believe that anything was better than facing her loneliness.

And now, what right did she have to a second chance? What right did she have to love, to forgiveness? She deserved to be alone.

The carriage slowed, and she realized with a start that they had arrived at home. Their new footman opened the door, and Harriet barely managed to step out before her composure cracked. Keeping her chin lifted, she strode inside, her boots clicking against the marble floor.

Mrs. Finch opened her mouth to speak, but Harriet did not stop. She could not. She moved swiftly down the corridor, past the grand staircase, past the portraits of long-dead ancestors from her mother's side of the family who had likely been better people than she was.

She barely made it to the painted room before her knees gave out.

With a muffled sob, she collapsed onto the settee, pressing her face into her hands as the force of her failure crashed over her. She could not hold it back any longer. The dam broke, and she wept.

The fire crackled in the hearth, filling the room with warmth, but Harriet felt only the hollow chill of loss. She had fought so hard to change, to become someone worthy of Sebastian's love. And yet, when it had mattered most, she had done what she always did. She had ruined everything.

A quiet movement stirred across the room, and she realized she was not alone. Evaline sat in her usual chair by the fireplace, sipping her tea. She had not spoken a word since Harriet had entered, but now, as Harriet lifted her head, she found her friend regarding her with calm, perceptive eyes.

"Well," Evaline murmured, setting down her cup, "your meeting went poorly, I assume."

* * *

Sebastian had barely seen the streets of London when his carriage rattled home. His jaw ached from how tightly he had clenched it, his hands fisting on his thighs as anger and confusion warred within him. The morning had unraveled everything. He had woken with Harriet in his arms, full of a hope he had barely dared to acknowledge, only for the bitter sting of betrayal to steal it away entirely.

Now, the only thing left was the certainty that he had to leave England.

The moment his carriage rolled to a stop, Sebastian shoved open the door and vaulted down, ignoring the footman as he stalked past. He strode up the steps, his boots striking the stone with hard, deliberate purpose. Campbell, the head footman who had recently been promoted to butler, inclined his head as he passed, but Sebastian did not slow.

"Milord—"

He did not stop.

Through the hall. Past Lorenzo, who had just emerged from the library. Up the stairs.

"Sebastian?" Lorenzo's voice carried after him, laced with confusion. "*Dio*, what now?"

Sebastian ignored him, reaching his bedchamber and throwing the door open so violently it slammed into the wall. He had to move. Had to pack. Had to put as much distance between himself and this place—between himself and Harriet—as possible before he did something truly foolish.

He yanked open a trunk, thankful he had insisted the servants not stow it away, and shoved folded shirts inside with far more force than necessary. The repetitive motions soothed nothing. His mind still reeled, caught between the sting of betrayal and the damned, infuriating truth that he still wanted her.

Even now. Even knowing what he knew.

A curse ripped from his throat as he tossed a waistcoat into the trunk. The door opened behind him.

"I assume you're fleeing the country," Lorenzo said dryly.

Sebastian ground his teeth, not looking up as he moved to his wardrobe. "Not fleeing. Leaving."

Lorenzo stepped farther inside, shutting the door with an ominous click. "I see. And what, pray, has prompted this dramatic departure?"

Sebastian grasped a stack of cravats, his hands trembling. "I have had enough of this godforsaken country."

Lorenzo hummed. "Fascinating. And does this sudden loathing for England have anything to do with Lady Slight?"

Sebastian stiffened. The cravats crumpled in his grip.

Lorenzo sighed. "You are not subtle, *amico*. You have returned looking like you might strangle the next man who speaks to you. What happened?"

Silence stretched between them.

Sebastian turned, exhaling sharply as he met Lorenzo's searching gaze. The truth burned on his tongue, his every instinct at war. He did not want to say it aloud. Did not want to acknowledge it. Because once he did, it would be real.

But Lorenzo was relentless.

"Sebastian."

The name was a command, sharp and unyielding. Sebastian's hands clenched. His breath came hard and fast.

"She's having an affair with my cousin," he bit out.

Lorenzo's brows lifted. "Which one?"

"Richard," Sebastian snapped.

A beat of silence. Then ... Lorenzo snorted.

Sebastian's glare could have stripped paint from the walls. "You find this amusing?"

Lorenzo held up a hand, still chuckling. "I find it absurd."

Sebastian scowled, turning back to his packing. "I saw them. Together."

Lorenzo's amusement faded. "Did you see them together, or did you assume?"

Sebastian tensed. "They were alone. She was distressed. He was comforting her."

Lorenzo sighed. "Sebastian—"

A knock at the door interrupted them. Sebastian exhaled sharply, grateful for the reprieve. He stalked to the door and wrenched it open.

Campbell stood there, composed as ever, giving Sebastian pause.

"Lord and Lady Saunton are waiting for you in the family drawing room, milord."

Sebastian stilled. Every ounce of breath left his lungs. The room seemed to tilt. Slowly, he turned to glance at Lorenzo, who had also gone very, very still.

Richard was here.

With his wife.

Waiting for him.

His grip on the doorframe tightened.

So. The guilty party had come to explain himself. Sebastian's jaw clenched as he forced himself to breathe. "Very well," he said, voice like ice.

Without another word, he stepped past Campbell, then descended the stairs with agitated strides. He would hear what they had to say. And then, by God, he would decide whether or not to break Richard's jaw.

Sebastian stepped into the family drawing room, his broad shoulders nearly brushing the doorframe. The tension in the room was palpable, thick as fog over the wintry Thames. Richard was pacing the length of the carpet, his movements restless, his cravat visibly loosened as though he had been tugging at it in frustration.

And Richard's wife, Sophia, sat primly on the settee, her delicate hands fiddling with her gloves. The firelight cast a warm glow over her flawless complexion, her red-blonde hair shining like burnished gold beneath the soft lamplight. She was dressed in a blue gown that complemented her striking blue eyes, which lifted to him the moment he entered.

Sebastian was momentarily struck by her serene beauty.

How could Richard—a man who had spent years as a notorious rake, but who now supposedly valued his reformed reputation—be so foolish as to betray such a fine female? A wife like Lady Saunton, graceful, mild, the picture of quiet dignity? The thought only fueled his anger.

He hovered near the door, his massive frame stiff with restrained fury. When a man was as large as himself, he could not afford to let his emotions overtake him. Losing his temper had consequences. He had spent years perfecting control, knowing that if he so much as shoved another man in anger, the force could send them sprawling.

But by God, he wanted to pummel Richard.

The pacing. The nervous energy. The guilty fidgeting with his cravat.

Sebastian's fingers curled into fists at his sides.

He waited. Waited for one of them to speak. Waited to hear whatever excuse Richard had prepared for his betrayal. But mostly, he waited because if he spoke first, he could not trust himself to do so without his anger boiling over.

Sebastian's brows lifted in surprise as the countess's voice, cool and unwavering, cut through the tension in the room.

"My husband has informed me of the misunderstanding that occurred at Hyde Park," she said, folding her gloves with precise movements before setting them aside. "He has explained to me at great pains that he cannot share the details of his conversations with Lady Slight. And I have informed him that it is time for Lady Slight to forgive herself and that you, Lord Sebastian, are the only one who can help her do so."

Sebastian stared at her. This was not the quiet, docile gentlewoman he had assumed her to be. There was steel beneath her polished exterior, a formidable strength in her tone that caught him off guard.

Intriguing.

He flicked a glance toward Richard, who looked both miserable and relieved that his wife had taken the lead in the conversation.

Sebastian's temper, which had been coiled tight as a spring, slowly began to ease. He stepped farther into the room, his large frame filling the space.

Sophia's blue gaze remained steady, assessing him with a frankness that left no room for pretense. "Sit."

He arched a brow. "I beg your pardon?"

"You need to hear the truth," she said, unruffled by his towering presence. "And you need to decide whether you are a real man—one who can take the good with the bad when it comes to the woman you love. Because people are not perfect, Lord Sebastian, and it takes strength to accept both their virtues and their failings."

Sebastian hesitated, then slowly sank into the nearest chair.

For the first time in hours, he was willing to listen. If he were honest, he was relieved that someone had appeared to take control of the situation that had been spiraling since he had awoken to find the painting hanging above his head. The countess made him, and apparently her husband, feel like a poorly behaved child with her firm tone, but if it calmed the

terrible tempest running through his large body, he was all
ears.

* * *

HARRIET CURLED DEEPER into the corner of her settee, her
arms wrapped tightly around herself as if she could hold the
broken pieces of her heart together. She should have known
better. She had played a dangerous game, and now she had
lost. Worse, she had lost him.

She had been granted a second chance at happiness and
had wrecked it as thoroughly as she had that final day
together when they had celebrated St. Valentine's. She was a
bad person to the core, and she was doomed to a lifetime of
unhappiness because of her terrible nature. Perhaps it was in
her blood, Bertram Hargreaves's ultimate revenge for trying
to escape his influence to become a better person.

The quiet crackle of the fire was soon drowned out by the
sound of determined footsteps. She barely had time to swipe
at her damp cheeks before the door to the painted room
swung open.

Evaline entered first, a determined set to her mouth.
Behind her, Finch carried a heavily laden tray, Jem trailing
behind with a second. And Belinda—Belinda, who should
have known better than to fuss over her—shut the door
firmly behind them, sealing her fate.

Harriet sighed. "I am fine."

No one responded. Instead, Finch set down the tray with
an air of finality, the delicate china clinking softly. Jem
hurried forward, arranging plates of refreshment and bowls
of sugar lumps beside the steaming pot of tea. The young
maid might not have perfected the etiquette of an upper-
class household, but she had certainly learned her way
around a tea tray.

The little York biscuits were delicate round confections, golden-brown and lightly dusted with fine sugar. Harriet had always relished their crisp exterior that gave way to a buttery, crumbly center, the richness melting on the tongue with just a hint of lemon zest and nutmeg. A plate of them sat in the center of the table, arranged neatly beside a dish of preserved cherries and a small bowl of clotted cream. They were the kind of biscuits that one could mindlessly nibble on while deep in thought, their sweetness offering a fleeting comfort. But today, Harriet doubted even the most perfect pastry could soothe the gnawing ache in her chest.

Evaline, Finch, and Belinda exchanged a look—one of silent conspiracy. Then, as though they were a single organism, they pulled chairs closer and sat.

Evaline sat poised on the edge of her chair, the very picture of refined delicacy. She was draped in a soft wool gown of dove-gray, its high waistline accentuated by a narrow band of embroidery, and the pale blue ribbons of her sleeves trailed as she idly toyed with the fabric of her skirts. Her fine-boned hands smoothed over the folds with an absent grace, as if she were composing herself.

Her golden curls, always so artfully arranged, framed her face like the delicate filigree of a porcelain doll, and her pale blue eyes—so wide and guileless—were filled with what Harriet suspected was guilt. When Harriet shot her an accusatory stare, Evaline threw her a small helpless smile, followed by a look of apology far too innocent to be genuine.

"I thought you needed reinforcements," she admitted, her voice as gentle as falling snow. "To aid you against your own decline."

Harriet exhaled sharply, glancing at the assembled women —Finch, Jem, and Belinda, all sitting together like a united front. It seemed her stubbornness had been outmatched.

Mrs. Finch sat with the air of a battle-tested general surveying the field, her generous figure unyielding as if she had been carved from the same stone used to fortify castles. She was a woman built for endurance, her ample frame wrapped in serviceable brown wool, the severe lines of her bodice accentuating the breadth of her shoulders. If Napoleon himself had stormed the sitting room, she would have met him head-on with nothing more than a sharp glare and an iron-clad sense of duty.

Her face, weathered by years of managing unruly taverns and unrulier patrons, was set in the stubborn lines of a woman who had never once lost an argument—nor intended to. Her mouth pressed into a thin, disapproving line, though her dark eyes, shrewd and knowing, carried a glint of something softer. Not sympathy—Mrs. Finch had no patience for self-pity—but an unspoken understanding. She had seen the wreckage men left behind, and she was not about to let Harriet sink beneath it.

With a decisive nod, she adjusted the folds of her apron as if preparing for war. "Right, then," she declared, her voice sharp as a musket crack, "let's get on wiv it."

Shifting her gaze to Belinda, Harriet saw not the woman her father had cast aside without a second thought, but one who had seized the opportunity given to her with quiet determination.

Belinda sat with her spine straight, her hands folded in her lap, the very image of composed elegance. Though she was dressed modestly, her natural refinement could not be disguised; she had a way of carrying herself that spoke of someone who had once been accustomed to luxury and had learned, through necessity, to survive without it. The firelight played over her dark brown hair, gleaming where it was pinned into a neat coil at the nape of her neck, and her hazel eyes—once dulled by resignation—now held a spark of purpose.

Harriet had given her a way out, but Belinda had taken that path on her own terms. There was no simpering gratitude in her expression, no trace of self-pity. She was a woman who had been wronged, yes, but she refused to allow the past to define her. She was forging ahead, stepping boldly into a new life, and Harriet could not help but feel a swell of admiration.

"Well," Belinda said, tilting her head slightly, her voice smooth and composed. "Are we to sit here all day, or shall we set about putting you to rights?"

It was a simple statement, but in it lay the firm resolve of someone who understood the necessity of resilience. Harriet had saved Belinda from ruin, but perhaps, in this moment, it was Belinda who might save her.

Even little Jem, the waiflike girl who had somehow wormed her way into Harriet's heart with her artless affection, had pulled a chair over—though it was far too large for her slender form. She sat with a resolute set to her face, her mop of unruly hair barely tamed by the simple ribbon she had tied it back with that morning. Her freckles stood out starkly against her pale skin, and her gray maid's uniform only emphasized the fragile delicacy of her frame.

Yet despite her diminutive stature, there was nothing hesitant about her presence. She had the air of someone who had made up her mind and would not be swayed, her hands clenched into small fists atop her lap as if she, too, were bracing for a battle.

Harriet almost smiled. Apparently, her status as an important viscountess was not sufficient to cower her own staff into leaving her to her misery. Evaline had invited them in with her dainty concern, so her band of rescues had all gathered—Finch with her unshakable stubbornness, Belinda with her quiet strength, and Jem, the smallest of them all, who had chosen to plant herself firmly in solidarity as though she, too, would stand guard against Harriet's despair.

Harriet stared at them. "I do not require a council of war."

"Nah, what ye need's a cuppa tea," Finch said matter-of-factly, pouring a cup and thrusting it into her hands.

"Ye should eat summat, m'lady," Jem added, her usual meekness replaced by quiet insistence as she nudged the biscuits forward.

"Men are cruel," Belinda declared, as if that alone would mend everything.

But Harriet's chest ached because she knew that was not true.

Sebastian was not cruel.

He had never been.

Most of what had gone wrong had been her fault. Or at the very least, a consequence of her own choices and the circumstances that had shaped her. Maybe the truth was that she had never deserved him. She had never been strong enough, never been honest enough, never been good enough. He had always been too good for her.

And now, she had lost him forever.

CHAPTER 14

Thin as a lobster I am grown,
Till scarce I by my friends am known;
I fix upon St. Valentine
To reveal this flame of mine.

The New Ladies' Valentine Writer (1821)

* * *

*R*ichard took a seat, his fingers twitching toward his cravat as he loosened it slightly, an old nervous habit Sebastian recognized well. He cleared his throat, casting a sidelong glance at Sophia before exhaling heavily.

"Some months ago ..." he began, but Sophia lifted a hand, her serene features sharpening with quiet command.

"Lady Slight's mistakes are her own to reveal," she said, her voice cool but firm. "We will not discuss the specifics of what prompted her to seek you out."

Richard pressed his lips together, giving his wife a wry

look. "Yes, well. Quite right." He turned back to Sebastian, squaring his shoulders. "What I can tell you is that Lady Slight approached me, asking for my help. She wished to"— he paused, searching for the right words—"become a better person."

Sebastian arched a brow, arms still crossed over his broad chest, unconvinced.

Richard sighed, running a hand through his hair. "She wanted guidance. To make amends, she said. To change her course."

The manner in which Richard said it—equal parts disbelief and rueful acknowledgment—had Sebastian narrowing his gaze.

"Go on," he said.

Richard huffed a short laugh. "At the time, I thought it absurd. Me? Mentoring someone on the path of virtue? You cannot tell me you do not see the irony." He gestured broadly to himself, a man who had spent his youth as one of the most notorious rakes in London. "I was hardly the model of good behavior."

Sebastian did not disagree.

Richard pulled a face, as if still baffled by the notion, and waved a hand. "I told her no, of course. Who was I to lead anyone toward redemption when I was still figuring it out for myself?"

"But then he told me," Sophia interjected smoothly, her voice mild but unwavering. She folded her hands in her lap, her blue eyes steady on Sebastian's. "And I reminded him that if he had chosen a different path for himself, he was in no position to turn someone away when they wished to follow his example."

Richard huffed, shaking his head. "Yes, well. She was annoyingly correct, as usual."

Sophia smiled faintly, but said nothing.

"So," Richard continued, leveling Sebastian with a look, "I wrote to Lady Slight. And I agreed to help."

Sebastian's jaw clenched. His mind whirled with this new revelation, trying to make sense of it against everything he had believed about Harriet. Had she truly wanted to change? Had the woman who had deceived him so thoroughly also spent months seeking salvation?

It did not erase what she had done.

But it complicated everything.

Richard exhaled, rubbing a hand over his jaw before meeting Sebastian's gaze. "Her situation was … more troublesome than my own," he admitted. "The things she wished to atone for were not straightforward. In my case, if I wronged a woman and it resulted in worsened circumstances, I simply made arrangements to improve those circumstances. It just took some ingenuity and some blunt."

Sebastian's brow furrowed. "And for Harriet?"

Richard spread his hands. "She is a woman," he said simply. "She cannot merely send a man some money to repair a situation. She cannot use her title, position, or influence in the same way a man might. And, besides that, the men involved in her past did not need anything from her. Each had profitable, successful lives."

Sebastian flinched at the implication, his mind immediately going to who those seven or eight men had been that Harriet had confessed to. He clenched his jaw, saying nothing.

"So eventually," Richard went on, "we settled on another approach. If she could not make direct amends, she could at least use what resources she did possess to help others, to ease her conscience. Not necessarily those she had wronged, but perhaps the more vulnerable who had been wronged by others. The forgotten." His voice dropped slightly. "Perhaps women, considering she learned her glib ways from her father. And women were the ones he had wronged most."

* * *

HARRIET INHALED SHARPLY, trying to steady her voice. "I just need some time to myself," she said, forcing the words out past the lump rising in her throat.

But to her dismay, the tears began to fall again. She pressed a trembling hand to her lips, ashamed of her own weakness. What a fool she was—foolish to have thought she could change her fate, foolish to have hoped for a future that had never been hers to claim.

If she had not lied about the painting, perhaps she would be on her way to Italy with Sebastian at her side. Perhaps she would have joined him in his home, walked through the grand halls where he worked, seen the great Masters for herself. She had dreamt of Florence once, long ago—imagined the golden light over its ancient streets, the rolling hills of Tuscany, the warmth of a land so different from England.

But it was all gone now. Lost because of her own lack of wisdom.

Harriet pressed her lips together, struggling against the loss that compressed her chest. She could see it so clearly— the sun-drenched streets of Florence, the ochre rooftops glowing beneath a sky so blue it would put the finest sapphires to shame. She had imagined herself walking arm in arm with Sebastian through the bustling piazzas, past merchants hawking their wares, and perhaps observing sculptors chipping away at blocks of marble that would one day become masterpieces.

She had imagined the museums, the frescoed ceilings, the smell of oil paint lingering in the air, the feel of his hand at the small of her back as they moved through galleries filled with the work of Botticelli and Caravaggio. At night, she had pictured candlelit suppers on a terrace overlooking the Arno, the warm Italian air carrying the scent of lemons and jasmine as Sebastian spoke passionately about his latest work, his deep voice full of the same excitement he had once shared with her in their youth.

And then, at last, she had imagined what it would be like to stand beside him in his home, to see where he lived, where he created, where he had built a life without her. She had imagined being a part of it.

And now, it would never happen.

She let out a broken laugh, wiping at her damp cheeks as the other women watched her in quiet concern.

"I thought I might go to Italy with him," she said softly, her voice raw. "I …" She hesitated, then shook her head. "I thought we could see Florence together. Walk through the Uffizi, explore the ruins of Rome, stand in the shadow of the Duomo." She gave a bitter smile. "But I have ruined everything."

Evaline shifted in her chair, her delicate fingers tightening around her teacup as though she longed to say something, but for once, she seemed at a loss.

Finch made a dismissive sound. "Bah. If a man really loves ye, he don't go abandonin' ye over just one mistake."

Belinda studied her carefully. "Did he say it was over?"

Harriet swallowed, glancing away. "He did not have to."

Silence settled over the room.

And yet, as she sat there, surrounded by the women who had become her own unconventional family, the grief did not feel as suffocating as it had before. The ache in her heart remained, but it was tempered by the reminder that she was not truly alone.

She would grieve for what she had lost.

But she would endure. What choice did she have?

A small shift on the settee drew her attention. Jem had moved beside her, her small frame barely making a dent in the cushion. Without hesitation, the girl reached out, her tiny fingers curling around Harriet's hand in silent comfort.

Harriet's heart turned over at the frailty of the gesture, at the simple kindness in the girl's touch.

She squeezed Jem's hand, finding solace in the realization that if she could not have Sebastian, at least she had helped these troubled women find a place in her home. At least she had done some good.

* * *

RICHARD SIGHED, rubbing the back of his neck before leaning forward, his elbows braced on his knees. "It did not take long for Lady Slight to realize just how insidiously her father had embedded himself into her life," he said, his voice grim. "The moment she started making changes, dismissing certain callers, altering her household expenses, it became apparent that nearly half her servants and retainers were being paid to report back to Bertram Hargreaves."

Sebastian frowned, his arms still crossed. "Her own father was spying on her?"

Richard nodded. "Not just spying—controlling her. She was his possession, a pawn to be maneuvered as he saw fit. Lady Slight believes he intended her to make a second match that would benefit him. The servants, those she had trusted, were feeding him details of her daily life, ensuring he always knew what she was doing, where she was going, and with whom. He had his fingers in everything—her finances, her household, even her very freedom."

Sebastian felt a fresh surge of anger flare in his gut. Harriet was a woman grown, a widow, and yet her father had treated her as though she were still an unwed debutante under his thumb. "So she dismissed them," he guessed.

"Nearly all of them," Richard confirmed. "It left her with a mostly empty household—no footmen, no maids save for a single scullery girl, no butler. Mostly just the men in the mews who do not access the house. But she did keep one person—her cook. An old woman who had served her since childhood and who she was certain had no loyalty to Hargreaves." He shook his head. "But even with Cook, she still had problems. The woman could no longer go to market herself, so Harriet went in her stead when the scullery maid had her day off."

Sebastian exhaled, pinching the bridge of his nose. "A viscountess forced to buy her own fish and bread."

Richard gave a small shrug. "It was necessary. And while she was there, she found someone who would shape the course of her decisions going forward."

Sophia, who had been watching them both in quiet patience, finally spoke. "This was when she met her first rescue," she said knowingly.

Richard nodded. "Aye. That was the day she met the battle-axe herself." He leaned back against his chair, his lips twitching with amusement. "Picture the scene—Lady Slight, dressed modestly, attempting to buy apples, when suddenly she hears a loud, no-nonsense voice berating a fishmonger for trying to pass off inferior haddock as fresh catch. And there stands a woman, built like a brigadier and twice as fierce, eyes sharp as bayonets, and utterly unimpressed by the poor man's attempts to defend himself."

Sebastian almost smirked despite himself. "You are speaking of Finch?" He had seen Finch in action. The description was all too fitting.

Richard smiled in assent at the guess. "She approached her, intrigued, and struck up a conversation. That was when she learned Mrs. Finch's story. She had been the wife of a tavern keeper—a successful one at that. It was she who had turned their business into a thriving establishment, managing the accounts, dealing with customers, ensuring the place remained respectable."

Sophia made a sound of disapproval. "And yet, despite all that, she lost it."

"Because of her husband," Richard confirmed. "A faithless, feckless bastard who, after years of living off her hard work, wagered the entire tavern away in a game of dice. And when the deed passed to another man, he abandoned her altogether, leaving her with nothing."

Sebastian's jaw tightened. "And what became of her?"

"She was reduced to being a mere barmaid in the very tavern she had once run. Forced to serve the new owner, to watch him reap the benefits of what she had built." Richard shook his head. "She had nothing left. No property. No security. Just her wits and her resolve."

Sebastian leaned back against his chair, considering. It made sense now, why Finch carried herself with such authority, why she seemed so ferociously loyal to Harriet. She knew what it was to have everything taken from her, to be left at the mercy of others. Harriet had restored something she had lost—dignity.

"So Harriet offered her the position of housekeeper?" Sebastian guessed.

Richard nodded. "And Finch, after a bit of skepticism, accepted. I do not think she trusted Lady Slight's motives at first, but she saw something in her, just as Lady Slight saw something in her." He gestured an open hand as if presenting an explanation. "That was when it started."

Sebastian frowned. "What started?"

"This idea of hers—that she could not undo the past, but perhaps she could do some good going forward. If she could not atone for her own mistakes, then perhaps she could offer a place for others who had been wronged. Women who had been cast aside, abandoned, or left with little means to make an honest way forward."

Sebastian exhaled slowly, his thoughts turning over. So Harriet had been trying to change, to build a better life. But why had she never told him? Why had she lied, deceived, and made such a mess of things?

And why, despite everything, did he still want to believe in her?

* * *

FINCH SNIFFED, folding her arms over her stout chest, reminding Harriet once again of a general surveying an ill-disciplined army. "All men are naught but shite," she declared with years of bitter experience behind her.

Belinda choked on a sip of tea, while Evaline politely hid a smile behind her teacup. Jem, wide-eyed, merely nibbled on a biscuit, absorbing the housekeeper's words as if they were gospel.

Harriet, however, merely sighed and rubbed at her temples, knowing better than to engage Finch in a debate when she was on one of her tirades.

"Oi'm sure Lady Slight did nuffin' wrong," Finch went on, her voice rising with righteous fervor. "An' if she did, it were only 'cause that man o' hers put 'er up to it. So, really, it's 'is fault after all."

Harriet opened her mouth to protest, but Finch was just getting started.

"Ye think Oi don't know 'ow men operate? Bah! Oi spent years servin' ale to the sort what swore undyin' love in one breath an' were slippin' a ring on some other wench's finger in the next. Sweet words, false promises, an' when they've wrung ye dry, they move on without so much as a backwards glance. An' let's not forget my own bleedin' 'usband—may 'e rot wherever 'e ended up—who took me life's work an' tossed it aside like a scrap o' spoiled meat!"

She gave a disdainful snort, as though just the memory of him were enough to turn her stomach. "Mark me, m'lady. Men'll blame ye for their own shortcomings, then leave ye to clean up the mess they made!"

Harriet listened to Finch's tirade, but inwardly she argued against it. Sebastian was not like other men. He had never been like the men Finch spoke of, had never been careless with her feelings or dismissed her as unworthy. Even now, after all the pain she had caused him, after the mistakes she had made, his anger stemmed from hurt rather than cruelty.

He had never abandoned her, not truly. Not when they were young, not now. Even when she had given him every reason to walk away, some part of him had still wanted to believe in her.

She had ruined that today.

"Mark me," Finch went on, still railing, "this is why a woman's better off without 'em. No grief, no betrayal, no bloody 'eartbreak."

Harriet exhaled slowly, turning her teacup between her hands. No grief? No heartbreak? Finch was wrong about that.

The absence of love did not protect one from pain. She had spent years keeping the memory of Sebastian at arm's length, believing she was guarding herself against heartache, but in the end, it had found her anyway. And it was a thousand times worse knowing she had done it to herself.

* * *

RICHARD LEANED FORWARD, his expression grave.

"I must ask for your discretion in this matter, Sebastian," he said quietly. "What I am about to tell you is not my story to share, but I believe you need to understand."

Sebastian, still brooding over Harriet's duplicity, gave a sharp nod. "Go on, then."

Richard hesitated for only a moment before exhaling and rubbing a hand over his face. "It is about Lady Wood."

Sebastian blinked in mild surprise. Lady Evaline Wood was an ever-present shadow at Harriet's side—polite, unassuming, and often overlooked in a room full of louder personalities. He had thought little of her, beyond the fact that she seemed a steadfast companion to Harriet, a chaperon with the proper pedigree. Now, Richard's tone told him there was far more to her story than he had ever suspected.

"You know that her husband died last year?" Richard asked.

Sebastian nodded. "An accident, was it not? A misfire?"

A muscle in Richard's jaw twitched. "Yes. An accident."

Something about the way he said it made Sebastian straighten.

Richard cast a quick glance at Sophia, who gave an encouraging nod before he continued. "Lord Wood was a gentleman, as you well know from his reputation. He was"—he broke off, shaking his head—"a monster. He had abused Lady Wood for years, being noted for his fists, and the last few weeks of his life he had kept her locked away in that house of his. I doubt she saw sunlight for the better part of a month."

Sebastian frowned, his mind sifting through the quiet observations he had made of Lady Wood over the weeks of their acquaintance. She had always been composed, measured in her words and actions. There was a delicacy about her—not of frailty, but careful restraint. Now, knowing what Richard was telling him, he understood why.

"She endured it for years," Richard went on grimly. "And when she was finally free, when he died …" He paused, swallowing hard. "I was there, Sebastian. Wood was drunk, and he had a pistol. We struggled, and it went off. The fool shot himself."

Sebastian's brows furrowed, but he said nothing.

Richard exhaled sharply. "Afterward, Lady Wood should have been free, should have been able to live on her own terms. But instead, she was left at the mercy of her husband's kin. They withheld her stipend, forced her to live as a poor relation in the very home where she had once been mistress. Where she had been manhandled. She should have been able to walk away and rent herself a new home, away from her nightmares."

Sebastian felt a slow burn of anger rise in his chest. It was a common-enough cruelty—widows cast aside, their security stripped from them the moment their husbands died. It did not make it any less despicable.

"I tried to help her," Richard continued. "Repeatedly. I offered her legal assistance, a place to stay—anything she needed. But she refused. She told me I had done enough by freeing her from her marriage."

Sophia let out a quiet sigh, shaking her head. "She did not trust men. Not after what she had been through. And I do not blame her."

Richard nodded. "Eventually, Sophia and I came to a conclusion. If she would not accept help from me, perhaps she would accept it from another woman."

Sebastian frowned. He already knew where this was going, and it was giving him a lot to think about.

"We turned to Lady Slight," Richard confirmed. "She had already begun this … this path of hers, trying to make amends. We asked her if she would extend an offer to Lady

Wood in our place. She did. And Lady Wood accepted. Apparently, Lady Slight was most persuasive."

Sebastian sat back, absorbing this revelation. He thought of Harriet and Lady Wood together, the way they so often moved in unison, a widow's solidarity that had seemed natural. He had questioned how Lady Wood had come to be under Harriet's roof. Now, knowing the truth, it cast the entire arrangement in a different light.

"Lady Wood reports that she is pleased with the arrangement," Sophia added. "She enjoys the company of another widow. And Lady Slight seemed pleased, too. It has been a transition for her—shifting from the shallow social obligations of her past to a life more meaningful—but together they have found some peace and become a good influence on each other."

Sebastian exhaled, rubbing a hand over his jaw. He was not certain what he felt. Shock, perhaps. Respect, even. Harriet, for all her flaws, had achieved the extraordinary.

And yet, the sting of betrayal still simmered beneath the surface.

"She never told me any of this," he muttered.

"Because if she told you the good she had done, she would need to tell you why she had made those changes. She would have to tell you about the bad," Richard replied. "I believe she has not because she has yet to forgive herself for her mistakes, so she assumes neither will you."

Sebastian's jaw tightened. He had no response to that.

"If you are the man I believe you to be, I think you can persuade Lady Slight that she has done enough," remarked Sophia. "It is time for Harriet Slight to let the past go."

* * *

The room fell silent.

Even Finch, usually so brash and full of sharp opinions, seemed to recognize that her earlier words had done little to ease Harriet's misery. The scent of tea and freshly baked biscuits hung in the air, but no one reached for them now. Instead, they sat together in uneasy quiet, all their efforts to lift Harriet's spirits having failed.

Finally, Evaline sighed, smoothing her skirts, her fingers toying with the fine embroidery as she searched for the right words. "Men are a prison," she said softly. "They trap your soul, repress your spirit. Cage you in a prison of expectation and disparate duty, while they carouse about and keep mistresses without a thought for the women they have bound to them."

Her words rang heavy in the air, and for the first time since their acquaintance, Harriet truly heard the bitterness beneath Evaline's composed exterior.

"I spent years locked away in a house that was never mine," Evaline continued, her voice steady but laced with pain. "Told when to speak, how to act, what to wear. Forbidden to leave without permission. I lived as a ghost while my husband dined at clubs, drank himself into stupors, and took his pleasure elsewhere. He was never reprimanded for it, never scorned. But I? I was expected to endure. Because that is the role of a lady."

She looked up, calm and unflinching. "Perhaps there is no place for men in our lives. Perhaps we do not need them at all. Look at what we have built together. This house is filled with warmth, with laughter, with friendship. We have each other. Why should we allow men to dictate our happiness when we have already found something far more lasting?"

Belinda nodded in quiet agreement. Even Finch grumbled her approval, though she busied herself with refilling her teacup as if reluctant to admit that Evaline had put words to that which she had long believed.

Harriet said nothing.

Because none of it was true about Sebastian.

He had never tried to cage her.

In their youth, he had encouraged her interests, treated her mind as an equal, invited her to explore the world with him, to share in his adventure on the Grand Tour. She had been the one to refuse. He had been the one to fight for the right to marry her all those years ago.

Even now—Harriet pressed her lips together, her throat burning—he had defied the duke, come to her the night before, clearly committed to a future with her. He had offered her everything, until he had seen the painting.

And was it fair to be angry with him for his mistrust when she had given him so many reasons to doubt her?

She had lied. Again and again, she had deceived him.

She had tricked him into a courtship.

She had hidden the truth about her past.

She had denied him the one thing he had wished for— honesty.

She could not blame him for being angry. She could not even blame him for thinking she was having an affair with Richard.

Because had she not already betrayed him once? Had she not taken his cousin Perry to her bed last year, leaving a trail of chaos until Perry had wed the country mouse and moved to Somerset?

The guilt of it crushed her.

Sebastian had every reason to turn his back on her. And he had not learned of Perry yet. At least, she did not think he had. And yet, selfishly, she still wished he would not.

CHAPTER 15

Your frowns I fear, your smiles I doubt,
Will ne'er to me incline;
The truth resolved to find you out,
I write, my Valentine.

The New Ladies' Valentine Writer (1821)

* * *

Sebastian exhaled sharply, running a hand through his hair. His mind was still reeling from Sophia's revelation. Harriet had been attempting to change—to atone. But what did that mean for them? Could he ever trust her again? Was there a future where he could look at her and not think of all the lies?

His gaze moved to Richard, who was watching him carefully. "And what about the girl? Jem, I believe Finch called her. Who is she?"

Richard's expression softened slightly, as if he had

expected the question. "A foundling," he said. "Lady Slight saved her."

Sebastian arched a brow. "Saved her?"

Richard nodded. "She was living on the streets, controlled by a despicable thief-master who used children as pickpockets. The usual scheme—take in the orphans, force them to steal, beat them when they do not bring back enough coin." His mouth tightened. "Jem was one of the unfortunate ones. She was caught by a clerk with her hand in his pocket. He was dragging her off to be arrested when Lady Slight came upon them."

Sebastian's stomach twisted. He knew what would have happened next. A child thief, particularly one caught red-handed, had little hope in London's justice system. She would have been sent straight to Newgate, crammed into a cell with hardened criminals, and treated with the same cruelty as an adult offender. If she were lucky, she would have been sentenced to transportation—to be shipped off to Australia like so much unwanted cargo. If she were unlucky …

He swallowed hard.

"Lady Slight paid the clerk off," Richard continued. "Gave him enough coin to silence his anger and take his grievances elsewhere. Jem was frantic, convinced Lady Slight had only done it to hand her over to someone worse. It took hours to convince her to board the carriage."

Sebastian could picture it too well. Harriet, in all her imperious splendor, taking on the role of a benevolent queen as she swept in to rescue a desperate girl. But this was not some grand social gesture made for appearances' sake. This was real.

"And then?" he asked.

"She brought her home," Richard said simply. "She and Lady Wood nursed her for a week. The girl had a fever, terrible nightmares. Likely half-starved before that, too. She pulled through, but as soon as she was well, she wished to leave. Return to the streets. The little one was too proud for charity, from all accounts, so Lady Slight had to persuade Jem that she was sorely needed as a chambermaid because Lady Slight had no servants to take care of her."

Sebastian rubbed at his temples.

It was almost too much to comprehend.

A barmaid turned housekeeper. A widow who had barely escaped her husband's cruelty. And now, an orphaned pickpocket who had been given a second chance at a respectable occupation in a good household.

A strange collection of people indeed.

And at the center of it all—Harriet.

Harriet, who had lied to him.

Harriet, who had deceived him.

Harriet, who had saved them all.

She truly was trying to change. He had always thought she possessed such potential, but there was no denying that Harriet had been rather selfish by nature when he had known her. This trouble she was taking to help women in peril was not carried out by the same girl who had always sought her own pleasures first.

* * *

JEM GAVE Harriet's hand a firm squeeze, her small fingers wrapping around Harriet's own with surprising strength for one so slight. Her big hazel eyes—too knowing for a girl so young—fixed on her with solemn determination.

"Men," Jem declared, in the same flat, matter-of-fact tone she might use to list items for the wash. "They beat ye if ye dinna steal enough. They take what they want if ye ain't quick enough to get away. An' a good blade's always a good idea." She gave a firm nod, like she was imparting the most sensible advice in the world. "Stick 'em in the leg. Right in the thigh. Then ye got time to run."

There was a moment of stunned silence. Evaline's gloved fingers stilled where they had been tracing a thoughtful pattern over her skirts. Finch, mid-sip of tea, gave an approving grunt, as if Jem had spoken nothing but truth. Even Belinda, who had weathered enough of life's cruelties to be unsurprised by much, blinked at the girl in surprise.

Harriet, however, felt her throat tighten as she looked down at Jem's small hand curled in hers. This thin, waiflike girl, who had stolen her way into Harriet's heart during her terrible fever, spoke as if men were merely another hazard of the world, like a carriage rattling too fast through the streets or a bitter cold snap that stole the warmth from your bones.

Jem had lived in a world where men were threats to be feared. A world where survival meant fighting back, running fast, or hiding well.

And Harriet, who had never suffered such things, but had known her own share of disappointments at the hands of men, had been inclined to agree.

Until now.

Her fingers tightened gently over Jem's. She did not speak, only stroked the girl's knuckles with the pad of her thumb, offering comfort in the only way she knew how. Jem had endured things no child should, and Harriet had tried to give her a home free of such fears. But those early years had left their mark. Yet even as sympathy bloomed in Harriet's heart, another thought followed swiftly on its heels.

Sebastian.

Sebastian, whose hands had never been cruel.

Sebastian, who had never used his significant size to intimidate, only to protect. Who had always been aware of his strength, careful with it, as if mindful that others were smaller, more breakable than he.

Even last night, when they had tangled together in the dark, his passion had never turned to roughness. He had been cautious even in the height of his desire, treating her with a reverence that made her ache now to remember it.

And what had she done?

Lied to him. Manipulated him. Used him.

She had thought herself clever, but she had been nothing more than selfish.

She did not deserve him.

Sebastian had spent years building a life of integrity, of art and purpose. And she? She was a scheming widow with a flexible sense of truth and a ruthless nature when it suited her.

No, she did not deserve him at all.

Harriet swallowed hard and looked down at Jem, who was waiting expectantly for approval of her tactics.

Harriet forced a small smile. "I sincerely hope you will never need to do such a thing under my roof."

Jem tilted her head.

"Still, 'tis good advice, m'lady," Jem said with a shrug, like it was nothing remarkable. "Ain't no man gonna chase ye proper with a knife stuck in 'is thigh."

Finch gave an emphatic nod of agreement.

Harriet exhaled, pressing a kiss to Jem's knuckles before releasing her hand.

If only all wounds could be healed so easily. Harriet found she was regretting how she had run off from Sebastian in the park. He had a right to his anger, and perhaps she should have stayed and explained herself. Perhaps he had deserved some answers after all the secrets.

* * *

Sophia grimaced, shaking her head as she looked to her husband. "And then there is Belinda Cooper," she reminded him.

Sebastian, who had been pressing the bridge of his nose between his fingers, froze at the name.

Cooper.

A chill ran through him as a memory stirred.

He had heard that name before. Recently.

His mind revisited the afternoon when Bertram Hargreaves had been waiting for them at Harriet's house, standing in her painted room with his hands clasped behind his back, his face carved into a mask of barely restrained fury. There had been a cryptic exchange. Harriet had been composed but dismissive, but Hargreaves—he had been searching for someone.

Cooper.

Then another memory surfaced. The remark about naughty novels that must not be found by a Miss Bélise Coupier, and his mind made the connection. Sebastian lifted his head slowly.

"You mean to tell me," he said, "that when Hargreaves came sniffing around Harriet's house, looking for Cooper, he was unknowingly looking for her lady's maid?"

Richard hesitated before giving a firm nod.

Sebastian absorbed this revelation, tension thrumming through his veins.

"Explain."

Richard sighed and leaned forward, rubbing his palms together before speaking.

"I was able to locate an address for Belinda after some effort—some rooms Lowe kept near St. James's Market," he admitted. "As soon as Lady Slight had it, she was determined to visit her."

Sebastian arched a brow. "Personally?"

Richard gave him a look. "Of course personally."

Sophia smiled faintly, shaking her head. "Once she sets her mind on something, there is no talking her down."

Sebastian resisted the urge to curse. That must have been the night he had followed her after visiting the museum. When he had thought perhaps she was meeting with another man. "What exactly did Hargreaves do to this woman?"

Richard's jaw tightened. "Belinda Cooper was a lady's maid who was acting as a chaperon for two girls when she met him. He seduced her, promised her security. For years, she was his faithful mistress. By all accounts, she genuinely loved the man."

Sebastian snorted, crossing his arms. "A rake like Hargreaves? I doubt he returned the sentiment."

Richard nodded grimly. "Indeed. When she aged out of his interest, he discarded her without a second thought. But it was not just that." His voice hardened. "He took back everything. The townhouse he had installed her in, the gifts, the furnishings, all of it. Even reneging over the modest settlement he had once promised her. One day, she was living comfortably, and the next, she was destitute."

Sebastian let out a sharp breath, anger prickling over his skin. He had never had much regard for Bertram Hargreaves, but this …

"What did she do?"

Richard's mouth pressed into a grim line. "With nowhere to go and no means of support, at her age, and with her reputation, there were not many options open to her. She was with Lord Lowe and one step away from ending up in a bawdy house."

Sebastian's stomach turned.

"And Harriet?"

Richard leaned back, running a hand through his hair. "Lady Slight was outraged. She refused to let it stand. She searched for Belinda relentlessly for weeks, even going so far as to brave her father's house to demand answers. When I gave the address, she promptly called on her and offered her an escape. And Belinda chose dignity over despair."

Sophia's voice was softer as she added, "That wretch, Lowe, had already laid hands on her, so when Lady Slight offered her a position as a lady's maid, she took it."

Sebastian sat back, processing this new information.

He had known Harriet was stubborn. He had known she could be reckless. But this ... this was different.

"She knew," he murmured, more to himself than anyone else. "She knew taking Miss Cooper in would create trouble for her. That Hargreaves would confront her, but she did it anyway."

Richard nodded. "She did, despite doing her best to avoid Hargreaves these past years," he confirmed. "Because she thought what he had done was very wrong, and for Miss Cooper, she was willing to put up with the troubles it would bring."

Sebastian exhaled through his nose. He should have expected nothing less.

That was Harriet, after all.

A force of nature. A woman who, for all her faults, had a mind of her own. But antagonizing her father? That showed a new level of courage she had not displayed before. The mere thought of upsetting him had been sufficient to make her tremble with anxiety as a girl.

A memory surfaced—Harriet as a girl, demanding that they stop to free a bird that had caught its foot in a snare. She had gone pale at the sight of the creature's frantic struggle, and when they had freed it, she had nearly wept. That was the girl he had loved. And now, it seemed, that girl was still there, buried beneath the mistakes and the lies and the years that had divided them.

Sebastian ran a hand down his face, releasing a slow breath. He had driven her off with his fury in Hyde Park, convinced she was having an affair with Richard. But now, as the truth unfolded before him, that certainty began to crumble.

Damn her. Damn himself.

He had to see her.

* * *

BELINDA, who had remained mostly silent, now set down her teacup with a deliberate clink and met Harriet's gaze with a steady, knowing air.

"You think he is different, but men are all the same, my lady," she said, her voice calm but edged with something raw, something deeply personal. "Even when you love them, even when you give them everything, they cannot be trusted. They will cast you aside when it suits them, and all your years of devotion will be for naught."

Harriet winced at the bitterness in her tone. She knew what had been done to Belinda—how she had spent over a decade loving Bertram Hargreaves only to be discarded like an old glove the moment he no longer suited him.

Belinda had every right to believe as she did.

And yet …

Harriet's mind turned to Sebastian.

His strength. His honor.

His unwavering, maddening, steadfast regard for her.

Through everything—through her betrayal all those years ago, through her scheming, through the lies and half-truths —he had still looked at her as though she was the girl he had loved. The girl he had once dreamed of making his wife.

It had taken only a few days for her to see the light of admiration return to his eyes since their recent reunion.

She swallowed hard.

"I have but one complaint about Lord Sebastian," she murmured, her voice barely above a whisper. "And that is his lack of trust."

The words settled over the room, a quiet, undeniable truth.

Finch huffed. "A man oughta trust th' woman 'e means t' marry, or 'e ain't worth the trouble."

But Harriet shook her head.

"No." Her voice was stronger now, conviction taking root inside her. "I cannot fault him for it. It is I who lied, who hid the truth or bent it. I am the cause of his distrust."

A breath shuddered through her as realization struck deep, shaking loose the last fragile justifications that tied her down.

"And it is I who must apologize to him."

A hush fell over the room.

Harriet lifted her chin, her pulse thundering in her ears. She had started on this path after Lily's heartfelt words, not a curse, but a blessing. And she had thought at the end of this road, however painful or difficult it may be, she might find someone for herself as Lily had. As that mouse who had married Perry had. But now she realized what she must have known all along.

She did not want someone like Sebastian.

There was no one like Sebastian.

She wanted Sebastian.

With all her heart.

She wanted to undo the mistakes of yesteryear and tumble into his arms. And stay there. Forever. As she should have done on that St. Valentine's Day.

But after all she had done to him, how could she ever win his trust? She did not even trust herself. Why should he?

The thought sent a wave of desperation through her.

No.

She would not let him slip away. Not again. She surged to her feet, fists clenched at her sides, resolve burning bright in her chest.

"I shall throw myself at his feet and beg him to take me back!" she declared, her voice shaking but firm.

And then—

A voice from the doorway. Low, familiar. Steady as bedrock.

"No begging necessary, Harry," Sebastian said, stepping into the room, his broad frame filling the doorway and conveying such adoration that she was stunned into incredulity. "You have always had me. And you always will."

Harriet gasped.

The world narrowed to him, standing there, looking at her as if nothing else existed. As if she had never shattered his heart. As if she had never once driven him away.

Her throat closed, emotion rising so swiftly it nearly knocked her breath away.

Sebastian was here. He was here. He had come for her.

And, in that moment, Harriet believed anything was possible. Even the possibility of forgiveness for a worthless life.

CHAPTER 16

Have pity on your constant swain,
And release him from his pain;
Cast him not like shells away;
But fix upon a joyous day,
When we to church shall trip away.

The New Ladies' Valentine Writer (1821)

* * *

Despite the impropriety of it all, the women rose to their feet as one, standing shoulder to shoulder with Harriet. Finch, naturally, was the first to speak, her stout figure braced like a general about to lead a charge.

"Well, m'lord?" she demanded, hands planted firmly on her hips. "Ye come stormin' in 'ere like some bleedin' conquerin' 'ero, but what I wants to know is—what're yer intentions toward our lady?"

Sebastian lifted a brow, clearly amused by the inquisition

but entirely undaunted. His gaze flickered across each woman before settling on Finch with a measured patience.

"My intentions," he said slowly, "are my own to discuss with Lady Slight."

Finch let out a huff, unimpressed. "Ain't good enough, m'lord. We all knows 'ow men work—ye'll say all them pretty things, make yer promises, then scarper soon as ye've 'ad yer fill." She folded her arms. "Oi'll not 'ave our lady left 'eart-broken on my watch."

Harriet, still reeling from Sebastian's sudden appearance and his words, barely managed to find her voice. "Finch—"

But the older woman was undeterred.

"Ye ain't got the foggiest what she's been through," Finch continued, her voice thick with conviction. "Ye don't know 'ow 'ard she's worked to turn things 'round. So if ye're just 'ere to muck about with 'er, ye can turn right 'round an' shove off out that door."

Sebastian did not so much as flinch at the scolding. Instead, he inclined his head, as though he had expected no less from the formidable woman. "I assure you, I do not intend to toy with her."

A delicate throat-clearing sounded beside Finch, and Evaline, ever the picture of grace and refinement, clasped her hands before her.

"My lord," she said, her voice smooth and composed but no less resolute, "it is not simply a matter of whether you intend to cause pain but whether you are prepared for all that loving Harriet entails." She tilted her head, scrutinizing him with an assessing gaze. "You may think you know her, but people change. Life changes them. You have spent years apart, and now you have only had a handful of days together. Are you certain you understand what you are asking for?"

Harriet's heart pounded. Evaline's words, spoken with quiet authority, struck true.

Did he truly understand?

Sebastian was silent for a moment. Then, at last, he spoke.

"I know her well enough to understand that I love her," he said.

A ripple of reaction passed through the room.

Harriet inhaled sharply, her stomach twisting into knots.

He loves me.

Finch and Evaline exchanged glances, but before they could respond, Belinda stepped forward, her gaze piercing.

"And yet you did not trust her," Belinda pointed out, her words laced with skepticism. "You accused her of unfaithfulness. You stormed out." She raised a brow. "What has changed?"

Sebastian's jaw clenched. "I was angry."

"That much was clear," Belinda murmured.

He rolled his shoulders, his tension visible. "I was angry because I have spent years trying to forget her. And the moment I stopped resisting, the moment I allowed myself to believe in a future, I discovered she had deceived me again."

Harriet looked away. He had every right to say it. Every right to hold that grievance close to his heart. But his next words made her breath catch.

"I left because I was afraid," Sebastian admitted, his confession settling over the room. "Afraid that I would never be able to trust her. Afraid that she would never trust me. Afraid that after everything, I had come back for a dream that had already crumbled." His voice turned hoarse. "But I was wrong."

A hush fell.

Harriet swallowed past the lump in her throat.

Sebastian took a step forward.

"Harriet, I know we cannot erase the past," he said. "I know we have made mistakes—both of us. But I also know that I am not willing to let you go. Not again."

Jem, standing by Harriet's side, her little hands balled into fists, finally spoke, her young voice quiet but firm.

"Then don't."

Sebastian turned his gaze to the girl, which Jem met without flinching.

"If ye love 'er, then stay."

The simple words, spoken with such certainty, sent a fresh wave of emotion washing over Harriet.

Stay.

She looked to Sebastian, her heart hammering. The room was silent, waiting. Waiting for her to decide. Waiting for her to believe. She took a shaky breath. And then, voice trembling but firm, she spoke.

"There are things I have done. Things you do not know about."

Sebastian's gaze focused on her, and he smiled in a way that made her heart flip over in her chest.

"When you are ready, you will tell me these mistakes that you regret. Until then, I accept you as you are because living without you is … I cannot do it again, Harry. It will kill me to walk away a second time, so take mercy on this wretched man who has loved you since the moment I first met you as a green youth in Wiltshire and have never stopped."

He stepped forward, respectfully making his way through the women who stood between them. Once he reached her, he lifted his hand to her cheek and tilted her head back to stare deep into her heart.

"Let me love you, Harry."

Tears spilled, but this time they were tears of gratitude. Gratitude for the man who knew her to her very depths. Knew her flaws. Knew about her secrets. And had always loved her anyway.

Sebastian used the pad of his thumb to wipe the moisture away from her cheeks, lowering his head to settle his lips against hers, and Harriet felt the pieces of her soul slowly pulling together into one whole. A flawed whole, but if a man as true as Sebastian could accept her as she was, perhaps she could, too.

"Right, then," Finch said, clearing her throat and folding her arms across her ample bosom. "This is all very sweet an' teary, but dinner ain't gonna serve itself, now is it?"

Harriet let out a breathless giggle against Sebastian's mouth, the tension of the moment giving way to sheer, giddy relief. The women chuckled amongst themselves before retreating, their skirts rustling as they dispersed, murmuring about roasts and puddings, no doubt eager to grant them privacy.

Sebastian lifted his head, gray eyes warm and fixed on her as the last of their audience slipped away.

"There are things to settle between us," Harriet said softly. "But"—she bit her lip, hesitant, but she knew what she wanted—"may I come to Italy with you? Perhaps we can wed in Calais?"

A slow, wondrous smile spread across his face. He nodded, then leaned down to kiss her again, more gently this time, as if sealing a vow.

Before she could take another breath, he bent and lifted her into his arms as though she weighed nothing. Harriet gasped, laughing as she instinctively clutched his shoulders. "Sebastian!"

"I have wasted enough time, Harry," he murmured, striding out of the painted room and toward the staircase.

Her mind whirled, half in awe that this was real. Could it truly be happening? The thought of leaving England—of starting fresh, of standing beside Sebastian in Italy, of finally being free of all the burdens she had carried—sent a thrill through her veins. Perhaps she might ask Belinda if she wished to leave England as well, to go where her past reputation would not hinder her, and she would be free to be Miss Belinda Cooper or Miss Bélise Coupier as she pleased, and Bertram Hargreaves's disapproving presence could no longer touch either of them. And, here in London, Evaline would take care of her odd little household in her absence.

Then, as the warmth of Sebastian's body pressed against hers, a more sobering thought crept in. She winced slightly, knowing that sooner or later, she would have to tell him everything. Confess her sins. Lay bare the worst of herself so she never again had to flinch at the shadows of her past.

It should be soon. It should be now. But just as quickly as the thought arrived, it was vanquished when Sebastian's lips found hers again, hot and demanding, scattering all reason as he carried her through the halls of her home. There was no past, no regrets—only the steady strength of his arms and the promise of new bonds, unbreakable bonds.

For, as evening approached, there was only them.

* * *

SEBASTIAN WAS EUPHORIC. All the doubts, the anger, the past arguments—none of it mattered anymore. Harriet had chosen him. She wanted to come to Italy. She wanted him.

For the first time since that fateful St. Valentine's Day, he was truly happy.

He held her close as he carried her up the stairs, savoring the soft warmth of her body against his chest, her breath feathering against his neck. She was his. After all the years apart, the regrets and misunderstandings, the barriers between them had finally crumbled. Whatever troubles they encountered, they would navigate them together.

Happiness was possible. Even in the bad times, even when life was imperfect, he would have her by his side. For years, he had hardened himself against hope, against the foolish notion that he could ever reclaim what he had lost. But now, for the first time in forever, he allowed himself to look forward to the future.

A future with Harriet.

Passion coiled hot and insistent through him as he ascended the last step, his grip tightening around her as he reached her rooms. He pushed the door open with his shoulder, stepping inside her private drawing room.

He had no wish to think of anything else. Not the quarrels. Not the past. Not even the painting that had begun the argument earlier this day.

There was only Harriet.

Harriet sighed against him, her soft body molding to his as he strode across the threshold of her bedchamber. He kicked the door shut behind them, blocking out the world beyond, leaving only the heat between them, the rapid beating of their hearts, the slow drag of breath as he inhaled the scent of her—warm, feminine, *his*.

But then, she stirred in his arms, shifting against his chest, pushing lightly against him. "Sebastian, let me down."

He hesitated. The last thing he wanted was space between them. But the quiet urgency in her voice cut through his desire. Slowly, reluctantly, he let her slide down the length of his body.

Her descent was agonizing. Every soft contour of her pressed against the rigid proof of his desire, her skirts rustling as she slipped down inch by inch, her lips tilted up toward his, their mouths fused in a slow, searing kiss.

Then, just as his arms flexed to pull her back, she broke away.

Sebastian exhaled sharply as she stepped back, escaping his embrace completely.

She turned, pacing across the room, hands wringing together.

"I do not want to bear the burden of my secrets anymore," she muttered, more to herself than to him.

Sebastian drew a slow, measured breath, willing his body to calm even as every muscle in him protested. He shifted, leaning back against the doorframe, arms crossed, schooling his expression into one of patience. But inside, he was aflame.

Every fiber of his being demanded that he go to her, pull her back into his arms, into the bed, into him.

But intrigue held him still.

Because this was important.

Whatever Harriet was about to say, whatever weighed on her, he needed to hear it.

Even if the only thing he truly wanted was to continue what they had begun the night before, to explore every inch of her again until there were no more barriers, no more lies, no more regrets.

Still, he forced himself to remain by the door, watching her intently.

"Then unburden yourself, Harry," he said, his voice low, rough with restrained passion. "Tell me everything."

Harriet licked her lips, her hands moving restlessly to her hair, disturbing the careful arrangement until strands began to slip free, mussing the perfect coif.

Sebastian's fingers itched. He wanted to reach out, pluck the pins from her hair, watch her glorious auburn waves spill down her back in a shimmering cascade. But she was pacing, her expression tense, her breath coming quick and shallow as if she were struggling to contain all the words rushing to escape.

"Where do I even start?" she muttered.

He said nothing. Just watched. Waited.

And then the words tumbled out, a frantic rush, as if she could no longer hold them in.

"The day I was supposed to meet you. The day we were meant to go to Calais," she said in a whisper, her fingers knotting together in a tight grip. "I-I was scared." She looked at him then, her blue eyes wide and pleading. "Not because I did not love you. Not because I did not want you. But because I was afraid that you could not support us if your brother cut you off. He was so dead set against helping us court that I was certain he would. But that was because it was what my father would do, and I cannot speak to the duke's possible actions in that event."

Sebastian listened, remaining silent.

"I was selfish," she continued, her voice thick with remorse. "I chose money and status. I told myself it was the practical decision. That it was for the best. That you would resent me when it became too hard." She gave a short, bitter laugh. "But it was never worth it. Not once."

She swallowed, bracing herself to continue her confession.

"My father …" She hesitated, then shook her head. "No. I will not blame him. The choice was mine. But he did whisper doubts in my ear. He filled my head with fears, coaxed me to marry Horace Slight because of the advantages it gave him. And I let him. I knew what kind of man he was. I knew I should have ignored his discouragements. But I listened, because it suited me to do so. To not show courage but to take the easy way out."

Sebastian's hands curled into fists. Not in anger—no, not even in frustration. But because the desire to throw her onto the bed, until every regret was erased, was nearly over-whelming.

But he understood. She needed this. Needed to purge these thoughts, to release them from the dark corners of her mind where they had festered for years. This was the new Harriet, embracing the difficult path that led to genuine rewards, so he remained where he was, watching her unravel before him as she had never done before.

She was ready to reveal her innermost thoughts and finally let him in. But in this moment, he knew that nothing she could ever say would make him rethink his choice to finally join with her. All the years of pain and loss had washed away while Sophia and Richard had revealed the real Harriet, the woman he had always known she was beneath the facade she had erected under her father's tutelage year by year. And now that he had finally found this woman, the real woman, he was never letting her go.

* * *

Harriet paused in the middle of the floor, her hands twisting together so tightly that her knuckles ached. The fire crackled softly in the grate, the only sound in the stillness of the room.

She peeked up at Sebastian. He was so still, his broad frame leaning against the doorframe, arms folded over his chest. He seemed calm—too calm—watching her with steady gray eyes that revealed nothing of his thoughts. He had shown no reaction to anything she had said thus far, simply listening.

Her breath quickened as she tried to think how to say what came next.

If he stayed in the room after this—if he did not storm out, if he did not look at her with disgust—then she would know. She would know that he would never leave her. That no matter what she said, what she had done, she would not lose him.

And yet, it was so despicable.

She swallowed, her throat tightening as she fought to force the words from her lips.

Just say it, Harriet. Say it before you lose your courage.

"But that is not the worst," she finally blurted, the words rushing out before she could stop them. "Last year, I had an affair with your cousin Perry."

Sebastian straightened, his arms uncrossing, a deep frown creasing his face.

Harriet's breath caught. *This is it. This is where he leaves.*

She watched in growing panic as he ran a hand through his golden hair, his fingers raking through the strands in that familiar way he always did when he was thinking, when he was troubled.

Her stomach plummeted.

Then he exhaled slowly, lowering his hand. He met her gaze, his expression indecipherable, but then, he nodded.

Harriet stared at him, stunned.

And then he spoke, his voice low but steady. "All right."

She blinked. "All right?"

Sebastian gave a small, weary nod. "It is not what I would have wished to hear, but ... I cannot say I am surprised. You were lonely. He can be charming." His mouth twitched with what might have been amusement in a different circumstance. "And he was utterly without honor, although I am told he is a very different man now."

Harriet released a shuddering breath, barely able to process his words.

He was not leaving. He had not raged. Had not recoiled.

And the part of her that had been bracing for his rejection —that had been certain of it—uncoiled like a spring snapping loose.

"You are not angry?" she asked, her voice tentative.

Sebastian ran a hand down his face, then sighed. "Oh, I am angry." His voice was rough now, his gaze sharp as steel. "But not at you. Not anymore." He shook his head, as though sifting through his thoughts. "I have spent years resenting the past. Resenting you. But the truth is, I left you to face England alone while I ran off to Italy. I should have fought harder for you. I should have made it impossible for you to doubt me."

Tears burned at the backs of her eyes.

"I did doubt you," she whispered. "I doubted that you could stand against your brother. I doubted that I was worth fighting for."

Sebastian took a step toward her, his voice fierce now. "You were worth it, Harry. You are worth it."

Her pulse slowed in shock, and then, she was in his arms.

Sebastian held her at arm's length, his strong hands firm but gentle as they rested on her upper arms. She could see the longing in his eyes, the way his gaze traced the lines of her face, the curve of her lips, but he would not allow her to press against him.

His voice was quiet but unyielding. "We should finish this, Harry. Tell me about Brendan."

Harriet blinked, stunned. A cold wave of dread swept through her, and she instinctively tugged away, crossing the room to wrap her arms around herself.

"Someone told you?" she asked eventually, barely audible.

Sebastian shook his head. "It was a guess." He exhaled sharply, rubbing a hand over his jaw. "Brendan did not say a single word during dinner last night. And he attempted to interrupt the duke when he thought his secrets were going to be revealed."

Harriet let out a short, bitter laugh, rubbing at her hair again, heedless of how she was mussing the already-loose strands. "Yes," she said hoarsely. "I had an affair with him." She hesitated before forcing herself to continue. "But that was not the worst of it."

She turned to face him fully now, her heart pounding.

"The problem was that he was here. In this house. When

his father was murdered." Her voice grew thready. "And I-I would not provide him an alibi. I was dismissive and selfish, and I refused to involve myself." She swallowed, shame thick in her throat. "Lily stepped forward in my place. She gave the alibi I should have given. And so they had to marry."

She braced herself, expecting Sebastian's anger, expecting his condemnation.

Instead, he nodded. Accepting the truth.

But she was not done.

"It gets worse," she whispered.

Sebastian's brows rose. "How?"

Harriet squeezed her eyes shut, willing herself to be brave. She could not stop now. She had to see this through, no matter the consequences.

"I was drunk. And miserable. And I could not understand why my lovers kept leaving me to marry unsophisticated girls." She let out a hollow laugh. "So I-I tried to seduce him after they married."

Sebastian stiffened.

Harriet forced herself to meet his eyes, her face hot with shame. "Lily caught me."

Silence stretched between them, thick and suffocating.

Sebastian's voice was quiet, but there was an edge to it. "And Brendan?"

Harriet's hands clenched at her sides. "He resisted me," she admitted. "He did not participate. He did not betray Lily. I was the only one at fault."

Sebastian was silent as he absorbed this.

Harriet waited. Heart hammering. Waiting for the moment he decided she was not worth forgiving.

The silence stretched so long that Harriet thought she might have lost all sense of time. Every muscle in her body was braced for his anger, his disgust, for the moment Sebastian finally realized she was too far gone to be redeemed.

But then …

He chuckled.

Harriet blinked, sure she had misheard.

Sebastian rubbed a hand over his face, shaking his head. "Well," he mused, his voice wry, "the duke's current resistance to you makes a great deal more sense now."

She stared at him, her lips parting in disbelief. "You are laughing?"

"I am," he admitted, amusement curling his lips. "Because I spent half the night trying to puzzle out why my customarily even-tempered brother was so damn stiff around you. Still. After all these years. And now I know." His gray eyes gleamed as he gave her a pointed look. "I also suspect this is what Sophia meant when she said your secrets were your own to disclose."

Harriet exhaled shakily, her hands still clenched at her sides. "Lady Saunton?"

Sebastian nodded. "She accompanied Richard to see me. To reassure me that I had not caught the two of you in an illicit assignation."

"And you are not angry?"

Sebastian's smile faded slightly, though not in disappointment—rather, with a quiet assurance that felt more certain, more enduring.

"I have been challenged," he said, his voice thoughtful. "Challenged to be the man you need. And after hearing all this, I understand why you began your quest for redemption and why you need a strong man who keeps his head. I committed to this role when I decided to return to you."

Harriet's throat tightened, emotion swelling inside her. She had expected fury. Or worse, pity. But Sebastian only saw her. And after everything, after all her mistakes, he still wanted to be the man by her side.

Harriet could scarcely breathe. She had prepared herself

for anger. For heartbreak. For the moment Sebastian would finally look at her and see someone unworthy of his love. But instead ...

"You forgive me?" Her voice was barely above a whisper.

Sebastian exhaled, his broad shoulders rising and falling. "It is not my place to forgive you, Harry," he said quietly. "I did foolish things when I was grieving us. You saw the error of your ways and have been making amends. I cannot hold these things against you when we were not together. I can only hold you to account for what you do moving forward."

Harriet swallowed hard, searching his face, trying to make sense of the impossible grace he was offering her.

"We were together," he continued, his voice rough. "And then we were not. I will not hold the last few years against you. I can only start afresh with you so we may continue our journey together."

A sob built in her throat, but she pressed her lips together, forcing herself to hold it in.

He was giving her a future.

A chance.

A beginning.

And for the first time in her life, Harriet dared to believe she might just deserve it. With another sob, she ran into his arms, and this time he let her. Sebastian caught her, his strong arms closing around her, holding her as if he would never let go. Her fingers clutched at his shoulders, at the fabric of his shirt, at anything solid—anything real—to anchor herself against the storm of emotion raging within her.

Then his head dipped, and his mouth claimed hers in a searing kiss. It was not gentle. It was not hesitant. It was everything—their past, their pain, their longing, their unspoken promises—all poured into the heated press of his lips against hers. Harriet melted into him, grasping at his nape, drawing him impossibly closer as her body sang with the relief of his acceptance, his passion, his love.

She had spent years running from the truth, but there was no running from this. She belonged to him. She always had. And as he deepened the kiss, groaning softly against her lips, she knew this time, she would never let him go.

CHAPTER 17

If firm respect can merit claim,
And amorous passion true,
Oh! Let them plead to thee, fair dame,
For these I feel for you.

The New Ladies' Valentine Writer (1821)

* * *

It had been hard to listen to Harriet's confessions, to imagine her with other men, to picture the pain she had suffered and the mistakes she had made. But now, standing here with her in his arms, he realized something vital—she had finally let him in.

She had not forced him to hear these hard truths from others, had not let him stumble upon them by accident. Instead, she had revealed them herself, laying her soul bare before him, trusting him with her deepest regrets.

And his very soul broke apart. Then reformed into something more resilient. Stronger.

Desire crashed into him, raw and unrelenting.

This time, when he kissed her, the depth of his passion was shocking even to himself. He pulled her hard against him, as if he could fuse them together, erase the years of separation and hurt.

The swell of her breasts pressed against his chest, her curves soft and yielding beneath his grip. Her hips nudged against his loins, sending fire through his veins, burning away all hesitation, all doubt.

He wanted her—had always wanted her—but this was different. This was need, aching and primal, fueled not just by desire but by everything that had come before.

His hands skimmed down her back, molding her to him, and when she moaned softly into his mouth, he lost the last of his control.

Sebastian had never kissed her like this before.

Not even when they had been young and reckless, tangled in stolen moments of passion.

Not even when he had held her in the dark, whispering his devotion against her skin.

His declarations were wild. Untamed.

Their lips clashed, parted, rejoined—breathless, desperate. Teeth scraped, tongues tangled, their shared hunger consuming them both. There was no more past, no more pain, no more regret. Only this moment. Only each other.

His hands roved over her, grasping the fine wool of her navy walking dress as if he could burn through it with sheer will alone. He could feel her body beneath—the swell of her hips, the arch of her back, the soft resistance of her stays binding her tightly.

It had to go. All of it.

With an impatient growl, he grasped the fitted bodice, fingers seeking out the row of tiny buttons. She shuddered under his touch, her breath coming in ragged gasps as she gripped his greatcoat and tried to drag it from his shoulders. The heavy wool refused to yield, caught against his broad frame.

"Off," she muttered between fevered kisses, tugging insistently.

With a hoarse chuckle, he tore his mouth from hers just long enough to shrug free of the greatcoat and coat beneath, sending them tumbling to the floor in a heap. She immediately attacked his waistcoat, nimble fingers sliding over the buttons, fumbling in her haste.

Sebastian had no such patience.

His own hands swept to her back, finding the row of fastenings running the length of her bodice. A series of pearly buttons, tiny and damnably intricate. He gritted his teeth, breathing against her throat as he worked through them, releasing one after another.

As he freed the last, the fabric slackened, slipping away from her shoulders.

Harriet let out a soft moan as he slid the gown down her arms, his gaze intent as the rich navy wool pooled at her feet.

She stood before him now in her petticoats, her chemise whispering against the fine linen of her stays, and the sight stole what little breath remained in his lungs.

He wanted to take his time. He wanted to soak this into his very being. But she had other ideas. Her fingers found the fall of his buckskin breeches, tugging at the buttons with a heated determination that nearly undid him. His hand covered hers, stilling her movements.

"Patience," he rasped. "I want this to last."

She made a sound of protest as he cupped her waist, his thumbs tracing the curve of her ribs through her stays. Slowly, with aching slowness, he ran his fingers up the boned fabric, feeling her tremble beneath his touch.

A flick of his fingers and the laces at her back loosened. Another tug, and the stays gave way completely.

She gasped as he pulled them from her body, dropping them atop her discarded gown. Her petticoats and chemise followed, the delicate fabric sliding over her hips, the lace-edged hem whispering against the wooden floor.

Sebastian could only stare.

She was exquisite. Last night he could barely make her out, but now she was revealed fully before him. He had always known it, had always remembered it, but nothing had prepared him for the reality of her standing before him now, bared to his gaze, the golden light of an early winter sunset licking over her flushed skin.

"God above," he breathed, his voice thick with awe.

Harriet's fingers trembled as they found his shirt, pushing it over his shoulders, baring the lean muscle beneath.

She had seen him before. Touched him before.

But never like this.

Never with this sense of inevitability, as if the world itself had led them to this moment.

She pressed a kiss to his chest, just above his racing heart, and he let out a ragged groan.

Enough.

He grasped her by the hips, fitting her softness to the hard planes of his body with a low groan of satisfaction. Harriet gasped as his fingers swept the length of her spine, coaxing her closer in a slow, inexorable pull.

She arched beneath his touch, her head falling back, offering herself completely. And Sebastian, undone by the sheer beauty of her surrender, could only hold her tighter, pressing a kiss to the hollow of her throat, his breath shaking as he whispered against her skin.

"Mine."

Sebastian slid his arms around her, one beneath her knees

and the other cradling her back. She let out a small gasp, her fingers clenching against his bare shoulders, but there was no protest—only the swift rise and fall of her breath, only the way her naked body molded against him.

He had carried her before. Across a dance floor. Onto a horse when she had twisted her ankle years ago. But this moment felt like the axis of his entire existence.

She was light as air in his arms, delicate yet strong, her warmth seeping into him where their bodies touched. His grip tightened, as if he feared she might dissolve into mist if he did not hold her securely enough. Harriet gazed up at him, her lips parted, her auburn hair cascading down her back in loose waves where she had mussed it. In the twilight, she was breathtaking.

He crossed the room with measured steps, savoring the way she curled into him, the feel of her uncovered legs against his forearm, the way her fingertips traced over his collarbone as though memorizing him. And then they reached the bed.

Sebastian lowered her tenderly onto the mattress, following her down as he braced himself above her. The sheets were cool against their heated skin, but she did not seem to notice. Their world was filled with the scent of each other, the feel of each other, the weight of his body as he hovered over her slight form, caging her in without trapping her, taking in the perfection of her rounded breasts.

His gaze swept over her, trying to etch the sight of her into his soul.

"Harry," he murmured, his voice hoarse with unspoken words.

Her hands reached for him, and with a groan of surrender, he let himself fall into her embrace.

Sebastian's mouth descended, claiming hers in a deep, consuming kiss. She met him with equal fervor, her fingers threading through his hair, nails scraping against his scalp as she arched beneath him. Their bodies tangled, pressed so tightly together that he could scarcely tell where he ended and she began.

Her scent—lavender and vanilla—wrapped around him, heady and intoxicating. He groaned, inhaling deeply as he traced the delicate curve of her throat with his lips, the soft skin yielding beneath his mouth. He tasted her there, slow and blissful, feeling the way her pulse thrummed wildly against his tongue.

Harriet writhed beneath him, her body a symphony of movement, her breath catching with each languorous stroke of his lips over her collarbone, her shoulder, lower across the bountiful breasts that had fired his dreams as a youth desperate to see them. To touch them as a lover would. His hands moved, roaming the silken expanse of her, claiming her in a way he had only ever dreamed of.

His name spilled from her lips in a hushed whisper, her voice trembling with need.

Sebastian shuddered, his mastery of self fraying even further as she clung to him. He wanted to taste every inch of her, suckle on those rosy nipples, taste the sweetness of the essence between her legs, to learn the way her body responded to him, to ensure she understood with every touch, every kiss, that she was his.

And tonight, for the first time, she would truly be his.

His hands slid upward to plump her luscious globes, strumming her nipples with the pads of his thumbs before he lowered his head to swirl his tongue over the pleading peaks, first one, then the other, while Harriet moaned and pressed up into his mouth.

Sebastian rose from the bed, the cool air kissing his heated skin as he stepped back. Harriet watched him, her lips parted, her breath shallow as he reached down and pulled off his boots, the heavy leather thudding softly onto the carpet. His fingers made quick work of the fastenings of his buckskins, and with a practiced ease, he pushed them down, along with his small clothes and stockings, until he was bare once more.

Straightening, he allowed himself a moment to enjoy the way Harriet's gaze was drawn—utterly helpless—to the rigid length of him. A slow, smug satisfaction curled through his chest as he noted the way her tongue darted out to wet her lips, her fingers twitching against the sheets as if resisting the urge to reach for him.

A playful smile curved his lips as he prowled back toward her, his muscles flexing with each movement, the firelight casting golden shadows over his body.

"See something you like, Harry?" His voice was a deep, knowing rasp.

She swallowed, her lashes fluttering as she dragged her gaze back up to meet his. "I think I may have forgotten how magnificent you are."

"Since last night?" Sebastian chuckled, lowering himself back onto the bed. "Then allow me to remind you."

Sebastian scarcely had a moment to revel in the sight of her beneath him before Harriet surprised him, shoving at his shoulders with unexpected force and rolling them until she straddled his hips, her pelvis coming down on his as she settled down, soft and wet meeting hard and dry. He let out a sharp breath, his hands flying to her waist, stunned and aroused by her sudden assertiveness.

She was the magnificent one. A conqueror. Her auburn hair tumbled loose from its pins, spilling over her shoulders in a riot of curls, her lips red and kiss-swollen, her chest rising and falling with rapid breaths.

"You think you can have all the fun, my lord?" she

murmured, trailing her fingers over his collarbone, down the defined ridges of his chest.

Sebastian smirked, his hands sliding over the curve of her hips. "By all means, have your way with me."

Harriet's gaze darkened with intent. Slowly, she traced his muscles, her fingertips featherlight, mapping the expanse of him as if she had lost her sense of sight and he was a landscape to memorize. He shuddered as she skimmed his ribs, the faintest whisper of touch enough to set his skin alight.

Her touch turned bolder, nails scraping lightly as she followed the indents of his abdomen, then lower still, to where the muscles tensed beneath her slow, teasing exploration. She took her time, smiling coyly, and Sebastian found himself entirely at her mercy.

He had thought he was the one in command.

But it seemed Harriet had other ideas.

Sebastian's breath came in shallow pulls as Harriet's fingers trailed lower, teasing the taut muscles of his stomach. Her touch was light—infuriatingly so—each delicate brush of her fingertips sending hot shivers racing beneath his skin.

He was used to control. To leading. To coaxing desire from the women he had lain with, using knowing hands and lingering kisses. But this—this slow, torturous exploration—had him undone.

Harriet seemed to sense it, her lips curving with a naughty smile.

"So very smug a moment ago," she murmured, pressing a kiss to his shoulder, then another to the hollow of his throat. "And now look at you."

Sebastian groaned, his fingers tightening at her hips, aching to reclaim his dominance, to flip her beneath him and drive her to madness as she was doing to him.

But then her mouth descended, pressing warm, open-mouthed kisses along the plane of his chest, tracing the contours of his chest with the tip of her tongue. He jolted when she caught his nipple between her teeth, tugging just enough to send a sharp, liquid shock through his veins.

His head fell back against the pillow, a guttural sound tearing from his throat.

"God, Harry."

She hummed in response, lips trailing lower, savoring him with playful licks and nibbles.

It was exquisite torture.

He had never been so completely at a woman's mercy, had never lain so utterly vulnerable beneath a lover's hands. Harriet was no meek, blushing maiden. She was fire and fury, a tempest of passion that threatened to consume him whole.

And he would gladly burn.

Her fingers trailed lower still, skimming his hip bones, her touch both treasuring and mischievous.

"You are beautiful," she whispered against his skin, and he nearly lost himself then and there.

No one had ever spoken those words to him.

Not like this.

Not in the hushed, awed way that Harriet did now, as though he were a marvel to be worshipped, as though she could never grow tired of exploring him.

His hands slid up her back, desperate to anchor himself, to hold onto something solid as she continued her torturous descent.

"Harry," he rasped, barely recognizing his own voice. "If you do not stop—"

"If I do not stop …?"

She lowered her head, her blue eyes dark with challenge as she swirled her tongue around the crown of his cock. He let out a strangled sound, half laugh, half groan, and gripped her hips, rolling them until she was beneath him once more.

Enough.

She had had her turn.

Now it was his.

Sebastian claimed her mouth in a kiss that left no room for resistance—just a deep, shattering need that stole the breath from them both.

Harriet arched beneath him, her fingers threading into his hair, tugging just enough to send a pleasurable sting through his scalp. His body was strung tight, his mastery fraying, his discipline barely holding by a thread.

"Enough of this torment, Harry," he murmured against her lips, the words a growl of frustration and need. "I have waited long enough for you."

Her lips parted, a soft moan escaping as he traced a slow, deliberate path down her throat.

And then, as though she sensed his intent, she shifted beneath him, her body a perfect, warm invitation. Sebastian inhaled her scent, then pressed his forehead to hers, his voice hoarse and raw.

"Are you ready?"

Harriet's hands slid down his back, nails biting into his skin just enough to make him shudder.

"I have never been more ready in my life."

Her words shattered the last of his composure.

And then there was only fire.

Only them.

Only this.

Sebastian crushed his mouth to hers once more, pouring every ounce of longing, of years lost and found again, into the kiss. But then, just as he was ready to take her, to claim her as he had dreamed of for so long, Harriet did something unexpected.

With surprising strength and determination, she twisted beneath him again, using his own momentum against him. In an instant, he found himself flat on his back, Harriet strad-dling him, her hair tumbling in wild waves around her face.

Sebastian blinked up at her, momentarily stunned.

A triumphant smile played on her lips as she pressed her palms to his chest, her touch featherlight yet searing.

"You think you are the only one who has waited for this?" she murmured, her voice husky.

A deep groan rumbled in his chest as she traced delicate fingertips along the taut lines of his stomach, her touch igniting a trail of fire in its wake.

Sebastian's hands moved to grasp her hips, but Harriet caught them, pressing them back against the mattress.

"Not yet," she whispered.

He let out a strangled sound, a mixture of a groan and a laugh.

"Minx," he muttered, but he allowed her this moment, surrendering to her touch.

Her lips followed the path of her hands, brushing over his collarbone, his chest, pausing at the scars he had earned over the years.

She kissed each one.

Sebastian's breath left him in a sharp exhale.

"You undo me, Harry," he admitted, his voice low and ragged.

She smiled against his skin.

"Good," she murmured.

And then she continued her curious exploration.

Harriet trailed her lips lower, her breath warm against his skin as she explored every sculpted plane of his body. Sebas-tian felt himself unraveling beneath her touch, his muscles tensing with every press of her delicate fingers, every sweep of her tongue.

His head fell back against the pillows, a deep groan spilling from his lips as she kissed down the center of his chest, her hands skimming along his ribs, his abdomen, before tracing the sharp cut of his hips.

"God above, Harriet," he rasped, his hands flexing against the sheets.

She paused, glancing up at him through her thick lashes, her expression a mixture of satisfaction and something softer—something that stole the breath from his lungs.

"You have always been majestic," she murmured, her fingers splaying over his taut stomach. "But like this ... beneath me ... completely mine to touch ..."

She lowered her lips to the curve of his hip, brushing a kiss there, then another, her tongue flicking out to taste him.

Sebastian's resolve frayed at the edges, his fingers gripping the sheets in an effort not to flip her beneath him and take charge. But damnation, he wanted to see what she would do next.

Her mouth continued its descent, her touch teasing, tormenting, until he was nearly shaking with the effort to remain still.

"Harry," he warned, his voice hoarse.

She smiled, wicked and knowing, and pressed her lips to the sharpest point of his hipbone, making his entire body jerk beneath her.

"You are playing a dangerous game," he ground out, his hands clenching into fists.

Her tongue darted out to taste him again and again.

"Perhaps I like danger," she whispered.

Sebastian swore violently, reaching for her, but she slipped from his grasp, laughing breathlessly as she pressed her hands against his chest once more, holding him down.

"Not yet," she teased. "I am not quite finished with you."

His chest heaved, his entire body drawn tight as a bowstring.

"Then hurry up and finish," he growled.

She only laughed again, and continued her slow, torturous trailing, driving him to the very edge of madness.

Then, when he knew he could not take another single second of her delicious torment, Harriet raised her hips and slowly lowered herself onto his throbbing length. Her slick channel closed around him, her tight heat driving him mad as he arched up to receive her, and she slid down until she was seated all the way to the hilt of him.

They both panted in unison, spellbound by the sensation of joining.

Then, ever so slowly, she gyrated against him, rubbing the center of her pleasure against his pubic bone and gasping as her head fell back to reveal the long column of her slender throat and she began to ride. Back and forth, she rode him with long strokes, squeezing his cock tightly with her strong, intimate muscles, and Sebastian groaned, torn between throwing his head back in ecstasy and watching her curvaceous body riding him.

As she picked up speed, grinding the apex of her crease against him, he feared he would not last at the sight of her taking her pleasure on him, her breasts swaying and bouncing with the motion of rhythmic undulation that drove him to the furthest edge of sanity, the sensation too much to contain. He strained for his self-control and groaned with grateful relief when he heard her muffled shriek of release and was finally able to let go, spending deep into her womb with a rush so intense, he feared he would pass out.

Harriet collapsed over him, their limbs tangled, their bodies soaked in sweat, and a curtain of red hair flowing in every direction. Sebastian raised a hand to hold her head to his chest and, in that moment, knew what it was to live in paradise.

CHAPTER 18

That which slew me can restore me,
Bid me with new ardor rise:
Then I still will fall before thee,
Captured by thy beaming eyes.

The New Ladies' Valentine Writer (1821)

* * *

DECEMBER 20, 1821

*S*ebastian sat stiffly in the drawing room of his brother's grand townhouse, his jaw tight as he stared at the Duke of Halmesbury. The atmosphere was tense, the silence thick with unspoken grievances. Beside him, Richard shifted, ever so slightly, but kept his focus on the duke.

Philip leaned back in his chair, fingers steepled beneath

his chin as he regarded them both. Sebastian knew his brother well enough to recognize the calculation in his gaze.

"So," Philip finally said, his voice cool, measured. "You wish me to grant my blessing on a marriage to a woman I have warned you against."

Sebastian's hands fisted in his lap. "I am not here to ask for your permission," he stated. "I am here to tell you that Harriet and I will be married. But I would prefer that you support us, that you accept her into this family as she deserves."

Philip arched a brow. "Deserves?"

Richard cleared his throat. "If I may, Halmesbury. Lady Slight has undergone a … transformation of sorts. I believe you are not aware of the good she has done these past months."

Philip's eyes flicked to Richard, assessing. "And what, pray, has she done to earn such praise from you?"

"Lady Slight sought me out in August. After the situation with Brendan. She asked for my help in pursuing her own road to redemption."

Philip exhaled, frowning slightly. He was clearly taken aback by this announcement.

"Truly? In what way?"

Sebastian exchanged a look with Richard and nodded. Harriet had given her consent to share some of her activities with the duke in an effort to mend things between him and Sebastian.

Richard leaned forward. "She has made it her mission to help those who cannot help themselves. To make up for her misdeeds. Women who have been cast aside. Servants who had nowhere else to turn. She took in Lady Wood when her own family would not aid her. She saved her maid, Jem, from life on the streets. She fought for Belinda Cooper when Lady Slight's father left her to ruin. And Finch, her housekeeper—"

Philip held up a hand, stopping him. He exhaled through his nose and looked away for a moment. "And you believe she has done this all out of genuine goodwill? A sincere desire to … change her behavior?"

"Yes," Sebastian said without hesitation. "I have seen it with my own eyes. She is not the woman she once was."

The duke was silent for a long moment. Then, to Sebastian's utter surprise, he nodded.

"Very well," Philip said. "You are determined, and I can see I will not sway you. If this is what you truly want, then I will not stand in your way."

Philip exhaled slowly, as if steadying himself, his fingers still loosely steepled beneath his chin. He looked past Sebastian, his gaze unfocused, lost in memory.

"For years, I have made decisions with the belief that I was acting in your best interest, but since your return, I have been reflecting on our strained situation," Philip said at last, his voice quieter now. "I believed I was protecting you. I thought I knew what was best." He paused, his mouth pressing into a firm line. "But I suspect now that I failed you, Sebastian."

Sebastian frowned, his back straightening. "What are you saying?"

Philip's gaze met his directly, his usually impenetrable mask giving way to raw regret. "I should have had more faith in you. More faith in your ability to choose your own path, to make your own future. You carved out a career in Florence, far from my influence." He shook his head slightly. "When I refused to support your courtship all those years ago—when I let my reservations about Harriet Hargreaves cloud my judgment—I was certain I was preventing disaster." His lips curved wryly. "And yet, all I did was ensure years of unhappiness for the both of you."

Sebastian's breath caught. Of all the things his brother

could have said, he had not expected this. Not an admission of fault. Not this … this understanding.

Philip sighed. "I should have listened to you back then. Stood beside you. But I let duty, and my own beliefs, dictate my actions. I forgot that you were my brother deserving of my fraternal appreciation, not merely a duty." He hesitated, then continued, "I do not wish to make that mistake again. I want to be part of your life."

Sebastian's throat was tight, his emotions warring within him. He had spent so many years resentful of his brother's interference. Had spent so much time convincing himself that Philip would never see him as anything but the younger brother, the reckless, impetuous spare who needed to be managed.

But now, now his brother was sitting before him, acknowledging his mistakes. Accepting them.

And deep within his chest, Sebastian's heart softened.

He did not hesitate. Rising swiftly, he strode forward, and before Philip could react, he grabbed him in a crushing embrace.

Philip stiffened in shock, his arms pinned at his sides. "Sebastian—"

"Shut up," Sebastian muttered against his shoulder, squeezing tighter.

For a moment, there was only silence. Then, with an exasperated sigh, Philip relented, his arms coming up to clap Sebastian on the back in an awkward, hesitant motion.

Richard, still seated, let out a low chuckle. "Well, this is unexpected."

Sebastian pulled back, clapping a firm hand on Philip's shoulder. "You were a bastard about it, you know."

Philip rolled his eyes, straightening his coat. "I am aware."

Sebastian grinned, warmth spreading through him. He could feel the past shifting, settling into something lighter.

Philip gave him a long look. "You truly love her, do you not?"

"With everything in me," Sebastian answered without hesitation.

Philip nodded. "Then I suppose you should marry her."

Sebastian grinned. "I intend to."

Philip exhaled sharply, shaking his head. "God help me, I am going to have to be civil to her, am I not?"

"Yes, you are."

Philip sighed. "Well, let us hope she does not make it too difficult."

Sebastian laughed, his heart lighter than it had been in years. He had gained his woman and his brother back, and it felt good.

* * *

WHEN HARRIET ARRIVED, she found herself standing before the duke, her heart hammering in her chest. His sharp gaze settled on her, obscure as ever.

"I hear you wish to marry in Calais," he said without preamble.

Harriet swallowed. "I …" She glanced at Sebastian, who gave her a small, reassuring nod. "Yes, Your Grace."

The duke inclined his head. "Then allow me to offer my assistance. A wedding, even in Calais, requires proper arrangements. I will secure a special license and accompany you across the Channel to see it done properly."

Harriet's breath caught. Her lips parted, but no words came.

A lump formed in her throat as she stared at the man who had been so cold to her for so long. And yet now, he was offering her not just permission, but his blessing.

Tears welled in her eyes. "I ..." She blinked them back quickly. "Thank you, Your Grace."

He inclined his head again. "You are to be family ... Harriet ... Philip is acceptable."

"Yes, Your Gra—" Harriet curtsied, then stopped. Straightening up, she stepped forward and stood on tiptoes to press a kiss to the duke's cheek. He was so tall, it landed on his jaw even as he leaned down to accept it. "Yes, Philip."

She dropped back and the duke smiled. It was stiff, but it was an improvement, and she was more than willing to accept the olive branch he was extending.

Sebastian reached for her hand, squeezing it in support. "Thank you," he said, his voice thick with emotion.

His Grace hesitated only a moment before extending his own hand. Sebastian clasped it firmly, a silent understanding passing between them.

It was done.

Harriet was going to be his wife, and his family would support them.

She barely remembered leaving the duke's townhouse, her mind a whirl of emotions too tangled to ... well ... untangle. The journey back to her own home passed in a haze, with Sebastian seated beside her in the carriage, his fingers wrapped around hers, anchoring her when she felt as though she might drift away on the tide of her own astonishment.

She had spent so long preparing for battle—for rejection, for scorn—that the sudden shift in fortune left her feeling weightless. It was done. Philip had accepted her. The duke—Sebastian's formidable, unyielding brother—had given his blessing.

And she was going to be Sebastian's wife. His partner. His travel companion. Her fingers tightened around his, and Sebastian glanced down at her.

"Are you well?" His voice was low, threaded with warmth and amusement.

Harriet exhaled a soft laugh, shaking her head. "I cannot believe I will stand beside you in Calais, repeating my vows with your family in attendance."

Sebastian lifted her hand to his lips, pressing a kiss to her knuckles. "That, my love, is every dream come true."

Her heart clenched painfully at the tenderness in his voice, the devotion in his eyes.

When the carriage rumbled to a stop before her town-house, Harriet allowed herself to be guided inside, her body and mind still reeling. Finch met them at the door, her shrewd gaze flitting back and forth between them before she gave a brisk nod, as though confirming an opinion to herself.

"Oi'll get summat brought to the painted room," she said.

"No need," Sebastian interjected smoothly. "We shall retire upstairs."

Finch's brows lifted, but she said nothing, merely gave another nod before sweeping away.

Harriet barely had time to register the meaning of Sebastian's words before he took her hand again and led her toward the stairs. Her pulse leapt. She climbed each step with growing anticipation, her fingers curled around his like a lifeline.

As soon as they reached her rooms and the door to her bedchamber clicked shut behind them, Sebastian turned to her, his eyes dark with desire. Harriet swallowed, heat coiling low in her belly as she reached for the buttons of her pelisse.

But Sebastian was faster, flicking them open. Then his hands came to her shoulders, slipping beneath the heavy fabric to ease it from her body. The wool slid down her arms, pooling at her feet in a whisper of fabric.

"You are wearing too much," he murmured, his voice

rough as he traced the line of buttons down the front of her gown.

Harriet shivered, her breath catching as he worked each one free, baring inch by inch of the fine chemise beneath.

The moment the last button gave way, Sebastian pushed the gown from her shoulders, leaving her in only the whisper-thin undergarment.

He took a step back, his gaze devouring her with such adoration that Harriet felt her knees weaken.

"You are glorious," he said, his voice barely above a breath.

She reached for him, fingers fumbling at the fastenings of his coat. "So are you."

Sebastian let her work, his breath coming heavier as she pushed the fine garment from his shoulders.

Then, in one fluid movement, he lifted her into his arms.

Harriet gasped, her fingers digging into the firm expanse of his shoulders as he strode toward the bed, his grip on her effortless.

She had always known he was strong. But now, cradled against him, she could feel it in every inch of his body—the raw, restrained power beneath the fine tailoring.

And yet, he handled her as though she were precious. As though she were everything.

He lowered her onto the mattress, face down, following her down with aching slowness, his weight settling over her back like the most exquisite cage. Harriet's breath caught, her hand coming up to trace the sharp line of his jaw, and relish the roughness of his stubble that he had shaved many hours earlier.

Sebastian caught her hand, pressing a lingering kiss to her palm.

"I love you, Harriet," he whispered.

Tears welled in the corners of her eyes, but she refused to let them fall.

Instead, she whispered back the only words that had ever mattered.

"I love you, too."

Sebastian traced his fingertips down the curve of Harriet's back, murmuring about starlight and silk. She lay beneath him, breathless and warm, her auburn hair spilling across the pillows.

Slowly, deliberately, he shifted, pressing a lingering kiss to the slope of her shoulder. Harriet shivered beneath his lips, her breath catching as he continued, his mouth traveling down the line of her spine.

His lips were fire against her skin, heated and sensitive to his touch. He followed the curving dip of her back, his palms smoothing over the curve of her waist as his kisses deepened, tasting as if worshipping her essence.

Harriet trembled, turning her head to the side as if to grant him better access, and he smiled against her lower back. She was helpless like this, unguarded, lost in the moment.

"Sebastian," she breathed, her voice hushed.

His name on her lips sent a fresh wave of longing coursing through her. Pressing one final kiss to the base of her spine, he whispered against her skin, "I will never tire of this."

He slid his hands back up, caressing her shoulders, drawing her close once more, ready to savor every moment between them.

Then she felt him leave the bed, and the sound of his clothing being removed made her shiver in anticipation.

"Take off your chemise," he commanded. Between her legs a thick sensation began to pulse as she struggled with the garment, eventually rolling off the bed in frustration to rip it off.

Sebastian chuckled, pulling her in for a deep kiss as Harriet grew ever more aroused, taking in his male scent and wondering what he would do next.

His mouth moved over her cheek to her ear, where he whispered, his warm breath stirring her hair, "Get on your knees."

Startled, she turned her head to stare up into his molten eyes.

"Get on your knees," he coaxed, his expression pure mischief.

Harriet licked her lips, the flames in her lower belly licking up until her entire body was on fire. Slowly, she turned to the bed and did as he had instructed, using her hands to brace against the mattress and revealing her naked buttocks to his gaze.

Sebastian approached, caressing his hands down her spine and down to cup her rounded cheeks. Then she nearly swooned when his blunt tip nudged against her swollen, throbbing womanhood, before sliding inside her with one smooth motion.

She gasped out loud, stunned by the size of him, how much she could feel him in the position, how deep he was buried, as if they were truly one organism. As he began to rock his hips and thrust into her, the sensation mounted. Each thrust was so glorious, so overwhelming, that it took all her willpower to push back against him instead of collapsing in a moaning heap of mindless pleasure.

When his hand came sliding around, seeking the center of her pleasure to touch her exactly the way she liked it, she bucked, ecstasy shooting out through every nerve as she rode the white-hot waves to her peak. But even when she shrieked her surrender, her feet arching in tortured pleasure, he was not done.

As he gripped her hip firmly with his large hand, his pace grew more frantic. Pounding into her to seek his own summit, his stamina and his strength were to be admired for their pure, powerful masculinity. Until finally he surged into her with one last thrust, a loud groan, and froze, his shoulders arched back as she felt the warm wetness of him spending deep inside her. She moaned anew as she took his seed and thought of the children she would bear him. They would enjoy a true marriage, the kind she had been so envious of.

Then he wrapped a muscular arm around her waist and rolled them as one into the bed. There they lay together gasping for breath, wrapped in each other's arms, and Harriet marveled at how close she felt to the wonderful man at her side. Her engaging in bed sport with the man she truly admired, whom she had revealed her inner secrets to, was beyond comparison to anything she had ever experienced. Even better than her first time with him years before because there were no more deceits between them.

They had laid their souls bare to one another and accepted the virtues and the flaws to form a true partnership. And maybe this was what fate had intended all along. To bring them back together where they belonged.

EPILOGUE

But vain the assistance that riches bestow,
The rapture that beauty imparts,
To soften the painful reflections of woe,
Or banish distress from our hearts.

The New Ladies' Valentine Writer (1821)

* * *

*S*ebastian stepped into the Scott townhouse, the sizable painting secure in his grip. Though it was not heavy in the conventional sense, it bore the full weight of his past, of his emotions, and of the mysteries it might reveal. He had no use for it—no desire to keep it—but the moment he had held it in his hands again, he had known precisely where it needed to go.

Lorenzo was already waiting in the library, his dark brows furrowed as he paced with restless energy. When he spotted Sebastian, his sharp gaze locked onto the painting, and his entire posture shifted from impatience to barely contained exhilaration.

"You have it," Lorenzo breathed, his voice thick with anticipation. He crossed the room in a few swift strides, barely sparing Sebastian a glance before reaching for the painting with near veneration.

Sebastian relinquished it easily, stepping back as Lorenzo cradled the wooden panel in his hands, tilting it toward the light from the tall windows. "*Dio mio*, Matteo's brushwork ... Look at the layering, the depth!" His fingers traced the edge of the frame, his eyes alight with admiration. "She is even more magnificent than I imagined."

Sebastian folded his arms, watching as Lorenzo drank in every detail, his joy palpable.

The painting was a masterpiece of quiet legend, its rich pigments lending vibrancy to the scene. Painted on wood, the four-foot-square panel depicted a woman standing in a moonlit lake, her form half-shrouded in the silvery mist rising from the still waters.

She was the Lady of the Lake from Arthurian legend, timeless and ethereal. Dressed in flowing robes of pale silver, the fabric rippling as if caught in an unseen breeze. Her auburn hair cascaded in waves over one shoulder, glinting with golden highlights where the artist had captured the illusion of light. But it was her expression that drew the eye—an enigmatic, knowing smile that hovered at the corner of her lips, as though she held a secret she would never fully reveal.

One delicate hand was raised, her slender fingers pointing toward the dark water below. The lake's surface was eerily smooth, reflecting the faint glow of a hidden moon, yet the shadowy depths hinted at secrets concealed beneath—secrets waiting to be discovered. Was it a treasure? A long-lost truth? The painting did not say, only invited the viewer to wonder.

The background was lush with flowers and verdant foliage, painted in exquisite detail. White lilies floated on the water, their pale petals luminous against the dark reflections. Wild roses climbed up a twisted oak on the right, their petals tinged with the same deep crimson as the Lady's lips. Fireflies dotted the dusky air, casting faint golden specks of light against the cool twilight hues.

There was a sense of serenity, yet also an aura suggesting the unseen. A hidden depth. The longer one looked, the more it pulled, as though the Lady herself were issuing an invitation—to step closer, to peer into the darkness, to uncover whatever lay beneath the surface. Perhaps that invitation was more than symbolic.

"She reminds me of Harriet," Sebastian murmured, half to himself.

Lorenzo, who had been studying the fine strokes of the Lady's flowing gown, glanced up. His eyes flicked between the painting and Sebastian before one dark brow arched. "Ah," he said knowingly.

Sebastian exhaled sharply. "Which is why I could not keep it years ago. But now it belongs with you, Lorenzo—Matteo's masterpiece."

Lorenzo studied him for a moment, then nodded, his fingers skimming over the delicate contours of the Lady of the Lake's face. "I will treasure it," he said simply.

Sebastian nodded, pleased with his accomplishment. But as Lorenzo continued his study, a slight frown tugged at the artist's lips. Something was wrong. Lorenzo leaned in, his expression shifting from admiration to curiosity, then sharpened. His fingers brushed over a particular section of the paint, assessing.

Sebastian frowned. "What is it?"

Lorenzo did not answer immediately. Instead, he turned toward the doorway. "We need sunlight. Come with me."

Without waiting for a response, Lorenzo strode through the house, carrying the painting as if it were a holy relic. Sebastian followed him through the back hall, out across the lawn, and into the garden shared with the miniature estate next door. The crisp winter air bit at his skin, and the midday light, though thin, would suffice.

Lorenzo set the painting against the stone bench that sat at the foot of the large ornate urn, which was bare of flowers for the season. Along the perimeter of the walled space, silent stone gods watched as Lorenzo angled the painting to catch as much sunlight as possible.

Sebastian watched, bemused, as his friend produced a fresh handkerchief from his pocket and, with delicate precision, wiped at a seemingly unremarkable section of the painting. The handkerchief came away with color on its pristine whiteness.

Sebastian leaned in. "What are you doing?"

Lorenzo huffed. "This oil—it is not oil."

He wiped again, more firmly this time. The sheen of the supposed varnish dulled beneath his touch, revealing a slightly different texture underneath. His eyes gleamed with excitement.

"It is tempera," Lorenzo murmured in awe. He straightened, staring down at the painting as if seeing it for the first time.

Sebastian blinked. "Tempera?"

Lorenzo turned to him, his expression alight with understanding. "Artists sometimes used this technique to hide things. Tempera is an egg-based paint. Messages. Secrets. It can be layered over oil to conceal what is beneath. But the nature of the paint—the way it dries, the way it absorbs light —it does not behave quite the same way."

Sebastian's sense of intrigue heightened. "Are you saying there is something beneath this painting?"

Lorenzo's lips curled into a slow smile. "That is exactly what I am saying. But only parts of it. Matteo wrote to his sister to point the way to this painting. And in this painting, he left a message. When we remove the tempera, we reveal the true oil beneath."

Sebastian stared at the Lady of the Lake once more, at her enigmatic expression, at the way she pointed down toward the water. A guardian. A keeper of secrets.

And now, perhaps, they were on the verge of discovering what those secrets were.

He stood with his arms crossed, watching as Lorenzo delicately brushed at the surface of the painting with his handkerchief, his dark brows furrowed in concentration. The afternoon light bathed the garden, filtering through the bare branches of the trees and lending an almost ethereal glow to the Lady of the Lake.

"See here," Lorenzo murmured, more to himself than to Sebastian, as he swiped another careful stroke over the lower portion of the painting. "The tempera layer is fragile, prone to flaking when dry. But look—beneath it, the colors are richer. Deeper. Oil paint. And I suspect something more."

Sebastian exhaled sharply, glancing between his friend and the painting. "You truly believe there's a hidden message?"

"I know there is," Lorenzo answered, his voice tinged with excitement. "The sixteenth-century Masters were clever, Sebastian. They used layers like this to obscure secrets, sometimes to protect knowledge, sometimes to conceal messages meant only for a particular viewer." He wiped again, and beneath the faded film of tempera, something more distinct began to emerge.

Sebastian took a step closer. His pulse quickened, curiosity warring with impatience. If Harriet had not kept the painting, if he had never demanded it back, they would not be here now, peeling away centuries of secrecy. His mind returned to the morning he had discovered it hanging over Harriet's bed. If—

"I say, what are you gentlemen up to?"

Sebastian started, instinctively adjusting his stance. Beside him, Lorenzo straightened abruptly, his fingers pausing mid-motion on the painting. Both men turned toward the voice.

Standing a few feet away was a young woman, poised and composed, with strikingly familiar features. Honey-brown hair, amber eyes, a confident posture, and an expression that was both amused and mildly assessing.

"Lady Campbell?" Sebastian asked, recovering, his voice tinged with wariness. He thought the viscountess was in Scotland with her husband.

The woman smiled, her eyes twinkling with mischief. "Ah, no. I fear you have mistaken me for my twin." She stepped forward, hands tucked into the folds of her stylish spencer. "Miss Henrietta Bigsby, at your service. I live next door. We share this garden with the Scotts."

Sebastian exchanged a look with Lorenzo, whose expression was still one of cautious surprise. But then his Italian friend shrugged and beckoned the young lady forward, apparently willing to share his enigmatic finding with her. Lorenzo did dearly love to explain art to a willing pair of ears.

Miss Bigsby stepped forward and tilted her head, her gaze drifting over the painting. "My, what a beautiful piece. But I suspect you two are more interested in what is beneath the surface, are you not?" She leaned down to examine the section Lorenzo had been rubbing with his handkerchief. "Whatever could you be looking for?"

* * *

Find out what happens when audacious Henri tries to
help Lorenzo in his quest. After encountering a
mysterious lord, a rescue turns into a kidnapping that
may unlock a great passion in The *Hidden Lord*.

DOWNLOAD TWO FREE BOOKS

Enjoyed the story? The adventure isn't over yet …

Subscribe to Nina's newsletter at ninajarrett.com and receive two novellas—absolutely free!

Interview With the Duke – What happens when an ambitious writer corners society's most elusive duke? Sparks fly in this witty prequel full of secrets, scandal, and charm.

The Captain's Wife – A runaway bride. A brooding army captain. And a reunion that could change everything.

Join thousands of Regency romance readers who love exclusive content, behind-the-scenes peeks, giveaways, and early access to new releases. Your next favorite story is just one click away.

AFTERWORD

Contrary to popular belief, Valentine's Day was not a holiday invented by Victorian greeting card companies. Its roots stretch much further back, entwined with centuries-old traditions of courtly love. By the early 19th century, the holiday was already well celebrated in England. Lovers often crafted handmade valentines, adorned with lace and verse. For those less confident in their literary abilities, publications such as *The New Ladies' Valentine Writer* offered ready-made poems and sentiments to woo the object of one's affection. While the Victorians later commercialized the practice, the impulse to express love through words and tokens was already thriving during the Regency era.

When writing historical fiction, particularly a Regency romance with a strong art and mystery component, balancing historical accuracy with narrative liberty is always a challenge. While I strive for authenticity, there are moments where small liberties are necessary to serve the story.

One such instance concerns Sandro Botticelli's *The Birth*

of Venus. The painting, created in the late 15th century, was housed in the Medici Villa of Castello for many years before eventually making its way to the Uffizi Gallery in Florence.

However, its exact placement by 1821 is uncertain. What is known is that by the early 19th century, many Renaissance masterpieces were being centralized in the Uffizi as part of efforts to preserve and showcase Italy's artistic heritage.

Given that Sebastian is a well-traveled art lover and connoisseur, it is plausible to assume that *The Birth of Venus* may have been accessible to him during his time in Florence. I took the liberty of assuming that he saw it there, as it is one of the most recognizable and celebrated works of the Italian Renaissance.

Another small but interesting historical detail is the capitalization of the word Mentor. Derived from a character in *The Odyssey*, Mentor was originally a proper noun, referring to the wise advisor in the tale. Until the mid-19th century, the term was often capitalized when used in English to describe a trusted counselor or guide. Only later did it become a more generalized term, losing its capitalization in common usage. In this novel, I have chosen to present it as it would have been written in 1821 as Mentor.

When the painting reveals its message, Lorenzo will need Henrietta's help to decipher its clues. But Henri's excursion to procure what he needs will turn out to be more perilous than they anticipated.

Soon, she is bound and gagged on the way to Calais. Lord Gabriel Strathmore has kidnapped her with no explanation. Which is rather infuriating because, until now, she rather liked the gentleman.

Can Henri and Gabriel come to terms before her reputation is ruined? And can they work together to solve the clues hidden within *The Lady's Hidden Secret* while avoiding the danger that it represents?

Find out in the next *Inconvenient Ventures* book, **The Hidden Lord**, in which Henri's bid to help uncover the mystery of Matteo's work takes an unexpected turn, and she just may be required to marry the dangerous Lord Gabriel to save herself from ruin.

ABOUT THE AUTHOR

Nina began writing stories in elementary school but took a long detour through real life before returning to fiction. After finishing her studies, she worked in non-profit outreach with recovering drug addicts—serving communities from privileged suburbs to the shanty towns of rural and urban South Africa.

Then she met a real-life romantic hero. A fellow bibliophile, he swept her off her feet, and she promptly married him and moved to the United States. There, she built a successful career as a sales coaching executive at an Inc. 500 company. Today, Nina lives with her husband on the sunny Gulf Coast of Florida.

Nina believes deeply in kindness, resilience, and the power of transformation. Inspired by the extraordinary people she's met across the world, she writes mischievous tales of bold choices, unexpected love, and the courage it takes to change. She tells these stories while sipping excellent coffee—and heroically avoiding cookies.

Join Nina's Newsletter at NinaJarrett.com for two free books, fun Regency content, announcements, and exclusive discounts.

Follow Nina Jarrett on your favorite platform.

ALSO BY NINA JARRETT

INCONVENIENT BRIDES

Five daring heroines. Five unexpected heroes. One scandalous series of love, redemption, and happily ever afters.

In this sweeping Regency redemption arc, five flawed men seek forgiveness and love—with the help of five extraordinary women. Each story stands alone, but together they form a powerful tale of legacy, loyalty, and the courage to change.

Book 1: The Duke Wins a Bride

Book 2: To Redeem an Earl

Book 3: My Fair Bluestocking

Book 4: Sleepless in Saunton

Book 5: Caroline Saves the Blacksmith

INCONVENIENT SCANDALS

A tangled murder mystery to unravel one romance at a time.

In the elegant world of *Inconvenient Brides*, five couples find love in the most unlikely places—while uncovering a mystery that could ruin them all. Each book delivers a satisfying, standalone Regency romance, but together they unravel a shocking murder that shakes the nobility. Only by the final page will the full truth come to light.

Book 1: Long Live the Baron

Book 2: Moonlight Encounter

Book 3: Lord Trafford's Folly

Book 4: The Trouble With Titles

Book 5: Lord of Intrigue

INCONVENIENT VENTURES

Five unlikely couples unlock a legendary secret.

In the glittering world of *Inconvenient Brides*, five unexpected couples are swept into a thrilling race to unravel a centuries-old secret. From coded paintings to Arthurian relics, each courtship reveals another piece of a legendary puzzle—one with the power to shake the British Empire ... or crown new heroes.

Book 1: The Courtship Trap

Book 2: The Hidden Lord

Book 3: The Phantom Romance

Book 4: The Rented Heart

Book 5: The Beloved Escapade

Printed in Dunstable, United Kingdom